Panopticon

Panopticon

David Bajo

UNBRIDLED BOOKS

Unbridled Books

Library of Congress Cataloging-in-Publication Data

Bajo, David.
Panopticon / David Bajo.
p. cm.
ISBN 978-1-60953-002-0
I. Title.
PS3602.A578P36 2010
813'.6—dc22
2010023985

1 3 5 7 9 10 8 6 4 2

BOOK DESIGN BY SH · CV

What we obscure becomes us.

Mil Mascaras

Panopticon

I.

*K*linsman arrived at the Motel San Ysidro on time, but the parking lot was empty and there was no police tape in front of room 9. The stucco walls of the single-story building were deep yellow in sunset, the roof postcard green. The neon sign had just come on, gaining full brightness with the sound of a lit fuse. He found the door to room 9 slightly ajar. He could only tell up close. He fumbled momentarily with the latex gloves he always brought to beat assignments but never managed to wear, then eased the door open.

The room was unlit and empty, with no signs of police investigation. Klinsman called Gina, his managing editor, hoping to catch her working late. She didn't answer. He flipped the light switch but nothing happened. He noticed that the cover and bulb for the overhead fanlight had been removed. A tiny square of black electrician's tape was stuck to the knob on the fan's pull-chain. Another piece was stuck over the door's peephole—on the inside. When he swung the door fully open to let in more light, Klinsman noticed yet another square of tape stuck to the inside doorknob.

He opened the heavy curtains to let in as much light as possible, a mix of neon and dusk and streetlight, and then the mass of lights from the Tijuana hills across the riverbed. When he thought about his past. It was that color, the light coming into room 9.

Klinsman tried his managing editor again but got no answer. He held her recorded voice to his ear, turned steadily, full circle, to examine the room. The doorknobs for the bathroom and the closet had black squares on them. The mirror on the dresser was draped with a towel. He tried the bathroom light and it didn't work. In the dimness of the shallow room he could see that the bulbs had been removed from the vanity light, with that mirror, too, covered by a towel. A toothbrush had been left beside the sink. Back in the main room, on the floor beside the dresser, he found a paper shopping bag containing all the lightbulbs, arranged on the bottom, neat as eggs.

He crouched on his heels and took his first picture, capturing the lightbulbs at the bottom of the bag. The double bed was made, but the thin cover, like milk skin, was wrinkled with the pattern left by a napping body, someone primly resting, gathering strength for a night out. With one arm outstretched, Klinsman held his camera above the bed and took a picture of the imprint. It was difficult to get the camera right above the pattern because the person who had been there had rested just off center. The pattern was intricate, swirled but contained like a fingerprint.

It was a woman. He could tell from the shape of the hips. Her hands had been clasped together over her stomach because he could see where her elbows had rested, little cups in the cloth on either side of her form. The cover was that sensitive, like a kind of photo plate, he thought, some silvery glass. Her heels, too, had left matching egg cups in the cloth. Klinsman took three shots.

He saw that it was time to leave for his evening assignment. He pressed the button on his camera and rotated a careful 360 degrees to get a panorama of the room. He lingered briefly on the blouse covering the TV screen but made sure he had enough memory in his camera left for the Luchadors in case he needed pictures for reference. The *Review* would send a good photographer to the Luchador event. Rita, he hoped, because she could be fun at that kind of assignment, make it not seem like work.

Klinsman closed the drapes, trying to leave room 9 in perfect order, rewinding his appearance. He even back-stepped to the door, checking to see if the industrial-grade carpet captured his footprints. There, then, imagining himself as intruder, Klinsman knew he had exposed himself to something and begun something, like Pandora taking the first full inhale of what she set free, Adam taking the second bite from the apple, feeling himself naked.

The light in the room was all artificial now: the neon from the motel sign, the sodium lamps from I-5, the veil of lights from the Tijuana hills, and that single collective amber borealis of humanity that forever hung above the landscape of his life, from these borderlands to the northernmost fingers of LA. He pulled the door closed but did not engage the lock, leaving it ajar again. As he had found it. Rewound.

2.

*C*afé Cinema was busy. Klinsman sat at the bar, turned toward the floor so he could watch the Luchadors play the room. They wore business suits and their brightly colored head masks, just like Santo and Blue Demon in the old Mexican wrestler movies Klinsman had grown up watching on Channel 12. Klinsman liked this troupe. They were guerrilla theater, an improv combo of LA's Culture Clash, Latins Anonymous, and Chicano Secret Service, but everyone knew them as the Luchadors. Sometimes they did scheduled events like this one, sometimes they staged secret impromptu events, and sometimes they blended one into the other. He had covered them seven years ago, one of his first assignments. It seemed fitting that he should cover them here, in the final week of the *Review*'s existence. Not much seemed fitting to Klinsman, so this was a rare moment. He wondered if Gina had given him this story as a gift, a bookend, a rare fit.

He sipped from his bottle of Tecate and guided the turn of his bar stool, imagining himself a kind of box camera, hollow inside, the images gathered, flipped, then righted. Los Abandoned played through the ceiling speakers, singing in their English–Spanish mix about being girls in barrios. *Nada mio es fake. Ven y tocame.*

The club was lit more than usual so everyone could see the Luchadors mixing with the crowd in different ways, chatting, dancing, demonstrating invented holds, performing little spontaneous skits. The main screen in the back and the smaller screens over the bar were all showing *Santo vs Blue Demon in Atlantis*, sound off. It seemed as if the Luchadors, or their doubles, had leapt from the screens and come to life among the crowd. They had finished their live overdub of the movie, where they had made the immortals from Atlantis into corporate heads overseeing the maquiladores, the beautiful double agents X-25 and Juno into the two current state senators, and the zombies into consumers. From the start, as always, Santo was there to fight for the people, those who had not yet become zombies. Blue Demon, his rival at first, later joined forces with his silver-masked nemesis to wrestle X-25 and then finally the immortals. Now Santo and Blue and X-25 and Juno were loose in Café Cinema.

One of the Luchadors in a silver head mask was dancing with three women. The women were young and writhing wildly, flinging their dark hair. The Luchador was intentionally dancing stiffly, like Santo in his movies, a muscle-bound pillar of righteousness in his gray flannel suit, mask on.

X-25, in her orange pantsuit, danced vaguely with two young men. Her gaze was distant, her steps minimal, allowing her to scan the floor, the café, the bar. Klinsman stilled himself, waited to be swept over, maybe catch her eye. She processed him without a blip, her gaze passing just above him.

Klinsman turned back to the bar and smoothed the cool lip of his beer bottle over his eyelids. He stared down at the brass bar top and noticed a fingerprint, neat and perfect, in the center of a water ring. The fingerprint was long, including the whorls below the second joint. The imprint of the woman who had rested so primly, so intentionally on the bed in room 9 flickered inside the hollow of his camera-self along with the rest of the images he had just gathered. She swayed like thin, dark seaweed between the figures of the Luchadors, her hips nudging them, her hair curling around their necks, her spiral fists up before her breasts, dancer, boxer.

When he looked up and faced the bar mirror, he saw that one of the Luchadors had taken a seat beside him. He wore a Blue Demon mask and a dark business suit with a thin '50s tie. The tie had a silk-screened flying saucer and a ringed planet on it. The Luchador was trim, not like the burly Blue Demon from Channel 12, and the elegant bones of his face were outlined on his silk mask. His lips were full, pushed into lushness by the blue mask.

"You're Del Zamora," said Klinsman.

The Luchador stared back with no reply.

"I didn't know you were with these guys again." Klinsman tilted his beer but did not sip. "I saw you with them a long time ago. Here. You've done well since then. I saw you onstage at the Globe. And in *Searchers 2.0*."

The Luchador nodded toward Klinsman's Tecate. "How much you pay for that?"

Klinsman eyed the bottle as though assessing its full value.

"Four fifty. Plus tip."

"Remember when you could get it in Baja for fifty cents?" asked Del. In the oblong opening of his mask his lips looked as soft and thick as sea anemones, supple and articulate with the tide.

"In Tecate," replied Klinsman, "during *feria* they'd pour it in the streets. When I was a kid I loved the smell so much. The town reeked of it, hops baking on the sidewalks."

"It looked green in the sunlight," said Del, squeezing a tiny smile.

Klinsman cocked his head, stroked his jaw. "But you're not from there. Or here. You're not even a real Mexican. You're mostly Apache or something. From New Mexico. Way back in *Repo Man* was when they turned you into a Chicano."

"I'm not Zamora."

"You are," said Klinsman. "I have no doubt. The mask only convinces me more. Highlights your features. Your voice."

"I'm Blue Demon," he said, lips moist with the truth.

3.

Someone wants to take our picture," said Blue Demon, nodding toward the space behind Klinsman.

Klinsman turned on his bar stool, Blue leaned in, and Margarita Valdez snapped the photograph. With a sideways bend in her wrist, she waved Klinsman out of the frame and then took a careful portrait of Blue Demon.

"Take off your mask," she said, lifting her chin.

"Then you won't know who I am," replied Blue.

"Besides," said Klinsman, "the rules are clear. You'd have to wrestle him. Pin him and then unveil him. Dig your fingers under his jaw."

"It's never been done," said Blue. "Not even Santo has beaten me that badly."

Rita looked at Klinsman instead, her black camera, with its fluted portrait lens, held aside but at the ready. She gazed oddly at him, lingering and with a hidden smile, as though catching him cheating, approving of it. She looked pretty whenever she did that, curvy, barely gathered. Her mouth formed a perfect ellipse, divided equally, full, a kind of emerging red. Her eyebrows were almost straight, never arcing, but lithe like something searching upward, or ready to search upward, above smooth and sleepy lids. A look of disdain appeared always atrigger in her eyes and mouth. Her black hair was gathered in a desperate failing ponytail, for her work, and this exposed her face to her subjects, its olive shape and color behind the free and springy strands.

When Klinsman and Rita turned in unison to address Blue Demon, they found him gone. Klinsman scanned the floor.

"There he is," said Rita.

He followed her gaze upward to the screen over the bar. Back in the *Atlantis* movie, Blue Demon stood with a woman at a cocktail party, planning something over martinis, same suit, same flying-saucer tie. Klinsman and Rita gazed at the screen together, necks bent like friends watching after-school TV. They got into the scene together, feeling their jobs slipping away behind them, their jobs ending after seven years. Seven days left. What were Blue and his striking accomplice planning?

"Why do the women take off *their* masks?" Rita asked as she and Klinsman watched together, drank their beers. "Why doesn't she wear her mask with her business suit? Like him? Why only the men?"

"Because the men are beastly under those masks."

"That guy we just talked to wasn't beastly. He was pretty. You could tell."

"He was Del Zamora," Klinsman told her. "I'm sure he was."

"Why are the men beastly?"

"Because they're actually wrestlers. Not actors. Which also explains keeping the masks on."

"They look like barrels wearing suits, with arms and legs."

"The women don't," said Klinsman as they continued to watch. The scene hadn't moved. Blue Demon and the woman were still chatting, their martinis unsipped. This was typical of these movies, the way they droned domestically between sudden outbursts of wrestling. "The women all are beautiful. So they take off their masks."

"They all look like Edwige Fenech. Mexican Edwige Fenechs. That actress in your Uncle Mir's *giallo* collection. How does she get her hair that high? How does she get her *chiches* that high? They're like rocket ships."

Rita scooped up her breasts and looked down at herself. Her camera clunked to her side, slung over her lens pouch. Her shirt was caught up in the straps of the pouch and camera, exposing the slope and curl of her waist above her jeans. Klinsman felt a sway inside him, seaweed bending.

"Can you come to San Ysidro with me?" he asked her. "After you're finished here? I know it's late. But I think it's important. It might be a story. Of some kind. I need pictures. Good pictures. I need you to see."

"Sure," she said, beginning to compose that look for him. "I'm finished here. Where we going?"

"San Ysidro Motel. Room 9."

. Her eyebrows leaned upward, her lips did something, fought gently against something, approved.

4.

*O*utside, the downtown air smelled of the bay, a barnacled hull. Rita and Klinsman shouldered their way through the 5th Avenue crowd to catch the southbound trolley. She got slightly ahead of him, always the photographer, always in front. She wore black boots, heeled to give her some height and vantage. Otherwise all her subjects would look nose-up and arrogant, she claimed. The black boots and jeans made her look *cholo*. "*Chola*," she would always say, correcting him. Then she would push her hip toward him, lifting, twisting a little, pinch a little flesh. "La la Cholitas. Never quite down enough for the clothes we wear."

She looked back to him as they neared the trolley. "We can take my car."

"You've been drinking."

"Only beer. And whatever was in those little green glasses the wrestlers were serving."

"I hate cars," he said.

"I hate the trolley this time of night. The *mozos* and sailors look at me like I'm a dancer going to the Bambi Club or something, with these cameras as props for some freak show. Not hot enough to work without props. You know?"

"I'll carry your gear."

"That will look much better."

They rode the trolley south to San Ysidro, Rita getting the window seat. She gazed at the blackness of the Pacific beyond the stretch of beachfront lights. She leaned her head to the glass and he watched the reflection of her face, her eyebrows slanted, melancholic, her rounded lips still as a single piano note. Sometimes she could catch sight of the waves, white and featherlike across the black shore. He wondered where she was, where she was going. He was surprised to hear his name.

"Aaron," she said, still gazing through the window. "You didn't call those people up north. You didn't do anything. Again. You didn't do anything. What are you going to do?"

"I'm going to travel Mexico. Then Prague with my uncle. See what I find. Write something."

"We're too old for those kinds of answers. We're already too old for what we do now."

"Having second thoughts?" he asked.

"Only for you. I like *my* plan. I leave for Manzanillo next week. Day after we finish here."

Klinsman was surprised, a wave suddenly lifting higher as it neared, doubling itself. "You've moved it up."

"Yeah." She rolled her forehead against the glass, closed her eyes. "I keep moving it up."

"You should've told me."

"I just did tell you. You're the first one I've told. *Chingadero. Chingadero* taking me to some motel on the border."

After the Palm City stop, the tracks bowed away from the sea and the trolley filled up more with Mexicans getting back across after very long work days. Most of them looked too tired to stare at anything, certainly not anything as complex as Rita, with her hair gaining more and more freedom from its ponytail, her brow mourning, her lips holding stoic and full.

Klinsman wished she hadn't mentioned Edwige Fenech back at Café Cinema because here the trolley was soaring above the land of his youth, where the old ranches and horse farms were now buried under the orange sodium lights of cheap subdivisions and strip malls with dollar stores in them. In his youth he'd read books in his room by the light of a TV, almost always set to Channel 12, almost always after 2 A.M., when he would wake for good and then wrestle insomnia until dawn. There were the Santo movies. And then there were the Italian *giallos*, dubbed twice-removed into Spanish, so out of sync that the voices seemed to float between the actors like noise clouds, sometimes drifting so far as to put women's voices over men's lips. But whenever Edwige Fenech appeared on screen, Aaron would thumb his place in whatever book he was reading. He would hear her voice or her music or catch the startling dark-pale contrast of her and sense that he should look up.

Some of the *giallos* were haphazardly edited for television, but many passed through unconcerned Mexican censors. Who would watch *Canal Doce* at 2 A.M.? Back then, Aaron felt he was the only one.

So he saw Edwige Fenech, all of her, when he probably shouldn't have seen her. It took a long time, well after he quit watching Channel 12 and all television for good, for him to realize that women did not look like her. Even through college, when he had moved just out of range of border television, her image had cursed him with a kind of relationship trip switch, a prompt inside him: *Time to end this. Time to draw back. There is something more out there for you.*

That *more* went well beyond Fenech and her mascara beauty, high raven hair, pale thighs, and rocket-ship breasts. Her characters were always so worldly, above all men, apart from all other women, but troubled with secrets as dark as her eyes. After he matured enough to cringe at his own superficiality, she still remained a shadowy impression, a promise at the door.

While doing a story on border radio and TV for the *Review*, he had been shown the storage room for the Channel 12 broadcast station in Baja. There he'd found an old cardboard vodka box containing the *giallos*. They were on old reel-to-reel videotape and had disintegrated well past salvage. He had dipped his hands into the broken and tangled strands of tape, twirled them about his fingers as though they were a lover's cool hair.

5.

Rita suddenly leaned upright and alert on the trolley seat beside him. She was lifting her chin and frowning in disdain at two *mozos* riding by the door. They were eyeing her and holding the pole suggestively between them, saying things just above a whisper. Passengers could catch some words, the right words.

Even if Margarita Valdez hadn't had some beers and whatever the Luchadors were serving in those little green glasses, even if she weren't in the last week of a job she loved, even if she weren't about to leave the country and go work for an expat paper in Manzanillo and take photos of things and people that really mattered, still she would have let the *mozos* have it. Klinsman could not keep up with her Spanish, could only jump to snippets here and there.

Her opening was perfect, winning the car first. "Fucking *mozitos*. You think these people need to hear your little-boy thoughts? Watch you jerk each other off on that pole between you? You think that's what they want? After a hard day's work? It's already tomorrow. They gotta go right back to work. Today. You think they want to see your liver tongues in these few minutes they have? Cocksuckers."

Somewhere in her scolding, Klinsman saw her glance briefly at another young man, a Latino, too, but dressed in a white shirt and thin black tie. He was watching her in a different way. Looking at her shoulders, part concerned, part measuring. And somewhere in her scolding she glanced again at the young man, just a splinter off her hard glare at the *mozos*, and called him something, too. Something odd. To Klinsman and his slow ears, it sounded like *Ojos ausentes salamandro*.

Rita kept jabbing at the *mozos* with her words, the passengers' eyes and smiles with her all the way to the next stop. There, at Iris Street, the *mozos* got off, probably not their stop, seeing as they looked dressed and awake for a longer night in the Tijuana clubs now that the American side was shutting down. The guy in the tie left, too, but not before looking back at Rita openly, thoughtfully adjusting his collar as though he were stepping out into a cold East Coast night.

Rita looked at Klinsman apologetically as the trolley picked up again, gliding them toward the border, over the lights of Otay, Nestor, and San Ysidro. Most of her hair had now sprung loose from her ponytail, a full lock of it draped down one side of her face and neck. Other strands wavered over her head, willowing down, brushing the tip of her nose. She blew at them.

Klinsman made a circling motion with his finger, moving his look from her hair to her eyes. "You want me to . . . ?" He made the little circling motion again.

She turned her head away and offered him her hair and neck. He gently gathered and clutched as much as he could hold in one hand and then removed the clasp. Before putting the clasp into the corner of his mouth like a cigarette, he eyed it carefully in the fluorescent trolley light. It was amber, like a bend of whiskey. It felt pearly against his lips.

With his fingers he combed and gathered more of her hair, pulling it to him. She relaxed her neck, letting his calm tugs loll her head. She closed her eyes, eased her lips out of their disdainful bend, almost opened them. So they were at their fullest. He watched the side of her face as he pushed his fingers up her nape and carefully raked the heaviest mass of hair, felt the bumps of her skull. His hand was buried up to his wrist in black coils.

"You're good at this," she said, eyes closed.

"I grew up with four older sisters."

"I hope you didn't do *this* with them."

"I watched them do each other's hair. When I was a boy. I believed I was getting a glimpse into another world, the one they really lived in, dreamed of. Their secret girls' world. I grew my hair long, too, but it wasn't the same."

"I'm sorry, Aaron," she said, letting her head fall back with the tug of his soft gathering.

"For what?"

"For that remark. Sounding that way about your sisters. I still have leftover sparks. From those fucking *mozos*."

He could feel her jaw moving with her words, his little finger slipping into a cusp.

"You said something else." Klinsman assessed the sheaf of black he had managed to bring under control, two fistfuls. "To that other guy. The one dressed like a waiter."

"I didn't see another guy. Just the *mozos*. Everything at the *mozos*."

"No. You glanced at that other guy, too. Twice. You knifed him twice. With words the second time. Something I couldn't quite understand. Something like . . . maybe like, 'eyes away, *salamandro*.' 'Eyes' you said for sure. That I could tell for sure."

"You watch me too much, Aaron," she said, keeping her eyes closed, her head almost back to his chest as he attempted the impossible, to set the amber clasp into her hair.

The trolley slowed as it neared the border stop, like something easing into its collapsed state. Rita sat neatly, her hair gathered, her expression smooth. They passed above Mt. Carmel, where Klinsman had gone to school. The asphalt playground formed a dark patch in the San Ysidro lights.

"You like riding this trolley down here because it puts you above everything," Rita told him, following his gaze out the window. "Everything you know."

"Everything I know is buried under lights and condos," he replied. "Save for a few things. That schoolyard. That smokehouse over there. That church."

"And the motel we're going to."

"What do you mean?"

"Don't play me," she said. "You told me once. You owned that motel once. You inherited it."

"Only for a month, Rita. As a kid. My father sold it for me. He used the money for my college. I never went to it. Except once after, with a date."

"Why are *we* going there?" she asked.

"I was sent there. This evening, on a damned beat call. I thought we stopped doing those. But it popped up on my billet. Just as I was heading out to the Luchador assignment. I haven't had to do a beat call in three years. I figured Gina was trying to jab me one more time. Before we're done."

"Gina sent you."

"It was just from the office. Gina's still gone. I tried calling her twice today. I don't think she's coming back. I think she's just going to wind it all up from wherever she's gone. Up north. Whichever job she picked up there. Typical of her to disappear on us like that."

"There's nothing typical about Gina," said Rita.

He told her about room 9, about the light, the tape, the covered mirrors, and the imprint of the woman on the bed. All he learned from the evening clerk was that two officers had dropped by before him, had seen nothing unusual for an empty motel room, and had assumed they'd received either a prank call or misinformation. The clerk wouldn't give Klinsman the name of the person checked into the room but did say that person was still checked in for the night. So Klinsman called the desk sergeant and used Gina's currency. Gina always made sure to portray the cops as weary but willing and bemused in the *Review*'s crime blotter.

The name Klinsman got was Marta Ruiz. No Marta Ruiz had been reported missing in San Diego or Los Angeles. Thirty-seven had been reported missing in Tijuana. Klinsman remembered two from grade school, three from high school, and two more from college. He had known none of them well enough to receive anything from them fourteen years later.

"But the room was open when I got there," he told Rita as they walked across the motel parking lot.

"Thirty-seven," she said, looking over her shoulder at the light-draped mesas of Tijuana. The neon sign shone on her lips like a prayer.

6.

*T*he door was exactly as he had left it. They knocked anyway, and after no response from inside, they gently pushed it open. He let Rita try the wall switch, then watched as she fished a grip light from her lens pouch and filled the room with an undersea glow. She had Klinsman reach up and clamp it to one of the overhead fan blades. She gazed at the room, brow flexed, seemingly unsure if there were really anything to see. He gently stayed her from absentmindedly sitting on the bed.

"No," he told her, then, motioning to the imprint on the milk-skin bed cover, "look."

The swirled form confused her further, lured her into bending over the bed, tiptoe, keeping her knees from brushing the cover. She looked as though she were about to dive in.

The grip light toplit everything, kept black the walls and floor, put Klinsman and Rita and everything in the motel room under a kind of bathyspheric probe.

"Put me on your shoulders," she told him.

He knelt and from behind put his head between her legs. He braced the tops of her thighs with his hands and stood, taking her weight as she clenched herself about his head. He felt her leg muscles like bands across his ears, heard the cupped rush in a seashell, thought for a moment it was her blood flow. She hooked her boots behind his kidneys, expert at this, like a circus performer, with a photographer's grace and objectivity.

"Hold still," she chided. She spun the fan to slightly off-center the grip light over the bed. The swirled pattern of the woman became even more distinct, the shadows deeper, the peaks glowing.

Klinsman straightened a bit, startled. His neck pushed into the zipper of her jeans.

"Hold still, *chingadero*," she whispered. She pressed her belly against the back of his head, leaned over, and took pictures of the imprint, no flash.

He tried to look up, inadvertently pushing his brow into her breasts. She tapped his throat.

"No. No. Still. I almost got it perfect."

He braced himself, her.

"How strong are you?" she asked.

"Pretty strong," he said. "Real strong."

"There's a lot of me up here."

"No. You feel good up there." He sensed what she was about to try. "Really."

She ponied herself up, digging the toes of her boots into his lower back, hardening her thigh muscles against his ears, and leaned way over, bending him with her.

She managed two or three captures before he lost his balance and let her fall onto the bed. After the mattress stilled, she smoothed the loose strands of hair from her face, lifted her brow, and opened her mouth like a boxer testing her jaw. She scooted herself back on her elbows and took in the room once again, the little squares of black tape here and there, glinting shardlike under the gauzy wash of the grip light.

"You were right," she said. "It's like a crime scene. But for a crime that never happened."

"Or one that hasn't been invented yet." He stretched out next to her, on elbows, shouldering her. He wanted to share her exact view of the room. He looked at the squares of tape. "They're like markers, no? For staging. Perspective. I figured you could tell."

"Yes," she said. "They look like that."

She removed her camera and lens pouch and placed them gently on the nightstand, rolling her hips away from him. She looked back over her shoulder at him, caught him looking, held still. He hooked his fingers about her hip and spun her to him, her softness tumbling up under him, her hair whipping in tails across his neck. They used their teeth to feel their way to a kiss, their tongues going into each other too fast, before first pressing lips.

She pulled away quickly and swung herself off the bed. He thought she was hurrying away, but she was only checking the door to make sure it was locked. Then she drew tight the curtain string, sealing the window completely. She removed the square of black tape from the little knob at the end of the curtain draw. She stuck it to the tip of her finger and waved it at Klinsman.

"We should keep one of these." She smiled and came back to him, jumping vigorously onto the bed, bouncing him into her.

He pulled her jeans down first, yanking them to the tops of her boots. She wore nothing underneath but her brown skin, paled there into a V, a milky outline. He put his head back where it had been before, when he'd had her on his shoulders. The light seemed to shudder. He kissed her thighs, holding them. She tasted like water from a metal cup, his tongue beneath the brim.

She tried to move her legs, raise her knees, lift herself more into his face, but she was bound by her jeans. She kicked at them, then at his shoulders, pulled off her boots and pants. He tugged her blouse over her head, thrashing most of her hair loose from its clasp. She pulled back, her lips parted. He removed her bra, eased it from her breasts, then kissed gently between them, grazed the stretch of his palms over her.

"Yeah," she said. "That's right. We have time. We have seven days. Somewhere between now and seven days is right for us, Aaron."

7.

*S*he held his hips firmly to the bed, hooked her thumbnails. He felt about to slide and skitter over the silvery bedcover, about to be pressed through surface tension. She pushed her hair over to one side as she moved her lips about him, hummed deeply, something he sensed to the base of his spine. Her tongue was rough in the center, soft at the edges. When she scraped her teeth against him, he almost let himself go, but she stopped him by biting down and creating a diverting pain, triggering something else in him. She drew off him, her lips remaining close, keeping him at bay.

He took deep, controlled breaths and tried to see behind the veil of light to the dark ceiling, but it appeared as though only black space loomed beyond. He imagined the two of them as sea creatures encased in white light on the powdery desert floor of the deep. Again she clamped her teeth into him when she sensed him about to lose control, then drew back, tapped him delicately with her fingers, blew a cooling breath. This calmed him for a brief moment. She glared up at him.

He reached down and took gentle hold of her head. He lifted gently and continued rolling her back, holding fistfuls of her hair, his fingers lost in there. He rolled with her, guiding her backward, himself over her. He straightened her leg, held her foot high by curling his fingers behind her toes, then drew his free hand along the back length of her thigh, the cusp behind her knee, the stretch of her calf. He pinched her Achilles, dug his fingernails in behind her toes. She turned her face to the side, into the swell of her hair, her throat stretched.

He eased his face down to her, guiding hands along the insides of her thighs, his thumbs pressing to find her pulse. He tasted her, water from metal again, still cool. He kept trying to do deliberate things with his hands and fingers, his lips and tongue, in order to steady himself. But it felt as though she were somehow still enveloping him. And putting the bridge of his nose against her, his tongue to her, only increased that sensation. He tried thoughts. *This is Margarita Antonia Valdez. My colleague. My friend.* This only made things more intense, made it real. A kind of distant rushing noise rose about him, as though the motion of their bodies had created a building static. He could feel it on his skin.

He gave up trying to distract himself, let something give at the base of him, a hard, sharp flint of pleasure, and hoped it might stay back a while. He glanced up. Wild tendrils of her hair seemed to be rising on the static, reaching toward the grainy light, probing a current.

Her taste, too, intensified things, fueled that building flinty stab inside him. It was a spark on his teeth, a pearliness on his tongue. He felt her foot brush his ribs, her heel digging back into his armpit. Then her thigh lay heavy over his shoulder as her foot pushed down along his side. He slid his hand along her side. She kneed her way beneath him, her toenails brushing along his belly. With her toes she found him, curled her instep around him, gave a little kick.

She brought her grip light into the bathroom with them and clamped it to a towel rack. This put a sideways glow in the small space. They left the towel draped over the mirror after considering it together with confused expressions. Before getting into the shower with him, she lightly adjusted the toothbrush on the sink counter, considering it with an inquisitive turn.

She pushed the shower curtain aside and stepped into the stall with him.

"Shower curtains," she said. "You ever see a shower curtain in Mexico?" She shoved it away.

The water hit their shoulders and spattered into the light, shooting high like sparks toward the dark ceiling, filling the little bathroom with glitter.

They cleaned themselves like athletes, not touching one another. She smiled at him as she washed her hair, let him watch her gather and sculpt its mass.

They returned to the bed, and he, reaching, sensing the world beneath him, fastened the grip light again to the overhead fan. While he was up there, he peeled the bit of tape from the end of the fan's pull-chain.

"Put that back," she said. "I already have the one."

This time they were more deliberate about things, their nakedness to the point. She rolled back the bedcovers, tightened the sheet. He reshaped the pillows. From either side of the bed they crawled toward each other. She shook her head when he tried to ease her back. Instead she laid him down straight, tucking his arms, stopping his hands. She stretched her length against him, her form into his. She swam onto him, her skin moving over him like a final, tactile shadow. She blew softly against his brow, smiled down at him, studied the edges of his thoughts.

Her wet hair fell heavily about his eyes, their faces held close together inside the damp black drape as she moved gently over him. This time Klinsman had nothing to struggle against. She felt new, unanticipated, a fragment of a dream yet to be remembered.

8.

*T*hey wanted to stay in the room for what was left of the night. The grip light was off, and the room was dark save for the glow of the motel's sign filtering through the edges of the curtain. They lay beneath the covers, their hands pressed to where the impression of the woman had been.

"You're worried she'll come back and find us?" Rita asked.

He fingered the sheet, pulled it up in little ridges between them.

"If she returned, what would she find?" Rita spoke softly, nosing the edge of the sheet, her legs moving beneath the covers, making a pleasant, sleepy sound. Her knee brushed his hip. "She would step into a motel room and find two people in a bed, sleeping, maybe screwing. So? And then of course we'd find *her*. And she could tell us what's up with the lightbulbs and the black tape."

"And the mirrors and the TV," Klinsman added.

"So we're good." She squeezed his hand. "Like this."

Rita slept deeply. A damp, soft breathing whispered from her lips, with only her chin and mouth discernible beneath the dark spools of her hair. Her shoulder rose and fell in a rhythmic shrug. Klinsman held his palm just above the rise of her shoulder, measuring the exactness of her breathing, the depth and thickness of it.

Klinsman never slept well, and his insomnia would rule this situation, armed with enough thoughts and images to deny sleep for the mere fragment of night remaining before dawn. Rita's heat bathed his face and neck, the iron-steam smell of her. He imagined her warmth and scent passing through a tear they had just rent in their friendship. He imagined the imprint of the vanished woman writhing gently beneath them, like involuntary movements in tired muscles, fingering his legs and shoulders.

He caught bits of half sleep, momentary dips into the same dream. The dream was a pale worry, an outline of the woman against a deep white, undulating in the color and contour of kelp. Each time he surfaced from this dream, the translucent amber of the kelp became the whiskey-colored clasp in Rita's hair. He would reach to his lips, imagining the clasp still there in the corner of his mouth.

They had known each other, worked together, grown to like each other over the course of seven years. So this would be easy for them, waking together, finishing off these seven days together. *Seven days is right for us.* They would have nothing to decide, could ride feelings like bubbles rising to the surface, heading breath-held toward open sky.

Del Zamora appeared in the last version of the dream, only his voice, really. But Klinsman could sense in the dream that Zamora had removed his mask, freed his lips. *Remember when you could get it in Baja for fifty cents? It looked green in the sunlight. You know this woman beneath you.*

This version startled Klinsman into permanent wakefulness, the heart-deep kind of quickening that fires all nerve endings. He slid up against the headboard as though pulling himself from a cold ocean dive. He heard the lonely clacks of the day's first trolley.

He wakened Rita, warmed his hand with his breath before gently tugging her shoulder, smoothing her hair from her face. Her body set itself beneath the sheets. She made a small questioning sound. Her hand moved downward over his stomach, found him.

"Good," she said.

They made love sleepily beneath the sheets, reaching to feel what they might find, cupping and grasping to tell what part of them it might be. He lay fully on her, she whispering an order for him to do that, to not brace his arms, to relax onto her. Her muscles, all along her, carried him. He barely came, a tug of a drawstring, the last of him. But she cried out, threw him upward with her body.

They dressed in the darkness of the room. They heard the shudders and blats of the first trucks on I-5, heading north, the only direction here at the very bottom of this longest of freeways.

Klinsman and Rita gathered their stuff, their captures of room 9, and walked into the dawn light of the parking lot. She swung her camera and bag over her shoulder, gathered her hair with both hands, the clasp held in her lips, ready. She took furtive strides next to Klinsman, some a little sideways, keeping him alert.

They found their bearings in the middle of the empty lot, a photographer and her journalist striding toward the day. They didn't look back toward room 9, never thought to wait for the figure of Marta Ruiz to appear.

9.

*K*linsman started some copy on the Luchadors story that morning at the *Review*, just feeling around for ideas on the keyboard. No one else was in the newsroom, though someone had arrived before him to turn on power, make coffee, put out baguettes and strawberries. He wandered from his copy, sat on the edge of the couch, fingered the coffee table as he looked over the sixteen empty desks, their flat screens like dark mirrors aimed together in a solar field. Only his at desk 7 was aglow and askew, foolish looking. Without Gina around, people weren't coming in. They were staying home, working or not working on their laptops.

The scent of the strawberries reminded him of the border, though the last of the riverbed farms had scooted north to the Otay years ago to avoid the polluted Tijuana. Strawberries, their scent in the ocean air, signaled the end of the rainy season. The grass along the freeways and on the hills behind the city would begin to yellow soon. Maybe one more rain would delay that turn.

The taper of the rainy season had always felt the most eventful time of year for Klinsman, a desperation lifted in him. It had to do with school's end, summer's approach. The days could still be different—cool and misty, rainy, hot and staticky with the Santa Anas, or infinitely blue, the Pacific horizon like a razor. Any chance he would have with a girl at school would be coming to an end, pushing him to be courageous, foolish, impossibly clever even, when he was lucky. This remained true from grade school through college. He was still programmed that way by this end of the season.

It no doubt had played a part in his reaching for Rita, his decisive and clear grasp of her hip. And it had him thinking perhaps too much about the motel. He was thinking beyond the thrill of it, the exciting notion that he and Rita were the ones who had committed the room's crime, invented the room's crime, finished things. He hurried back to his desk to tap some more lines of the Luchador piece, thoughts of room 9 alight in his fingers. The call had been for him. The door had been left open for him. This had to be the case.

Some of the copy was about Del Zamora, and he knew Gina would edit it even if it somehow passed fact check. So he typed one more line to be cut: *You know this woman beneath you.*

When he came to the press floor first and early like this, he fell easily into believing he was in the true heart of this city, removed from the tourist spectacle of the Gaslamp and Old Town. It was part of Gina's design for the *Review,* for all of them. Outside, the Boulevard ran due east from the edges of downtown to the foothills of the Cuyamaca Range, straight through endless miles of work and dreams, cultural blends and barriers. When alone like this, Klinsman could feel the Boulevard's waking buzz, a wire always seeking full connection, popping here and there, up the way or back against the sudden rise of downtown. The temperature rose ten degrees if you moved from the sea air of the west end to the smoggy push against the desert hills of the east. In that rise of heat you could get a loan, your car fixed, a good or bad haircut, a hooker, a book, a drink, coffee, or drugs; you could quit a day job, play a gig, or speak Spanish, English, Vietnamese, Tagalog, and then a different-sounding English and Spanish.

At desk 7, Klinsman always felt off-kilter, as anyone would at the four middle desks: 6, 7, 10, 11. No one could be at the precise center. Gina was at 10, an over-the-shoulder glance at Klinsman's 7.

The overhead lights were still off, the only other glow coming from the rest-area lamp in the back. He returned to the couch for the fourth or fifth time this new morning. In the coffee-table spread someone had left a hard end from yesterday's baguettes just for him. His favorite breakfast was black coffee and a hard roll. He felt sorry for, the only one of the sixteen desks to have no job prospects after next week's final issue, the only one who was still coming to work on time. The perfume of the strawberries made him want to go outside, ride down to the border, see the bullring at the sea's edge.

Klinsman sensed movement, a gray blur at the upper edge of his vision, and looked to the monitor above the back door, which scanned the entryway outside. In the monitor stood Oscar Medem, encased in the webby light of the cheap security. The grainy capture, the camera's struggle to make sense of the contrast between Oscar's dark skin and light shirt, reminded Klinsman of the stock footage so often seen in Santo movies. Oscar might have been thinking something similar as he eyed the little outside screen that showed what awaited inside. Gina's sense of balance again, her tilt on the collective.

Oscar entered and moved along the edge of the desks, arms folded, that marching stride he had, watching Klinsman smell a strawberry. The act of keeping a secret hung on Klinsman's shoulders, kneaded along the muscles of his back. He must have shifted his posture. Oscar, he could see, had been about to say something, something maybe about the strawberries, but then he closed his mouth, reasserted his honest gaze, and tightened his arms about his chest. He tilted his head as though Klinsman were something new, something exotic and behind bars. Klinsman would have to tell him about Rita, but now felt too blunt, too soon. It would have to be sometime before Rita divulged anything. If Rita told first, Oscar would be hurt, betrayed even. Such was the timbre among the desks, especially those at the floor's heart—Oscar, Gina, Klinsman, Rita, 6, 10, 7, 11.

Oscar proceeded into his routine, walking the row to his desk, checking any open pages or notes or photos on other desks along the way, picking up fallen pens. He looked back at Klinsman in quick glances, selectively, as though Klinsman were one in a crowd.

He punched in his jump drive, bringing his screen to light, then slung his messenger bag over the back of his chair. He set his notepad to the right side of the keyboard and his green metal water bottle to the left. Without sitting down, one arm braced on the desk edge, he visited his home page—the site of a journalist in El Paso, the woman who'd written the first book on the Juárez femicides and who was still keeping tabs on those kills. The one journalist trying hard to keep it real, the one who was not going to let it all disappear into wrong metaphor and the wash of drug violence from here to there. She was Oscar's hero, Klinsman's demon.

Oscar folded his arms across his chest again and stepped to the side of his screen so Klinsman could get a look, a hard look at the pink cross in the sand and the incredible number below it counting the bodies found in the desert. Then he freed his arms like a boxer stepping back, Ali into the ropes. His t-shirt hung loose and threadbare about his shoulder muscles, a silkscreen of an extinct frog spread across its front. Worry passed over his face, the waver of flame light.

Klinsman had met him six years ago on a story at the Tijuana Cultural Center, an exhibition called "Africa's Legacy in Mexico." It was a photography show touring the world, offering portraits of black Mexicans, *pardos*, the descendants of slaves. Oscar was finishing up his studies at UNAM then. The university had sent him up to Tijuana to follow the show as it crossed the border into the States.

Oscar was himself a *pardo*. Among the portraits in the exhibit he looked as though he had stepped from a frame to wander stunned through the press party in his t-shirt and jeans. Klinsman brought him to the *Review*, and Gina hired him and helped him get his green card. She told him to learn to flatten his expression, told him his face was too forthcoming, all his features like living clay. She wriggled her fingers above his cheekbones. If you can't do that, she told him, then maybe try looking happy when you're sad, surprised when you're bored. Don't let your subjects get ahead of you. She made him into the best investigative reporter.

Oscar gathered himself—leaned against a desk and hooked his thumbs into the belt loops of his jeans. He faced Klinsman, drew the soft morning light of the pressroom floor into thoughtful shadow and flush. Klinsman could see his own copy on the desktop in front of Oscar. Then it blinked away, disappearing into screensaver.

"What are your three?" Oscar asked. He knew what Klinsman's three assignments were. Oscar knew everybody's assignments, often better than they did.

Klinsman answered anyway, in this quiet but demanding light. "She has me doing three old stories." Remaining at the back, on the couch edge, he nodded toward his screen. "The Luchadors' show last night. Then park surveillance. And then this little blotter piece at Motel San Ysidro." Klinsman shrugged but felt secrecy and guilt weigh on his shoulders.

"Why's that one old?"

Klinsman shrugged again, trying harder to seem casual. "I don't know. It just feels somehow like walking into the past. Maybe it was just the light."

"Old like stale?" asked Oscar. "Or old like something deep?"

He always sounded as though he knew your answers. So Klinsman gave him something new, something not wholly considered.

"I found a woman. A kind of woman, I mean. Someone found and vanished at the same time. On the bed. From the bed."

Oscar appeared skeptical, an unusual expression for him, a glare to his eyes.

"I know her and don't know her—at the same time," Klinsman said. This didn't help. "I'll show you," he said. He stood to walk toward his desk.

Oscar leaned back on the desk edge, elbows into his sides, again into the ropes.

"Why do you keep doing that?"

"What?" asked Oscar. "Doing what?"

"Leaning away. Like you're staying out of a circle. *My* circle."

Oscar looked to the side as though catching an eavesdropper, then straight at Klinsman. "There's trouble about you, Aron." *Ahrone*, he pronounced it, trilling the r once.

10.

*K*linsman told Oscar about the tag sending him to room 9, then about his first visit there. He told him he planned to go back today and ask around, try to find out who the woman was. Marta Ruiz. And then he asked, "Why do you sense trouble about me?"

"You look like you're hiding something from me," Oscar replied. "Right when I came in you looked that way. Hiding your lips behind a strawberry like that. People who really have something to say always do that in interviews. Rock their bodies a little like something's trying to get out, guard their lips." Oscar crossed his arms over his chest and gripped his shoulders. "Maybe it's just me."

They finally moved toward one another, among the desks, and stopped at number 7; Oscar straightened Klinsman's screen so it was in formation with all the others. Klinsman leaned over his keyboard.

"Let me show you the room. I took a 360. It's not very good. Rita will have a better one."

"You took Rita?" Oscar backed away.

"The second time."

"You went back?" Oscar stepped sideways, getting behind Klinsman's shoulder.

"I had to go cover the Luchadors with Rita. So then I took her back to the motel with me to get better pics." Klinsman opened his photos. The 360 of room 9, lit poorly with duskglow, grainy, moved across his screen. It paused on the blouse covering the TV, slowed over the bed. The tape pieces were difficult to discern. They looked like tiny blank squares in the screen, glitches in the display.

The light of the capture played across Oscar's face like pool reflections, his sad eyes lifted.

"See the tape pieces?" Klinsman pointed to the screen, fingered the surface. "We figured they were markers. Like stage markers. Or marks for a shoot."

"Or they could indicate blind spots," said Oscar. He touched the screen along with Klinsman. "Where they are seems darker. See? If you were filming or photographing this, you'd want to know those. Rita would've figured that. She didn't say that?"

Klinsman shook his head and watched the screen with Oscar. Their faces were now close, shoulders touching.

"How was she?" The breath of Oscar's last word brushed Klinsman's neck.

Klinsman felt a deep blush cascade through his entire body. Startled, he tried to think carefully about his next gesture, his next move, to quell any twitch for Oscar to read. He scratched his head.

"What do you mean?"

"How was she acting there? Was she acting funny? You know how she gets when she starts figuring things out ahead of you? I hate how she does that. I hate when she gets ahead of me. Gina says never let Rita get ahead of you. Then you'll always know you're at the front."

"No," said Klinsman, relieved. "She wasn't funny. I was hoping she'd be in now so we could see her pictures of the bed."

Oscar straightened and backed away a little. "You sure no one was there? No one real, I mean?"

"Yes. I was alone." Klinsman gazed over his shoulder at Oscar. "We were alone."

"Alone." Oscar put a hand on Klinsman's back and guided him into the chair, squared him in front of the screen. "Alone," he said again. "Let me show you something. But you have to close your eyes until I'm ready. For the full effect. Yes?"

Klinsman closed his eyes. He heard Oscar click once at the keyboard and twice with the mouse. Then Oscar moved to each desk, one after the other, performing the same quick action, one click at the keyboard, two with the mouse. It sounded like a mechanical waltz, fading then nearing as Oscar glided from station to station.

When he was done, he stood behind Klinsman and guided him into a standing position, turned him a bit. Still from behind, his breath on Klinsman's nape, he covered Klinsman's eyes with his fingers. Aaron imagined the fingers as clay, the slate-colored stuff dug warm from the riverbed.

"Now look." Oscar opened his fingers suddenly.

All the desk screens were on, clicked to their camera capture utility. Each one caught the empty room from a slightly different vantage point, but in ordered succession. It was like what you see when you hold a mirror to a mirror, an infinite telescoping of images. A few of the screens caught fragments and wholes of Oscar and Klinsman.

"Amazing," said Klinsman, swaying himself to make his image fold across some of the screens. "But so?"

"So we all sit here, all the time. On camera. Most of us don't even know we have cameras on our PCs. Little rectangular eyes." Oscar pinched his finger and thumb around an imaginary marble. "Staring."

"Only if we activate them," said Klinsman. "Like you just did."

Oscar shook his head. "I didn't activate the cameras. I only activated the screens, switched view options. The cameras are always on, Klinsman. Always, because they are really just lenses. Lenses with tiny filaments, nerves, taking in, sending out."

Oscar was obsessed with secret apertures, the detritus of abandoned lenses, cheap and random eyes left by amateurs and pros, voyeurs and snoops of all types, to catch what they could. He liked finding them while researching stories. He liked collecting the newest kinds at tech conventions he covered.

Klinsman scanned the desks. He noticed one screen still black, or maybe gone black.

"One isn't," he told Oscar.

Oscar's gaze followed Klinsman's to the blank screen.

"Number II," said Klinsman.

"Rita."

II.

W hat does it mean to call someone *salamandro*?" he asked Oscar as they watched the fifteen remaining screens, one at a time, go into squiggles and patterns of saver mode.

"I hear it sometimes around the campuses. State, UC. It's new. A *salamandro*'s a *mozo* spending too much time in their cave, under rocks, watching their screen. Turning white from it. Even if you're like me." Oscar rubbed his jaw, pushed his dark skin. "Why? Someone call you *salamandro*? One of the Luchadors last night?"

"No." Klinsman nodded to desk 11. "Rita used it. I think that's the word she used. Her Spanish is too fast. She was scolding a kid on the trolley. A guy watching her too much. Dressed strange. Like a waiter from the '50s. When I picture him, I see him in black and white."

"Rita used it?" Oscar lifted his chin, scowled a little. "How was she with the Luchadors?"

"Okay. Her usual good. Having people pose, then taking shots in between. The real ones. Mixing. You forget what she is, even with all that equipment hanging from her."

"Yeah," said Oscar. "But I mean was she different with any of the Luchadors? Was she keen on any of them?"

"Maybe," replied Klinsman. "One of them. I'm pretty sure it was Del Zamora."

"Zamora's not helping Culture Clash anymore."

"He was last night. I'm sure it was him, behind the mask."

"You're seeing things," said Oscar.

"I *am* seeing things. All the Luchadors seemed different."

"Different how?"

"Even more mixed into the crowd. More than usual." Klinsman pictured Santo thickly dancing with the club women. Remembered X-25 in her orange pantsuit, barely shaking her hips, scanning the room. "More *in*," he explained to Oscar. "*Blurred* in. Like they were sucking you into the screen with them. Almost."

Oscar looked intently at Klinsman, tasted something.

"Why?" asked Klinsman.

"Nothing."

Klinsman tilted, watched his image fragment across the screens. Then he looked back to Oscar.

"Your three. What are your three tags?"

"The clothes mountain out near Tecate. An old story like yours. Then the Juárez benefit up in La Brea. Again. But I did ask Gina for that one."

"And the third?"

"Gina didn't give me one. I'm waiting for the third shoe to

45

drop. It's put me on edge a little. About everything. Rita. You even. And with Gina being gone like this. Staying gone. What's she up to, you know? What's she up to?"

The desk screens began blinking into sleep mode, going blank in perfect order like dominoes.

They went outside to climb the landing, one floor above the late-morning traffic of El Cajon Boulevard. The T-shaped North Park sign spread its arms, looking quaint and somehow stunned by what had grown around it over the decades. Klinsman loved all such signs along the Boulevard, their grand arching, their neon script, the crumbling stucco of their bases, like fragments of aqueduct in ancient cities.

Oscar squinted at the sun over the eastern hills. An ocean breeze this far inland made the sky feel even more blue.

"It'll be even nicer in the borderland," he said.

"The strawberries are out." Klinsman visored his hand above his eyes, mildly watching the Boulevard, counting good car, bad car.

"But forget about the strawberries," said Oscar. "For once, Aaron. Forget about the strawberries and all the things you used to see and taste and smell down there. Go down there and try some things. One thing that always works for me. Get things wrong. When you talk to the clerk, get things wrong. People love to be right, love to correct."

"Any clerk at the Motel San Ysidro would be all over that, Oscar."

Oscar shook his head, bit his lower lip. "Even if that happens, keep going. If he's on to you, watched too many cop shows, then he'll slip into his role. Really. It's even better when you get them to slip into their role. Direct them. Milk them."

"Want to come along?" Klinsman asked.

"No. I got my old piece. That mountain of brand-new clothes, last year's lines, piled into an old airplane hangar. You buy Chanel and Prada and Gap and Kmart, all mixed together, by the pound. You go in like a miner." He exaggerated his accent on the brand names, making the last one seem the best prize.

Klinsman looked down at his own clothes, fingered a faux-pearl button on his Western shirt, thumbed the silhouette of a cowboy galloping past cactus across a sunset.

"Maybe I'll find something there for you," said Oscar. He put his hand on Klinsman's shoulder. "You do fine."

In the Motel San Ysidro parking lot workers were stacking mattresses from the rooms, tilting them together on end like giant books. They had taken nightstands and bureaus from most of the rooms and arranged them in stacks for hauling, fitting the cheap matching units together, snug as Lincoln Logs. It unnerved Klinsman to see the mattresses and furniture laid out that way in the morning sun, years of intimacy and secrecy, night stuff, whispers, mechanically exposed to the day. A man from a city truck was spray painting green and orange marks on the asphalt.

"What's going on?" Klinsman asked him.

The guy wore his yellow helmet at an absurd slant, embarrassed maybe. He kept looking down at his work, at the measure of his strokes. The paint hissed, then flicked, hissed, then flicked.

"Getting set for a teardown." He glanced at Klinsman—blue eyes under hard black brows, deep laugh lines that only made it seem he was done laughing forever—then he back-stepped to his next target on the asphalt.

Klinsman stepped with him. "Think I could check one of the rooms? I think I left something last night."

The guy shrugged and sprayed two lines, one green, one orange, deftly working the toggle switch on his paint torch. "Most of the doors are open. But if it was worth anything, you won't find it now."

Klinsman found the door to room 9 wide open, a yellow bar of sunlight across the colorless carpet. One of the movers resting on some stacked furniture briefly eyed Klinsman. Still wearing his clothes from the night before, his TJ Western shirt untucked and wrinkled, his hair dirty and mussed, Klinsman must have looked the part, a drifter wishing to retrieve his wallet, hoping desperately that woman hadn't stolen it, hadn't wanted him for that. Not just for that.

Inside, the room was gutted except for the bed frame and mattress. He could imagine the yank of the sheets from the skewed position of the mattress. The black tape piece from the fan's pull-chain lay on the carpet. Some of the other tape pieces, from door-knobs and curtain pulls, had fallen also. The bag of lightbulbs was gone, and so was the toothbrush.

I was alone. He crouched near the foot of the bed, looked carefully around the room. *We were alone.* Something was missing from the wall, near the light switch. On closer look he figured it was the thermostat, one of those old round dial types with the glass center. Its two thin sensors dangled from torn plaster, wires skinned and curled at the end. He checked the two rooms on either side of number 9 and found the thermostats still there. Three of the movers were now watching him.

Klinsman pretended to leave, went instead to the back, used a rain gutter and honeysuckle trellis to climb onto the roof of the motel. He was careful not to walk above the lobby, where the clerk might hear him as he made his way up the pitch to the top. He sat on the ridge beam, where he could think and breathe a little.

Who would take an old thermostat? He couldn't recall if it had been there last night but was pretty sure he'd have noticed if it wasn't, his eyes keened by the odd tape pieces and covered mirrors. Rita could have doubled back on her own to take it. Oscar could have hurried down in his truck this morning, ahead of Klinsman's trolley ride. Or the woman on the bed. She could have returned for it. Maybe nobody in particular had taken it. Maybe it had just been erased, vanishing as so much of this landscape had vanished, sometimes in sweeps, sometimes in bits.

He imagined himself a gargoyle on the ridge beam, crouching, familiar, knowing. The ocean breeze was stronger down here in the South Bay. A pond smell was heavy in the salt air, which meant the tide was in full ebb, sucking the Tijuana sloughs with it, walling the waves up high. Glimpses of the breakers' white blown-out tops feathered between the far beach houses and dunes. The bullring, marking where the Mexican beach began, looked like a flying saucer landed at the sea edge. Everyone described it this way.

The lowlands between him and the sea, where Aaron had once ridden his Stingray bicycle and played among the little ranches, farms, dairies, ponds, swamps, and graveyards, were now covered with dun-roofed houses and condos and licorice-colored streets and cul-de-sacs. The long slab of the Tijuana mesa rose sharply from the ocean, then ran east seemingly forever, split once by Smuggler's Gulch, immediately south of him. No one called it that anymore. They called it Goat Canyon. But no goats or smugglers ever passed through that split in the mesa these days. Only rancid black and chemical-yellow trickles from the *colonias* and maquiladores came through, finding their way to the riverbed.

In the motel parking lot below, the movers were hauling bed frames, snagging them together, metal clanging. The man from the city truck was still spraying his green and orange marks on the asphalt, occasionally eyeing the Mexicans.

From his satchel Klinsman withdrew his spiral notebook and jotted down his thoughts about the thermostat, put in a reminder to scan for it in the captures he and Rita had taken. Then he sketched a pull-chain and a doorknob, one pair with tape squares on their ends, one pair without. He darkened the tiny circles at the centers of the last two sketches, the pencil lead forming a reflective slick.

He fought against reverie, against indulging more in the views, sounds, smells, tastes of the past, against the strawberries for which Oscar had chided him. He noted the factory outlets built along the riverbed to the east, where some of the strawberry fields had been, asparagus fields, too, where on hot days he could lie within the green ferns, look at the blue sky, the black turkey buzzards circling, and listen to the stalks growing. So fast, yes, he could *hear* them sprout and stretch.

I could hear them, he wrote in pencil.

Klinsman climbed down from the roof, smoothed himself, and entered the small lobby, surprised to find the clerk manning the counter as though nothing were happening. He was a bony guy with dentures that were too big for his mouth and horn-rimmed glasses that seemed to crash down on his face, making him grimace and wince around his shiny incisors. He wore a polyester guayabera the color of soap. You could get the shirts for three bucks along the walk to Revolución, amid stands hawking tire-tread sandals and paintings of Elvis on velvet. It looked good on him, right and safe.

Klinsman told the man who he was, that he was doing a story. "On your motel. We think it's a landmark."

The clerk wrinkled his nose. Klinsman feared the heavy glasses would tumble from the old guy's face.

"You mean before the teardown?"

Klinsman rubbed the back of his neck as though he were tired, chewed imaginary gum.

"Yeah. Before that. When is that again? Exactly?"

"Three days. They're not supposed to be gutting the place yet. I'm supposed to be here running the place as usual. Right up to the end. But they asked if they could sneak in early, and I said to hell with it."

"No one's been checking in, huh?"

"Oh, yeah. Some yesterday even. But to hell with it."

"Room 8?"

"Three, 5, and 9. I like to space them out in case they want to make noise."

"Lonely men down from LA."

The clerk weighed and bounced his dentures with his lower jaw. His pale arms hung like sticks from the stiff sleeves of his guayabera. "No," he said, getting his teeth right. "And a woman."

"Yeah," said Klinsman. "Marta Ruiz in room 9."

The clerk leaned his head way back, trying to get Klinsman within range of his bifocals. He sneered his upper lip above his dentures, where it stuck.

"An old colonial like you, up from Guadalajara," guessed Klinsman. "Come to stay here one more time."

"Nah," he replied, his throat rattling, then clearing with the long sound. "A pretty Mex. Your age. Standing like you. Just like you."

Klinsman looked down at himself. "How am I standing?"

"Like someone who owns the place."

"A pretty Mexican? How pretty?"

"Very pretty. Like cactus pear. With dew on the needles."

Klinsman had to brace his boots apart. "But not named Marta Ruiz."

"Nahhh." He pushed his big glasses into place, where they balanced fleetingly before sliding down one notch. "Something else, I'm sure."

"Something prettier," said Klinsman. "Like cactus pear?"

"Yeahhh." He rattled it out long. "With red in it."

Klinsman rubbed the back of his neck again, bowed away from the old guy.

"Where'd you get that shirt?" the clerk asked as Klinsman turned to leave.

"Next to the place you got yours."

Klinsman started to push open the glass door, step into the sunny parking lot, where one of the workers was singing a Oaxacan lullaby, about a coatl who loved a mountain cat.

"You still have the scar?" the clerk asked from behind.

Klinsman turned, keeping the door ajar, letting in the lullaby, the part where the coatl gets rejected and vows to travel the world. He looked at the clerk, who was tilting his head way back again, getting Klinsman into focus.

"The snakebite," said the clerk, drawing out the last syllable in a kind of reenactment.

Klinsman pulled up his pant leg, hitching it above his boot edge so the clerk could maybe see the two red puncture scars along his shin, innocent as desert flowers.

12.

At the age of nine, in a paradise of sorts, Aaron Klinsman was asked to help hunt down a subspecies of *Crotalus lepidus*, a type of pit viper, what everyone on the ranch came to refer to as the big Mexican rattlesnake. His father, the only real doctor in the borderlands at that time, had gotten a special deal on some irrigation pipes from one of his patients on the Mexican side. The pipes arrived on a flatbed, where they waited unattended until the family had finished Saturday lunch. Rust and Baja powder had cast the pipes the color of sunburned flesh. They lay like giant straws, the ocean wind playing organ notes through the hollows as Aaron and his eight older brothers and sisters stood watching the winch hook find its way to the first pipe.

As the first pipe was tilted upward by the winch, a great shushing sound came forth. Instead of dirt or water or rust, what flew from the downward end of the pipe was a six-foot snake, striped in green, gray, and black, thick as a bread loaf. When the snake came free, it formed an S in the air, caught the afternoon sun in the silver ladder of its belly scales, and fell dead in the weeds by the reservoir. Its body whumped like a feedbag on the hard summer sedge.

Klinsman's sister Connie ran to the snake first. Quickly she was there, kneeling, petting its spade-shaped head, trying to quiet the angry glare in its eyes. Alejandro, the ranch hand who had shown them all how to shoe horses and lay pipe, arrived next to take gentle hold of little Connie's wrist and make sure the snake was as dead as it appeared. He flopped the upper jaw and nodded.

They all stood back a little at the raising of the next pipe. Again there came a sound, a similar hushing but much softer and slower. What came forth from this pipe amused the brothers and sisters but greatly concerned Dr. Klinsman and Alejandro. It seemed at first a snake, of similar length and color as the other. It too formed an S in the afternoon sun as it came free. But it floated on the air for a moment, flicked its tail in the breeze, rose a bit as though it were the ghost of the snake before. When it fell, it settled like a falling kite without a sound and lay delicately on the tips of the brittle summer grass.

Aaron was the first to this one, beating Connie by a step to stroke the translucent scales. It was the hollow skin of another snake, perfectly formed and intact, with a piece of the rattle caught on its tail end. It felt like something from the sea, cool and moist as kelp. He wanted to put his arm in it.

The snakeskin was carefully mounted on the wall of the barn attic. The Klinsmans had fashioned the barn's upper floor into a clubhouse, complete with pool table, dartboard, refrigerator, water spigot, and daybeds. The western window of the big A-frame had a spectacular view of the borderlands and the Pacific. You could see the sunset over the Coronado Islands. Most of the redwood barns of the borderland ranches had spaces like this, rustic dormers for hired hands, migrant workers. The Klinsman children considered themselves ranch hands, so this attic was theirs.

The four oldest brothers were named after the Book of Daniel. Dan, the oldest, organized and led the snake hunt. He used the snakeskin mounted on the wall as his point of reference, often stroking its scales with his fingertips as he instructed his brothers and sisters on the dangers of this particular subspecies of pit viper, its speed, its utter lack of hesitation, the intensity and complexity of its venom. He was already in college, premed, as all his younger siblings would be, until the last of the nine—Aaron—broke tradition.

During formal phases of the hunt, they were instructed to search in assigned pairs. The oldest in each pairing was to keep a half step in front while searching and also while overturning any object that could cover a possible hiding place. Aaron was paired with the youngest of the first set of brothers. Azariah believed everything was a game, or so it seemed to Aaron. Not yet in college, Az wore his hair in an unfashionable crew cut but got dates anyway. He liked Aaron because the little boy was always up for his elaborate games and designs—designs that often played out for days, weeks, or the length of a summer.

The set of four sisters, born in sequence after the set of four brothers, was named after the Immaculate Conception. Perhaps their mother, who had taken charge of all the naming, had hopes that these names, their stories, would somehow fortify her children. Mary, the oldest, used her name and her position as the middle child to claim a position as lieutenant in all family decisions and events. Thus, she stood second in command to Dan on the snake hunt. Mary would not touch the skin, though. She paired herself with Connie with the expressed purpose of keeping the littlest sister, not quite eleven, from running all about the ranch in hopes of catching the giant *Crotalus lepidus* first. Connie bounced on the daybed as Dan and Mary gave their instructions until Josephine calmed her by putting a pet rat into her hands.

Aaron, who was not named after the Book of Daniel or the Immaculate Conception or the story of Moses, stared fascinated at the snakeskin on the barn wall. He imagined it on his arm like a sleeve, watched the barn light glisten on the green, gray, and black scales, which were as large and inviting as nickels. Unattached to any set or book, he remained a free radical among his siblings, was not even assigned a room or bed, was left by his mother to find a nook and pillow each night in whatever room would take him. His father, for once claiming rights at his final child's birth, had named him on the day Hank Aaron had set the home run record.

As adults twenty years after the hunt, Jo and Liz, who eventually used their premed degrees from UC to become animal behaviorists, posted old 8-mm footage of six-year-old Connie wearing a bull snake around her neck as she walks the north fence line. Dappled light sifting through the eucalyptus adds flicker and grain to the silent footage, making it seem even older. Just as Klinsman warned his sisters, soon after they put the footage up on their sites and spaces, the clip quickly made its way around the web. How could it not? In the footage little Connie's image is ethereal as she walks calmly toward the camera, letting the snake coil around her, nosing her throat and shoulders.

The ranch hunt for *Crotalus lepidus* posed a great challenge for Dr. Klinsman. Only one of his children, the middle one, Mary, feared snakes. She was in fact the only one who was not fascinated by them—fascinated by all animals, really. So by having them organize the hunt, partake actively, Dr. Klinsman made the ranch safer. Except during formal hunting, no one was allowed to go off pavement unaccompanied. Awareness of the snake remained high.

A herpetologist from the zoo conducted a couple of fruitless searches. He told them the snake could live in this climate only for about two weeks, that the cool ocean nights and mornings would be the viper's undoing. He was very confident. Jo and Liz, already on their way, apparently, questioned him intently. Connie told him it could live forever. She pointed to the skin mounted on their clubhouse wall. The herpetologist seemed surprised at the skin's length, the nickel-sized scales. He went silent and left soon after that. "Good luck," he said to them.

Two chickens disappeared. The horses neighed most nights. But no traces were ever found, no signatures appeared in the sand and dust. During the summer months on the ranch, it was not unusual for foxes to come out of the dry riverbeds seeking food and water. Perhaps they had taken the chickens. And so, after three weeks, the formality of the hunt dissolved. All precautions were lifted.

The snake became a phantom, escaped from the skin of the physical world. For all except Alejandro, who continued to work the ranch armed with a staff he had fashioned from eucalyptus. It had a forked end.

The snake hunt became a game, especially for Az, who took his assigned partner, Aaron, with him on exaggerated expeditions stocked with stolen beer and hard rolls from Tijuana. On what was to be the last of these play hunts, Az and his little brother began near the house, just off the driveway, where Alejandro was repairing an irrigation stanchion. Their mother claimed she could see Alejandro and her two sons from the kitchen window.

They began at the doghouse, which was used not to house the ranch Labs but to store irrigation repair tools. Az, who even as an adult could not explain why he confused game with reality, suggested to Aaron that they raise one end of the doghouse, look under there. Alejandro, just off to the side, stood suddenly, just as Az and Aaron took their prescribed positions—older sibling to the fore, younger a half step back and to the side.

Az was laughing when he lifted the end of the doghouse, laughing at little Aaron's formal and sincere stance, still following the rules of the barn. Alejandro was moving toward them deliberately with his staff, speaking calmly in Spanish, a crease in his dark brow.

Aaron saw the snake first. It appeared unreal to him, an oversized and gaudy plaster sculpture of a Mexican pit viper, a thing from the movies. Its head was raised. Its rattle sounded. Aaron imagined the clacking of a projector, still not grasping what was immediately before him.

His older brother's move to save him was probably what caused the snake to strike. Az fearlessly tried to grab the viper by the neck. In what seemed to all of them like a blip in the daylight, a jump in the reel, the big Mexican rattlesnake struck, burying its fangs into the flesh around Aaron's shinbone. The pain slammed upward, hard through him like the bell of a carnival game.

He fell back into his brother's arms. The snake remained attached to his shin, stretching itself outward, unfurling its splendorous length. The rest of the scene for Aaron went silent as he seemed to lose his hearing to the upward rush of venom. Alejandro threw aside his staff and grabbed the snake by its fat tail. He waited a second for the snake to dislodge its fangs and go for its next strike.

The last image Aaron saw was Alejandro swinging the snake in a long and powerful arc swiping the summer sky. The centrifugal force stretched the viper to its full length. The gray, green, and black stripes looked like a breach in the sky, the tattooed knuckles of something great trying to push through. Aaron's vision went black with the thud of the snake's body slamming onto the summer hardpan.

13.

On her somewhat neglected site Concepcion Klinsman posted a video pan over the photograph of the Klinsman children holding the dead *Crotalus lepidus* that had struck their little brother. The children stand shoulder to shoulder, the snake lain across their outstretched arms. Missing from the photo are Dan, who felt too old to be in the picture, Mary, who took the photo and wasn't interested in handling the snake in any way, and Aaron, of course. The snake itself, still fresh and supple, appears to be lounging like something royal in the children's arms.

Az, his smile a grimace as he fails to hold back tears, balances the tail end and rattle, which hang like a shucked ear of corn from his hand. The other children smile easily as they stand barefoot in their summer shorts, taking up the middle length. Connie cradles the viper's anvil head, cooing a lullaby, it seems.

The photo was taken just before they handed the body over to the herpetologist from the zoo. It was Jo and Liz who decided on this, rejecting various plans to bury the snake, burn it, skin it, or eat it. The herpetologist rushed down from his lab as soon as he received the call, eager to study this durable and resourceful sub-species, a viper able to summer in the borderlands.

Twenty-six years later the neglected scan was picked up by several grandchildren, Connie's nieces and nephews fascinated by their rogue aunt who had gone to live deep in the Amazon to work in a dental clinic. From those posts, the scan and photo migrated across hundreds of sites. Klinsman often tried to find it through different kinds of searches, but it remained very easy to find if you simply searched "kids holding big snake."

Dr. Klinsman brought Aaron home from the emergency room, refusing orders to leave the stricken boy in the hospital for over-night observation. Dr. Klinsman was one of the last physicians to make house calls. He still carried a black house-call satchel. When opened, it smelled of leather, alcohol swabs, and crushed pills. You could close your eyes over the opened bag, imagine yourself healed.

He set his son up in the barn clubhouse, reclined him on a daybed, which he positioned so Aaron could gaze out over the bor-derlands and the Pacific. Dr. Klinsman expressed many arguments in favor of this decision. It would comfort the boy, let him believe he was out of danger in this space of revelry. The other kids could keep easy vigil during the day, shooting pool, throwing darts, lis-tening to records, letting the summer breeze in through the feed door. At night Aaron's mother and father took turns staying with the boy.

On only two occasions was he left alone. Soon after Aaron was propped up in the daybed, Alejandro and Dr. Klinsman whispered together at the bottom of the loft steps. Alejandro was telling the doctor what he knew about the snake. The venom coursing through Aaron, though it clutched speech from his throat, sharpened his hearing, his ability to hear and understand Spanish.

"It will not kill him," Alejandro softly told Dr. Klinsman, "but it will ruin his life. That's what they say about this snake. That's what has always been said about this snake."

The two men shuffled out the door. Aaron could hear the scuff of their boots over the barn floorboards, the crunch of their heels in the dirt. Unmoving but for his eyes, which also felt honed by the venom, Aaron gazed at the twilight sweep before him. The flattened lights of Nestor and Imperial Beach, the black ocean, the sky like dented steel.

"They say," he heard Alejandro whisper, "that he won't have his life. That he will have instead the snake's life. He'll shed his skin and then be ready to live some more. Yes?"

The gentle *yes*, Aaron knew, was Alejandro comforting Dr. Klinsman's tears, tears he never showed his son. Aaron lay stiffly, finding that any small movement created stringy tugs throughout his body, all centered on that constriction surrounding his swollen throat. He imagined himself a crumpled and tangled marionette, but with eyes that flicked and focused easily, painlessly.

Two movie drive-ins were in his view, the South Bay and the Big Sky. On summer nights the Klinsmans would bring popcorn and blankets out onto the barn roof and watch the movies, filling in the dialogue on their own, discussing what might be happening on the silent and distant screens. They had binoculars for the good parts. The South Bay Drive-in still stands and flourishes, perhaps the last of its kind in the entire country. The Big Sky was felled soon after Aaron's recovery, taking with it—it seemed to him—what was supposed to be his life.

What the little boy saw that evening on the two drive-in screens, which stood equidistant between the Klinsman ranch and the Pacific Ocean, was not the second-run movies that were supposed to be showing that night. What Aaron saw with his venom-sharpened eyes was the two lives that lay before him. On the Big Sky, on the right-hand edge of the window's view, ran the life he was sure he was supposed to live. There moved the adult Aaron Klinsman, a physician in a dark suit and tie, a stethoscope draped about his neck, his groomed hair parted neatly. A woman from the movie, played by Molly Ringwald, had somehow become his wife, older, in pearls and a skirt. They appeared to be discussing important things, like buying a car and having children. They held cocktails in stemmed glasses. This was who Aaron was meant to be.

On the South Bay screen, to his left, ran something that oddly terrified him, that would have made him scream if his throat were not constricted by venom. It was a simple close-up of how Aaron Klinsman knew he would look at the age of thirty-five. He appeared handsome enough, sincere in his gaze, a smile ready on one corner of his lips. What was terrifying to the little boy was knowing how correct this future version of him was.

The other time he was left unattended during his barn-room recovery still remains a point of contention within the family. Through his medical connections on both sides of the border, Dr.

Klinsman learned of another child Aaron's age who had survived a *Crotalus lepidus* strike. The plan was to have this little girl come to Aaron's bedside and show him that everything would be all right. The girl, Aracely Montiel, was in Aaron's third grade class at Mt. Carmel, had recently been transferred there. Aracely had been bitten in Jalisco, where the snake was indigenous. In fact the snake-bite, the Montiel family's realization that their daughter could go for a walk in their town and get bitten by such a monstrous pit viper, had been the primary reason for their move to the border-lands.

Everything about Aracely Montiel became vague and remained so for Aaron until he finally befriended her in seventh grade. But even then, and in the ensuing years of high school, only certain aspects of her became clear. Some say the visit was called off by the family when certain Montiels found out. Dr. Klinsman claims that it was neither confirmed nor canceled, that he had just put the word out hoping it would get to the Montiels' private physician. It was never even clear on which side of the border the family resided.

Most of Aaron's siblings claimed the visit was a venom dream. Dr. Klinsman agreed at first but years later was convinced by Aaron that the visit did actually occur. His mother insisted it was a dream, that nothing so remarkable in her son's recovery could have occurred without her absolute knowledge of it. Aaron knew it was not a dream. He had only one recurring dream during his recovery. It was stark and indelible.

The dream was always accompanied by the near sound of surf and the distant rattle of the snake. The image was the one Aaron actually saw when he was bitten. The viper's fangs were plunged into his shin, its angry glare exaggerated by the downward slant of its anvil brow. Its body seemed to trail back into the summer sky, splitting the blue, its tail almost infinitesimal as it probed back into the depths, hooking and rattling. And Aaron felt as though the sky, or something dug into from behind the sky, were being pumped into him.

14.

*E*ven after she befriended Aaron in seventh grade, Aracely Montiel never confirmed or denied the bedside visit. When he first reminded her of it, asked her about it in the school lunch yard, she said nothing. The next day she said she didn't know, maybe she had just dreamed it the night before, a dream induced by Aaron's question. Subsequent dreams on following nights, of her own snakebite and Aaron's, only served to bury her true memories. But Aaron knew it.

He lay in his sickbed, unable to sleep, the insomnia that would plague him for the rest of his life already set in at the age of nine. The final late showings of the South Bay and Big Sky drive-ins had flickered off, quiet flames blown out by ocean wind. The flat sweep of borderland lights seemed to shimmer beneath the air, like pebbles on the bottom of a clear stream.

Aracely rose step by step through the floor entrance to the loft. It pained Aaron to crane his neck to see who was coming. He was still hoping to receive a first visit from Az, to hold his hand.

Aracely's skinny little frame lifted quietly into the attic, almost too light to creak the sensitive floorboards. She wore her Mt. Carmel uniform, white blouse, green plaid skirt, and green knee socks. Her black hair was pixie-cut, bangs even as a comb over her brown forehead. Her dark eyes seemed amused. They always seemed amused, he would learn in their later friendship. At nine she had just gotten her real smile, a smart white challenge to everything she said, you said.

Her voice had an intermittent crease in it, an extra curl to the r-sound, sharpening all the words around it. Her English had no accent.

She stood at his bedside, looked him over, lifted her brow at the view he was afforded.

"I know you can't talk," she said. "I couldn't speak for a whole week."

Aaron moved his eyes, a kind of nod.

"And it hurts for you to move anything."

He felt tears welling, prayed against them, against the horror of letting a girl—a girl in his class—see him cry.

"Here," she said, "I'll show you something." She pressed her thumb gently into the soft crook of his elbow. Her touch felt cool and deep against his fever.

"It doesn't hurt here," she said. "Feels kind of good even. And it doesn't hurt here."

She moved her thumb to the hollow of his collarbone. From there the coolness of her touch seeped downward through him, a momentary current against the venom. She raised her foot to the edge of his bed, pushing her knee toward him. She carefully rolled her knee sock down her skinny brown shin and showed him the fang marks. They had become flowerlike scars, tiny rose tattoos.

"They'll itch for a month," she told him. "Go ahead and scratch, no matter what they tell you."

She tilted her head, kept her knee toward him. "Did they tell you?" She challenged her words with a smile, the first time for him. "Did that Mexican guy out there try to tell you? Tell you it won't kill you? But it will ruin your life?"

Aaron shifted his gaze slightly, a shimmering.

"That's what they say where I'm from," she said. "Where the snake's from. But you have to know Spanish to get it. You speak Spanish?"

Aaron looked down at her scars, then back to her eyes. She recited the saying in Spanish, the quirk in her voice gone without the English r-sound.

"See?" she asked. "They use the word *arrasar*. Which doesn't have to mean *ruin*. Like in English. My nurse told me. After she found me crying through my swollen throat. *Arrasara*. Almost my name. *Arrasara*. It will raze your life. You know what that means? You know what *raze* means?"

She pressed one cool thumb to the crook of his elbow and the other to the hollow of his collarbone. She smiled some more, her new teeth, her woman's teeth.

The last time Klinsman ran an image search for Aracely Montiel, a year ago, he found only one. It was a photograph of her with two other women at what looked like a fund-raiser. The women were dressed formally, with thin silver necklaces, looking like support-ive wives. Ara's hair was cut short again, the way he had first seen it but with the bangs swept back, matronly. Her smile was the same, too, unmistakable. The caption was brief, locating the event in Jalisco and not naming any of the women.

Except for Connie, Klinsman's sisters continue to argue that Ara's bedside visit had to have been a dream. That it occurred so late—after the drive-ins had finished!—served as one obvious clue. How would a nine-year-old girl from a family like that be allowed to do such a thing at such a late hour? And the uniform? This was Liz and Jo's favorite challenge to the reality of the visit. Even if she had somehow managed to be out after midnight, the idea that Aracely was still wearing her school uniform, the only way Aaron had ever seen her to that point, clearly indicated dream and fan-tasy. He had probably seen the fang marks on her shin in the schoolyard. Aracely was a fever dream, they told him.

She was your body healing itself.

15.

From Motel San Ysidro he traveled one trolley stop north. Pressed amid Mexican passengers heading toward noon jobs, Klinsman called up the billet on his notebook. The next assignment left for him by Gina, listed after the Luchadors and room 9, was for him to do that story on park surveillance. This puzzled him, even after speaking with Oscar. The story *was* old. The *Review* had run a number of pieces on the various impacts of public security cameras, one story by him, others by better street reporters. London had its Ring of Steel, and New York was unveiling its own version. Several movies and novels had already saturated media with the subject, had shown how frightening it was that the average American was recorded two hundred times per day. No one seemed frightened.

Heading into the morning in Amsterdam, you could stroll past a sidewalk projection and wave to pedestrians in Tokyo, heading into the night, waving back just the same. You could get to know someone that way, someone on the other side of the world, passing by her life-sized image every day, maybe develop a crush, exchange a look, tip hats.

Maybe he was supposed to put some cultural spin on the subject, to make it into something that might be viewed as art. To consider the possibility that the city was inadvertently composing a true portrait of itself with its myriad devices for self-surveillance, with its cameras above freeways and traffic lights to catch speeders and red-light runners, with its sonar and visual sensors gridded about the borderlands to monitor illegal immigrants and smugglers, with virtually every public space and every place of economic exchange under a collection of online eyes.

But even that angle felt tried. Perhaps for his finale Gina wanted him to give what she called "that special Klinsman twist" to the entire landscape of his work for the *Review*. This was to be his summation, his farewell to covering the eccentricities of his homeland. There was no way to confirm this. Gina was gone, not there for anyone, it seemed.

He looked over the passengers, tried to see between those who had to stand in the overstuffed car. His shoulders were pressed by commuters on the seats next to him. His wrists were forced into angles above the keyboard, his fingers brushing the keys. He spotted the security eye atop the front bulkhead of the car, the lens as nonchalant as an eight ball. Someone had drawn a bit of graffiti beneath it, a black-marker rendition of a blunt-tailed reptile nosing the dark glass.

He looked for one of Rita's *salamandros*, some paling Latino youth oddly dressed, someone briefly out of his cave. But everyone he could see was dressed for work, their eyes glazed with the inevitability of it, the breadth of it. They could see the ocean.

He got off the trolley at the Iris Street station and walked to Silver Wing Park. The giant metal wing was propped on end, reaching high enough from its hilltop perch to require an aviation light on its tip. Klinsman sat in its shadow, beside the stone monument commemorating Montgomery's first fixed-wing flights in 1884. The Otay mesa slope the aviator had used was now this park, a wide sweep of lawn that blended into Little League and soccer fields. Klinsman noted one camera mounted on the bottom of the wing, two above the basketball courts atop the slope, three above the distant parking lot on the far end of the park. The cameras looked like storks, poised and waiting for prey above shallow water.

With his notebook he activated interface software from Viper Lab, a variation on VideoJak and UCsniff. It was an update on the program Oscar had given him the first time he had covered park surveillance. Oscar had gotten the information while covering the Defcon conference in Vegas. "The software's there for us. For you. For free," he told Klinsman, trying to get him to go deeper on the park story. "A kid can do it. Actually, kids are the ones doing it, most times."

The main difference between him and Oscar had something to do with faith. Klinsman had faith in technology, a blind faith, like most people. Oscar didn't; he needed to know how things work, so maybe he could rework them, or make them work better for his purposes. But Oscar had an odd faith in people, some people, those few who could follow their own unique imaginations. Those few open to the ideas and imaginings of others but able to stay true to their own visions and creations. The journalist in El Paso who kept vigil on Juárez. Gina, with her gift for leading and then letting go. Rita, whom Oscar almost feared because he had so much faith in her aim, her art. And Klinsman, for no reason other than his befuddled, bejumbled, insomniac view of this city, what it had been and what it had become.

Beneath the loom of the wing monument, Klinsman jacked his way into the security feeds and brought up an image from one of the far parking lots. Except for the playground, which was alive with toddlers and moms and *nanas*, the park was empty because school was in session and the neighborhood was at work. On his screen Klinsman could see his own tiny self on the hilltop opposite the parking-lot camera, a hunched silhouette against the blue sky, a man about to be crushed by the silver wing tilting over him.

He clicked around for another view, not knowing which camera corresponded to which number. His image leapt forth, caught, it appeared, by the camera fastened beneath the wing. He saw a man with disheveled hair, an unshaven jaw creased by lack of sleep, dressed in a Western shirt from Tijuana not tucked in. If it weren't for the laptop glinting in the sun, he could have been taken for a noontime park regular, concerned as a toad.

He walked the mile north to the next park. This one was a sloped rectangle of grass surrounded by a sea of sand-colored rooftops, treeless housing tracts. This one had no name but was commonly known as Ranch Park, after the ranch that lay beneath it, the Klinsman ranch. On the courts men on lunch break were playing Mexican basketball, nine-on-nine, everybody in. Their calls were sparks of sound in the ocean air, seagulls hailing one another.

Klinsman noted two cameras above the courts, two more perched atop seedling light posts. This park was newer than Silver Wing, and its cameras were smaller, sleeker, little black domes looking like forgotten thermos caps.

He sat on a stone picnic bench and clicked into the cameras. He called up the basketball courts, watched the games, the ball swimming over a mosh pit of dark arms and heads. He clicked around, searching for the view holding himself. Except for the basketball game, the park was empty and still. Finally he reached the camera aimed at his bench.

He wasn't there.

16.

It was like looking into a mirror and seeing everything but himself. Klinsman felt this sensation as an upward rush through his nerves, like that hot push of venom. At first he sensed himself erased, then somehow sucked underneath—to the place this park used to be, to the time when he ran the fields, racing his youth, his brothers and sisters. This spot, this stone bench, marked where they used to have tomato fights after the last harvest, ducking and firing among the endless rows, soaked and smelling sweet with rot. The gull-like cries from the men playing Mexican Nines only enhanced that feeling, echoes draping him.

Not far from his bench, work had been done on a sprinkler. A worker had peeled back the turf and neatly piled a small amount of excess dirt to be removed later. Klinsman fetched a clump from the pile and brought it back to the table. He sat and eyed the clod as you would a precious gem. The dirt just beneath the topsoil of the ranch was this hard red composite, a little brighter than brick, a little duller than blood. When Viking sent pictures of the Martian landscape back to Earth, Connie said the rocks looked just like the clods she liked to throw at him right after the deep fall plowing. Klinsman placed the red clump carefully beside his laptop. The online feed still showed him disappeared.

He straightened his shoulders, looked away from the screen and into the blue above the far ocean, blinked, sought reason. The screen remained the same when he looked back, this stone table and bench empty, its shadows cast the same way on the grass, the same sprinkler cap to the side, the same dandelions quivering in the sea breeze. He waved his arms, trying to make himself appear. He clicked around to the other cameras, found the game of Mexican Nines. He clicked his way back to the near camera and still found himself gone.

Now a coldness slithered in him. He wanted to call Rita. He wanted to call Oscar. He wanted to call his brother Azariah. Or even Connie, so far away. He lifted his cell and crooked his thumb.

A shadow fell over him, paused him.

A young man stood above him, close enough to shield the noon sun.

"Don't do that," he said with a slight Latino accent, not enough force on his T's. "You lose connection."

Klinsman placed the cell down gently beside the laptop, maintaining connection. On the screen the man, like Klinsman, did not appear. This made him feel a little better.

He looked the young man over, angling off the overhead sun to get a better close-up. He was far too skinny for the dark suit coat he wore. The coat had stylized shoulders, razor sharp at the corners, sliding. His black hair was mussed and barely shifted in the breeze, and his lips hung slightly parted, as though he had allergies. He wore thick-rimmed glasses, chef's pants, and mismatched shoes, one brown loafer, one black wingtip. He had a newly sprung mushroom color and smell about him.

"Could I?" He nodded to Klinsman's laptop, open to the sky on the stone table.

Klinsman offered with his hand, and the youth hunched eagerly toward the screen. His hands were long and thin and moved like dragonflies over the keyboard. His touch was very light, making almost no sound, the burble of a little stream.

The game of Mexican Nines came up onscreen. One more flit and burble over the keys and the players disappeared, the courts empty but for the shadows of backboards and hoops.

Klinsman scrunched his brow.

"It's just yesterday's feed," said the young man, adjusting his glasses. "*Mixto.* Mixed in." His throat was the color of the inside of a seashell.

Klinsman's brow remained furrowed. "But the passive feeds . . . you can't get the old feeds."

The young man looked at him, then at the game of Mexican Nines, then at the empty courts on screen.

"But *you* can," said Klinsman.

The youth shook his head. "No. Not me."

Klinsman looked him over again, starting with the mismatched shoes, ending with the pointed shoulders of his jacket. Klinsman switched to Spanish, ending with the plural "you." "*Tú, no. Pero ustedes, sí.*"

The young man gazed steadily at Klinsman, breathed gently through his lips.

"You *nombre?*" asked Klinsman.

"Douglas," the young man replied. "Douglas Cook. We want you to leave us out of your story."

"What story?"

"The third one on your list. Your last story."

"How do you know my list?" Klinsman stood, keeping one knee on the bench, a hand over the keyboard. The *mozo*'s eyes were very dark, very steady.

"How I know where to find you?" The young man opened his thin hand, like spun sugar. "Like this? Right here, *ahorita?*"

"Who is 'we'?" Klinsman looked around, at the sky, at the empty grass of the park where the barn used to stand.

The young man smiled, an almost flat spread of his lips, amused at the very ends. "That would put us into your story."

"I won't put you in." Klinsman gazed steadily at him. "As you will see. I don't even want to write the story. I'll make one up. Like I always do."

Klinsman held his fingers above the red dirt clod. "See? For me, it's more about this. What's underneath. That's what I'll write about."

The young man picked up the clump and held it to the sun-light. Then he slipped it into the pocket of his coat, nodded once, and turned to leave, hunched, hands slung into pockets.

"But what could you do if I did?" Klinsman asked. "If I did put you into the story?"

Douglas Cook, a trembling compass needle, spun toward the laptop. His fingers flashed over the keys, thumb stinging once at the end. The image of their park bench returned to the screen. In this one the young man appeared, in the same coat but with his mismatched shoes reversed. Klinsman was not there.

17.

*K*linsman walked north along the park's length to another stone picnic table that marked the spot where he had been bitten by *Crotalus lepidus*. The scar on his shin did not throb, the way Rita had said it should when he'd first brought her to this spot. She had made spooky motions with her fingers beside her ears, her wild black hair adding to the effect. He felt nothing as he sat on the tabletop, boots to the bench. He was numb but shivering like something in bad reception.

He thought of the border legends all the kids used to talk about in the schoolyard. The ones they used to scare themselves. The ones parents used to warn their daughters. Owls, goats, pigs, cows, half-human, unnamable creatures who haunted the border. The cloven-hoofed man who danced with you, seduced you, took your soul. Connie knew all the legends, taught them to her little brother. Rita knew them, had shared her versions with Klinsman.

He left a message for Rita, then one for Oscar. He tried calling Gina.

The thinnest twirl of sea mist hung in the blue sky. He could still smell the ebb tide, the sloughs being sucked into saltwater, breathe it in slow, full intakes. The clack of the trolley sounded too near as it echoed off the Tijuana mesa, a sharp metal sound over the hum of I-5. The sweep of rooftops surrounding the park seemed long dead, an ocean of fallen leaves.

He struggled to stay in the moment, tried to shake his head clear. On his laptop, which he balanced on his knees, he clicked around the park feeds until he found the one aimed over the sidewalk Douglas Cook had taken, running along the southern edge, heading east into a housing tract. The *mozo*'s figure, a tall splinter of shadow, moved down the very center of the sidewalk, listing slightly—with thought, with worry, with plans. At the first corner, still just visible, it turned north and disappeared into the neighborhood.

Klinsman began writing his fake story, the one about how surveillance technology was forming the city's self-portrait. Gina had taught him to begin stories on location, to get at least a little down.

But on his battered spiral notepad he wrote about Douglas Cook and the game of Mexican Nines. And about how he was shaking and how that shaking made his scribbling even more illegible. He sketched Lechuza, the giant owl who sucked the toes of infants, then the wild boar that once haunted the asparagus and artichoke fields, then a goat skull, then a cow skull. And he sketched the whorls on the bedcover of room 9, letting them swim more on the page, rise through the lines.

––––––––

Not long after Aaron had recovered from the snakebite, Uncle Mir had come for one of his extended stays on the ranch. At the end of that stay, Uncle Mir had killed a man. Only Aaron understood this.

Aaron's father, though he was a physician, believed a ranch should be worked. The family farmed tomatoes in the lower field, keeping the ranch alive and bringing in some needed income. They needed workers to do it well and so hired migrants like everyone else. Alejandro served as foreman, using his experience to make the crop extremely high and good. When Aaron was too little to help haul the irrigation pipes into place among the endless rows, he would ride the swing and watch the workers move among the vines with his older brothers and sisters. The most mesmerizing form of labor was the dusting of the vines.

The workers—expert migrants only—would don gray protective suits and helmets and strap the crankdusters to their backs. They looked like deep-sea divers walking in slow motion through the vines, the white dust trailing behind them as though caught in a current.

If you farmed in the borderlands back then, you brokered everything, including people, through a man called Julián Cabeza de Baca. Dr. Klinsman called him the Necessary Evil. But his brother Jaromir called C de Baca more than that. Uncle Mir often stayed for entire seasons, traversing from the ranch to his room in Tijuana's Hotel Cesar, where he insisted he could lie low but readily visit the States. Dr. Klinsman seemed to take him seriously, but Mrs. Klinsman did little more than humor her brother-in-law.

C de Baca's full worth became known only after his death, when all of his holdings, on both sides of the border, had to be divided up. "He could have bought the city," Dr. Klinsman declared when the number made the papers.

Once Aracely told him about C de Baca. They were still in seventh grade at Mt. Carmel, still dressing in uniforms. She called him on the phone after school from her aunt's, and, as they always did, they met at the back fence of the ranch, in the distant corner beneath the shade of a single, cloud-shaped eucalyptus. A picked-over tomato crop was rotting on the vines, the smell lying thick and low under the sea breeze. The story of C de Baca was still being spun across the borderlands, a lunchtime favorite in all the school-yards and halls.

"You know those stories you hear about the devil in TJ? The ones where the young woman dances in the most popular club, with the best-dressed man, and then looks down, after it is too late, to see his cloven hooves? They're about Cabeza de Baca, I know. I saw him there, all dressed in black silks and fancy boots, choosing young girls to dance with. The people who watch over me in those clubs made me stay away. They said he uses the girls later to take care of his anger, his desire, or his hunger. Sometimes all three, hunger last."

"But he died," Aaron told her. "I watched him die."

"They say he is a twin, that he has a brother who stays on the Mexican side while he stays on this side. They never die. But they also say there is only him, that he can be two at once—this side, that side. Do you believe that, Aaron?"

In Spanish she could make it seem like the past was the present, or that there really was no difference.

On this side you wouldn't have known C de Baca was worth so much unless you knew him. He dressed like a painter, looked starved, in baggy linen pants and tire-tread sandals from Boulevard Revolución. In winter he wore potato-sack shirts with the packing-company logos still on them. In summer he wore soccer t-shirts, like many of the migrants he brokered. He smoked all the time and loved to work on trucks. He'd spend hours beneath a truck—any truck he could find, sometimes on the Klinsman ranch. His skinny ankles and sandaled bony feet would lie still, as though he were sleeping beneath the warmth of the engine. But you could hear the soft clunk of his tools, and the cigarette smoke would trail its way through the angles and wires of the motor. Dr. Klinsman couldn't keep him off the ranch, not when his workers and his irrigation pipes were out there. And not without consequence.

But Uncle Mir banned C de Baca from the kids, especially from Aaron and Connie. After Aaron survived the snakebite, Mir grew even more protective of the youngest two. And he managed to make them the best archers among the nine children.

Once, while they fired arrows at straw targets, he told them about C de Baca. "He, men like him—and they are always men—command the world with what they can provide. They don't live inside it but swirl like buzzards above it, dipping in when they want. *Want*," he said, angrily releasing an arrow. "That is what they do. Want."

Standing tall above them, he drew another arrow from his quiver, his loose hair tumbling about his eyes. He considered the shaft's trueness, wondered about his next words to his niece and nephew.

"After they get what they want, they eat it."

He quickly drew the bow, took aim. "But sometimes there are others—much more like him than they can sometimes stomach. These are men and women who also dip like birds into this same world. They sometimes can do things to stop the buzzards." He let fly the arrow but did not watch it strike the center of the target, did not watch it shudder with perfection.

When Chavez and the Tortilla Priest came through to talk to the workers and serve them mass, C de Baca's trucks would show up right before Communion, and the men and women would rush from the gathering, racing to the flatbeds that promised work. Worse, he practiced an old trick, an evil trick that everyone knows. He called *la migra* after the work was done but before the wages were paid. He didn't need the money. He just did it. He ate the juiciest tomato afterward, while watching the holding vans roll away. He let the juice and seeds spill down his chin.

Once he pulled that stunt on the Klinsman ranch. He knew it resulted in painful separations, crushed dreams, ruined lives. He relished the fact that it resulted in death even, and would have watched that death if he could. He ate his tomato and watched Jaromir this time, not the holding vans. But everyone could see that C de Baca's call had been aimed at Jaromir.

When he found out *la migra* had been called, Aaron's father offered to pay all the wages. "I will see you burn in hell," he said, jabbing his finger into C de Baca's birdlike chest.

The flat look delivered by C de Baca was a death sentence, not for the doctor but for one of his children, most likely Connie. At least that was what Mir told Aaron, many years later, when he asked his uncle about it. When Klinsman, the young journalist, accused him of what happened next.

True to his nature, C de Baca showed up on the ranch the next day while a new batch of migrants added more strings to the vines, the crop so plentiful. He lay beneath one of the flatbeds, softly clunking his tools in the warm shade of the engine. The cigarette smoke curled its way up through the metal channels. C de Baca's sandaled feet wiggled proudly a little this time, waving, it seemed, to anyone who passed.

As an adult, as a journalist, Aaron Klinsman couldn't convince himself that a man like C de Baca, a mechanic of such expertise who could casually smoke beneath a motor, would make such a foolish mistake. They said it was a fuel line that came loose and doused him with the fires of hell.

The flames blew out from beneath the flatbed with a thudding boom in the summer air. The smell of cooked flesh swept along the front edge of the firewind that rocked Connie and Aaron. They were standing at a safe distance with Alejandro, who had taken them just to that spot, just at that moment. Jaromir was on a flight back to Prague.

Everyone on the ranch, even the workers out among the most distant vines, heard the screams. The drawn-out, dying screams of a desert raptor. The tire treads of C de Baca's sandals burned with a red flame, pouring two parallel lines of black smoke straight up into a pale sky.

Still sitting on the park table, Klinsman set aside his battered notebook and returned to the laptop. If Douglas Cook and his *ustedes* were checking—him, his stories—then he wanted to make sure they saw what real journalists could do. He called up Oscar's home page, let them see how insignificant his own stories were.

In her vigil on Juárez, the El Paso journalist writes about men like C de Baca, how they harvest innocent girls who must make the dark commute to the maquiladores on the city's desert outskirts. But she doesn't write of legends or walk through dreams or fashion the crimes into distant metaphor. She names her suspects and walks the dangerous night streets and rides the midnight buses that take the girls to their terrible fate. She goes to the shallow graves in the sand, sees the bite marks on the flesh, the triangles branded on the necks. She writes of the lives of the girls, too, the ones they lived while working for their families and the ones they might have lived.

18.

After leaving the park Klinsman returned to the *Review* and waited for Rita. Someone had eaten all the strawberries and bread from the coffee table, but the place was still empty, all sixteen screens black.

On screen he quickly rechecked his 360 of room 9, looking for the thermostat. The wall was mottled and smeary with the neon evening glow, shadows and bright spots pulsing. But he could see the round metallic form of the thermostat there beside the light switch, that familiar shape, easily overlooked. It remained familiar because it did not have a square of black tape stuck to it. It was just plain, forgotten. But it was there.

Klinsman tried to catch a nap on the couch but fell instead into a furtive set of half sleeps filled with fusion dreams of Douglas Cook helping John J. Montgomery with his fixed-wing glider, helping him run it down the green slope of the Otay mesa, into the ocean wind that carried Klinsman above the wild borderlands. Each lifting woke him.

He heard someone come and go, a polite coworker who knew of his struggles with sleep. The steps were tiptoe light, the rustling of papers apologetic, the clicks of a pen as distant as stars.

Rita Valdez awakened him with a light kiss on his forehead. Without opening his eyes, without surfacing completely, he could sense her, the sound of her breath, the little hmm after her kiss. The scent and warmth of an ironed shirt.

"Sorry," she whispered. She touched her forehead to his, her eyelashes brushing his cheekbone. "You were finally sleeping. Dreaming. But I don't have much time. I have to get out to Oscar and take pictures. So." She kissed his forehead again, maybe sensing he was slipping back to his dreams.

Eyes still closed, he dreamed a kind of thought, a black climb toward all the bright images disappeared by her lips. He always wanted something from those dreams, felt he needed their forgiveness.

She took him to her place. Only minutes away, her house was in the Heights, a fragment near downtown that used to be a rough part of the city, wasn't anymore but would soon be again. Neighbors still kept the old barbed wire up. Rita's aunt had left her the place, a little redwood Victorian scrunched in with others like it, with scalloped walls and sagging ridge beams and brick chimneys like crooked fingers. Inside, it was the same as Tia Coco had left it, with green-striped wallpaper and oval rugs, wainscoting and floor-boards almost black with age, crucifixes with holy-water cups. Rita kept change, keys, chocolate, and paper clips in these cups, which were in every room and along the dark, narrow stairwell. All the curtains were heavy with dust. If pushed aside, the curtains released dust motes like spent magic into the sun shafts. "I like them like that," Rita would explain if she caught anyone staring.

She led him up to her studio, the only room in the house with any upgrade, the only one she seemed to live in. It had a small bed and fridge. The walls were new and white and speckled with push-pins, and the windows had electronic blinds she could adjust with a remote.

Afternoon light slanted through the blinds, striping the bare wood floor, Rita, too, as she stood hands on hips, sizing him up. Then she framed him with a squaring of her thumbs and fore-fingers while he sat on the edge of the daybed. Her hips were cocked, and one heavy parenthesis had come loose from the gathering of her hair, the light like water in the long black curls. Disdain heavied her eyes.

"What's wrong, Aaron? Why are you over there? Why aren't you standing with me in this wonderful light? Why did you ride in my car all tucked into the corner like you were getting dropped off at school?"

"Nothing. Nothing's wrong. I'm just not sleeping."

She ignored this, adjusted the frame of her fingers. "You need me to leave? Right now instead of next week? Will this be too much for you? These days we have left to face each other?"

"No," he replied. "They won't be enough."

She gauged the truth of this with a slide of her frame. She stepped closer, stripes scrolling over her.

"Did you go back?" he asked, stopping her. "Without me. Did you go back to the motel room?"

Still looking through the frame of her fingers, she squinted at him. He thought she would get angry, but the question appeared to intrigue her instead, maybe even impress her.

"Why would I do that?"

"To go there alone. Without my weight. See what there was to see without me in the way. Take your own shots. Like you do. Like Oscar says you do."

She shook her head, then sharpened her look. "Did *you* go back? Alone. Without me?"

"Yes. But it is my story."

"You and Oscar," she said, dropping her hands, her arms stirring the blind shadows. "Your stories are my stories. No?"

"Did Oscar go there? This morning?"

She lifted her brow. "You told him about it?"

He shifted on the edge of the daybed.

She didn't step back, but she seemed to retreat into the lines of shadow and light, to collapse away from him. "About all of it? Us?"

"No. Not that. Just the room, the figure on the bed, the tape and everything. I showed him the 360 I took."

She angled her hips more, one boot aimed to the side, toward the window light. Maybe some anger rose somewhere in her. It was always hard to tell, her features so readily drawn to it. "Why would you think I knew about Oscar? About him going back there?"

"I met one of your *salamandros* today," he told her. "They watch us." He looked over at her computers, the huge screen of her main and the laptop opened beside it like a child. A shaving mirror stood propped to the side, a small pewter-looking thing with a baroque frame, something to undermine the technology. "They watch us with our own cameras. You know this."

"Of course I know this. I'm always catching them stealing my pictures."

"They know you," he said. "And they know me. How come they know me?"

"Of course they know you," she said. "You did that story."

"Why didn't you tell me?"

"*Tell* you." She widened her stance, hands to hips again. Another parenthesis shook loose from her hair. "Tell you what? That there are a bunch of *mozitos* in this city holed up in their basements spending their days and nights watching other people live?"

"Your camera's off. The eye on your computer. At work. Oscar turned them all on for me. Number 11 stayed blank."

"You and Oscar stay the fuck away from my desk."

They remained still, he on the edge of the daybed, she standing in stripes of light. In some way, a stack of mirrors, she appeared myriad. He felt as though she were coming at him, her look pencil sharp, her lips flushed, the aftermath of her words a hot-wire scent in the air. But she stood motionless. She stood so motionless she could evaporate into slices of light and shadow. He would be left reaching.

Rita fastened her photographs to the wall, shoving the pushpins forcefully into the corners of the prints she had made for him. She stood on tiptoe in her boots to get the pictures up high, to leave room underneath for something tall. Even from across the studio, he could see how much better her shots were than his. The three slanted rectangles hung clear as windows into another room. They were shots of him sitting at the bar with Blue Demon, taken from behind when Klinsman was unaware. Even from a distance he could see how she had angled her lens so that the bar mirror let the viewer see both sides of the men.

He hurried across the room to them. She looked over her shoulder at his approach, drew a sudden breath as if he had surprised her, as if she had forgotten he was back there watching her angrily push her pins. She drove a pin into a corner of the fourth picture, the shot of him and Blue Demon sitting at the bar facing the camera, posing together. The pictures almost dizzied Klinsman, made him wonder if he had been in a Luchador movie, Blue's sidekick against Santo. Rita stabbed a pushpin into the heart of the final picture, reaching on tiptoe. He wanted to put his hands to the exposed impression of her spine, burn his fingers there.

"Oh, fuck it," she said. "Screw you and Oscar for messing with my desk. *Chingaderos*. I was going to lay these out nice for you to see. To see my good work for you. But now—fuck it."

He stepped gently to her, hands to the backs of her shoulders, thumbs pressing lightly. She leaned her forehead to the wall and curled back to him a little. She put her hands to the wall, just below her chin, fingering the plaster. The photos above them rattled as he spun her to face him.

He put his lips to hers, soft and open, not pressing. And he spread his arms out over the wall, feeling the coolness with his palms. He held himself that way, a veil containing her against the plasterboard. So when she moved she squirmed against him. She slid her kiss to the bend beneath his lips, then to his chin, his throat, his neck. Her elbows and breasts, knees and thighs moved along him as he kept her gently webbed against the wall, something turning in chrysalis.

She tapped her forehead twice against his collarbone and then whispered into his shirt, her breath passing through to his skin, like a fold in his heartbeat.

"I don't have time for this. Any of this."

He eased away.

"I have to get out to Oscar," she said. "Before the place closes. Before my light is gone."

"I'll ride with you."

"Oscar said not to bring you."

"Bring me anyway."

"Maybe," she replied. "But let me show you something. Why we came here."

She pushed him aside, taking him by the shoulders to clear him away from the wall space. Then she unrolled a poster-sized photograph, taller than herself, and pinned it neatly beneath the arc of other pictures. It was a blow-up of the imprint of the woman in room 9. Rita had deepened the contrast. The satin cover appeared liquid, melted and silvery. The folds and indentations deepened.

The soft peaks of the curving lines looked suddenly abandoned, licked upward, releasing, already pleading for return.

Klinsman back-stepped away from the life-sized portrait. The farther back he went, the more he could discern the swimming form of the woman, some sea creature lurking and swaying beneath Blue Demon.

"My gift to you," said Rita. "Come with me or stay with her."

19.

He rode with her, like one of her bags thrown in against the door. She drove fast on the 94 East, trying to make up time lost messing around with him. But her fingers touched the wheel delicately, and it was a good time of day to head into the desert hills, with the sun at their backs, its late-afternoon slant deepening the scrub and rocks in front of them, sharpening their horizon, blueing it just above the most distant mountains.

Her scent filled the car, a metallic friction, the smell of guitar strings. He peeked at her in moments, turning a blank gaze back to the pale landscape whenever she caught him.

"You always have people drive you," she said, watching the road, "so you can look at them. I don't care for it."

He didn't reply. He eyed parts of her, where he imagined the coppery air of her. The inside of her arm pressing against the side of her breast as she eased the wheel. The crisscross of her shoulder straps, the bra green, the blouse black, her brown shoulders round and confident. If he could have brought himself to reach across and touch her, if she would let him, he would lightly brush two fingers along her nape, just below the great lift of her hair, where he might trigger its fall.

"I'm trying to figure how far ahead you are," he said.

"Way far ahead."

"I think it was you," he told her. For courage, he stared at the desert hills along the border. "On the bed."

"It certainly was me."

"I mean before that."

"Before that?" She gripped the wheel, knuckles paling. "You sit there, with me right here beside you." With her free hand she pulled her blouse top down and away. "In the flesh. And you think of *that*. The wrinkles left by a woman on the bed before us?"

She adjusted her blouse and bra, switching hands on the wheel. She blew at some black coils tumbling free as loose thoughts above her eyes. "Didn't we erase her, Aaron? Didn't that do it for you?"

He put his head to the window. The desert hills were flattening to the south. The train tracks here resurfaced from below the border, coming out of a small mountain tunnel to curl into the scrub and sand and rocks. Everything out there was still, a diorama, where one might expect a stuffed and marble-eyed coyote.

"Still," he said, "if it wasn't you, then who was it? What do you think happened?" He hoped that by superimposing her on the bed in room 9—on the bed before they had used it—he could let her see that she was part of his need to know.

She hit the brakes suddenly, hurtling him forward, and swerved her car into the sandy shoulder. They skidded to a halt, tires coughing, and from behind their dust cloud swept over them, shrouding them in a brown veil, in a gauzy light. Rita undid her seatbelt, released it with a whipping sound, and got up swiftly on her knees. She clambered to him, over him, put a knee into his belly and grasped his chin. Her grip crushed his cheeks to his teeth as she shook his head. Her breath poured over his face, and her hair came loose from its clasp, bouncing heavily against his neck, catching him in tendrils.

"Nothing happened," her breasts heaved against his throat as she maintained her grip on his chin. "Until *we* happened. Yeah, something clearly was supposed to happen there. But it didn't. It was abandoned. Only marks left. Yes?"

With her grip she shook his head once more time, then put her hands to his shoulders, all her weight in his lap, her knees hurting his ribs. She dug a boot tip beneath his groin, just threatening.

"I hold my face to yours," she said, her breath in his eyes. "My eyes to yours. *Como este.* A tongue-reach away." She put the tip of her tongue briefly into the dent above his lip. "And tell you this: I don't know what was supposed to happen in room 9. What did happen, I loved.

"I know what you know. If you would just quiet your thoughts. If you would just untangle them." More of her hair fell about his face and neck. The dust settled around the car, letting full sunlight back in. "I know that everything we saw that night was probably not what it seemed. I know that our city watches itself more than it knows, helped along by a bunch of *salamandros*—boys—who are not sure of what they're doing. Does that *really* put me ahead of you, *cabrón?*"

Against him, lifting him, he felt the squirm of her foot inside her boot.

"Now you drive, *cabrón*," she told him. "The rest of the way. I want to get some shots of the train from the car. When it catches us. The driving will help straighten your thoughts."

Klinsman drove. Rita had her window down and was getting pictures of the distant train that ran with them across the high desert, skimming the border. Taking peeks away from the road, he would look at the flat of her back twisting, at the way she got her legs and boots beneath her as though she were ready to spring out the window. Her hair was cinched tight against the blast of desert air. The train she was shooting, the San Diego & Arizona Line, dipped for a long stretch into Mexico. It brought the clothes to the warehouse Oscar was covering. Except for the yellow-and-black engine that appeared bright as a toy on the chalky landscape, the train looked brief and shabby, reluctant with its gray and brown cars in tow.

His gaze fell to the small of her back, exposed with the lift and twist of her effort. When she finished with her shots of the train, she raised her head and shoulders into the desert blast. She pulled the clasp from her hair, going with the whip and direction of the wind. With eyes and lips closed softly, the brown curves and planes of her face were open to the desert, a fearless tilt to her chin.

He felt a break within his chest, caught himself thinking they should just drive off together like this, knowing how she would rightfully scorn such a young and fruitless notion. Dig a boot heel into him.

20.

When they arrived at the warehouse, the desert heat was filled with the musk of spring, the thought of hard new leaves, chuparosa, and cactus flowers. Oscar was in the shaded east side of the old airplane hangar, playing soccer with his son, Artie, and some of the workers who had brought out their kids, too. The hangar shadow stretched long across the asphalt and into the sand and scrub. The boys and girls wore oversized jerseys they had gleaned from the piles inside the hangar. The men, including Oscar, wore very nice silk shirts tied into bandanas about their heads. Oscar stood goal in front of the hangar wall. Each time one of the kids fired a shot past him, the corrugated metal clanged and then warbled like a saw blade.

As they approached the game, Rita took one sidestep away from Klinsman. When he gave her a quizzical look, she returned an apologetic smile and pretended to search through one of her shoulder bags. He knew her cameras were at the ready.

Oscar spied Klinsman and kicked an attempt high over the

game. The kids stood still and watched the ball arc over the asphalt and tumble into the sagebrush, beyond the edge of the shade and into sunlight. Klinsman gave chase. He jogged into the brush, enjoying the stretch and motion after the car ride, the talcum feel of the air and the sandy paths. The ball skittered over some pebbly hardpan and spun to a stop beneath a creosote bush.

Oscar, running up behind his wild shot, surprised Klinsman and beat him to the ball. As Klinsman reached for it with his hand, Oscar nabbed it with his foot, flipped it upward off the tip of his shoe, tapped it high with his knee, eased it once on the top of his head, then let it fall into his arms.

With an overhead in-bounds pass, he flipped the ball toward Klinsman but launched it well over him, as though he were a defender. Klinsman jogged to retrieve the errant throw.

The ball had come to rest near what looked like a sprinkler, something you'd expect to rise from a suburban lawn.

Klinsman picked up the ball and stared at the device. He began to crouch for a closer look.

"*Cuidado, cabrón,*" said Oscar. "You'll bring the tonks out here."

Klinsman stared at the thing, which upon closer inspection appeared spindly and alien.

"Is it a camera?"

"Worse," said Oscar, maintaining distance. "Or better. Depending. If you look like me, if you look like you. It's immersive media. Laser trigger, heat and motion sensor. The wetbacks call them 'spider eyes.' They're laid out on a chessboard from here to the border, from Yuma to the sea."

"I don't see where the camera could be."

"They're just remote lenses, not cameras," Oscar said flatly. "I tell you to forget the idea of camera. You only need something to gather and construct images. No one needs a fucking camera." He motioned toward the asphalt game, where Rita had taken his place at goal to face the kids and workers and another ball. "Except her."

The two men looked at Rita. The sun hung just above the bow of the hangar, dipping into the city haze, beginning to orange.

"Get it, Aaron." Oscar crouched and scooped up a handful of sand and pebbles, let it spill and sparkle in the yellowing light. "We are the cameras. All this needs is a lens, a tiny, tiny chip, and two little filaments. A little glass BB and two silk threads. A spider's eyes and feelers. All you need is feed in the air." The last of the dust, the finest powder, drifted like smoke from his hand. "Our air is full of invisible feed, here for the taking. We are the cameras. We put the shit together and make it visible."

"Is that what you're really doing out here?" Klinsman asked. He didn't know what he wanted to hear and feel from Oscar. There was sublimation in Oscar's crouch, the way he remained down there, looking up at Klinsman, in his shadow. Klinsman let the soccer ball ride on his hip, pinned casually there with his wrist.

"I'm out here doing the story on this clothes mountain," Oscar replied. "Just like Gina ordered."

"But maybe bringing my story along."

Oscar, lips tucked, nodded toward the desert. "Yes. Yeah. I swung by the motel on the way here." He continued watching the desert, east along the border, which formed a thin gray sound wave over the bare hills. "I took the thermostat from the room. I thought you'd be there. I waited a bit, then had to leave." He finally looked back to Klinsman.

"Why?" Klinsman asked. "Why did you go?"

"It was a freeway thing. You know?" Oscar straightened from his crouch. "North to the 8 or south to the 117, both shoot east. I was thinking about the 360 you showed me. You know how you think better about something when you're not seeing it? When you're just picturing it? *Imaginando*. I was thinking about those tape pieces. Where they were. How they were, putting them in their places. Only then did I think where they weren't. They seemed to be stuck on everything. The doorknobs and pull-chains and peep-hole. So why not on that thermostat? I nabbed it while I had the chance."

"You could've called."

Oscar shrugged. Artie called to him from the blacktop game, and he looked over his shoulder, then back to Klinsman. "You're here. And I haven't had much of a chance to look at it yet. I'm not hiding anything."

The kids and the workers were getting distracted by the two men in the desert bush. To them, it must have appeared as if they were getting ready to fight, Klinsman set to drop the ball, Oscar to duck in *vato*-style, under the chin.

"I'll show you after—in a little while," said Oscar. "See what we find. But I got to finish out here. Get back in the warehouse, see the workers close things up, with Rita getting shots."

"What will we find?" asked Klinsman.

Oscar took the soccer ball from him. "A thermostat. Probably."

"Maricónes," Rita's voice called to them from across the asphalt and scrub. "Come play with us, too." It chimed in the quiet air, the color of the falling sun.

Oscar leaned on one side of the hangar opening while Klinsman leaned against the other. They were facing in, watching the workers tuck and neaten the heaps of clothes using rakes and garden scoops. Oscar sent little Artie across to Klinsman, bearing a gift. It was a Western shirt embroidered with orange trumpet flowers and their green vines. The small buttons were yellow glass lozenges.

Klinsman thanked the boy and slung the shirt over his shoulder. Artie hurried back to play among the clothes mountains, which ran in tall lines the length of the hangar floor. The two men watched Rita wander alone in one of the valleys, taking pictures. She aimed her camera toward the rafters. There, the workers over the years had draped banners tied and twisted from unwanted clothes. The clothes hung like crepe paper and flags among the metal girding. The most colorful and gaudy of all past fashions, they caught the upward stream of sunlight coming through the hangar windows, filtered everything and everyone in funhouse splashes.

Rita arced her body to aim her lens directly overhead. She toed one boot tip forward, and her hair draped the S of her back. Yellow and red light played over her brown arms and throat.

When Klinsman looked away, over to Oscar, he found his friend staring at him.

"You be careful." Oscar nodded toward Rita.

Klinsman felt himself blush. "What do you mean?"

Oscar measured him steadily, as though he were telling Klinsman about himself, but he spoke of her. "You think right now she's shooting that stuff up in the rafters. But she's getting us, too. That little cheap-looking digital on her hip is on, aimed right at us. Her big fancy camera is making all that noise, all those fake clicking sounds. But that quiet little thing on her hip, with the indicator light punched out, is getting us."

Klinsman spotted the little gray rectangle at Rita's hip.

"She already has you looking at her," said Oscar. "You looking at her in that way. That way you just were. She'll take those captures, still them, sharpen them, move in. All the way into your eyes maybe. And know exactly how you're feeling. Maybe better than you know."

They watched her climb the slope of one clothes mountain, still looking through her camera, aiming upward, along the crest where the window light was forming a horizon of colors atop the clumps of shirts, dresses, pants, skirts, and robes. She kept herself steady as she climbed, like someone walking in deep snow.

"I want her there," said Klinsman. "When we look at the thermostat. When you take it apart for us. She gets to be there, first thing."

Rita, sensing their gaze from her perch along the slope, aimed her camera squarely at them and took a picture, a lingering capture that stilled them, silenced them, pushed them back.

The workers had closed up the hangar and left. Big evening shadows covered the desert flats in broad sweeps, but you could still see outlines of sunlight on the mountain ridges to the east. Oscar, Rita, and Klinsman stood near the open tailgate of Oscar's truck. He had backed it up to the scrub at the edge of the parking lot so Artie could play in the sandy spaces between creosote bush and ocotillo while they examined the stolen thermostat.

Oscar shoved at his satchel. "Ay. I forgot his snack."

Rita offered an orange from her bag. "I have this, if he wants. But it's got a *saldito* in it." She tossed it to Oscar.

"He loves *salditos*." Oscar almost smiled at Rita, then brought the orange to Artie, who was fixing a sort of camp beneath the fountain stalks of an ocotillo. The green stalks were covered with tiny red flower buds.

Klinsman and Rita watched as Oscar showed his kid the slit in the orange where Rita had inserted the *saldito*. As a child Klinsman would watch the ranch campesinos pull apart their oranges during afternoon break, revealing the sunburst colors made by the little salt-cured plums tucked inside. The taste was an intense clash of salt, bitter, sweet, and sour. It woke you up, spiked your blood. At the end you could chew the plum seed and pulp like a cud of tobacco.

Artie had his dad split the orange for him. Oscar dug his thumbs into the slit and pulled the fruit neatly in half. The center was dark purple, lightening to red along the edges. He handed the halves delicately to Artie, so as not spill a drop, then rejoined Rita and Klinsman at the tailgate.

They did not go about the business at hand. They watched Artie fix up his camp beneath the ocotillo, setting a flat stone for himself and another to his side. He placed one of the colorful orange halves on the empty stone.

"Who's that?" Rita asked softly, watching the boy adjust the orange half for his imaginary friend.

"PJ," said Oscar. "He's new. I think it's a he. His teacher at school is working with his J sound. So that's one reason for the name."

Klinsman inhaled the desert air, the stone-baked scents, let himself be fooled into thinking it could just be like this for Rita and Oscar and him, watching and caring very simply for a child who was learning to make sense of the world, to sound out his Js correctly, to enjoy the desert. That there was no important truth to find, no knowledge to rescue, no artifact to disassemble, no story to compose with word and picture, nothing buried.

Rita took up her main camera, the black thing with the fluted lens, and began making adjustments for distance and light. Her aim was the space on the tailgate where Oscar would examine the thermostat. She also gauged Oscar's profile, then Klinsman's. She let the camera linger on Klinsman, wordlessly, then flipped it around so he could see the capture of himself on the viewscreen. But he looked at her face instead, her sincere, almost worried gaze. Frustrated, she pushed the image closer to him, gripping the camera with both fists. He ignored it and continued to look at her, at the dark and quiet exasperation in her eyes. Somewhere on the periphery of his vision the screen holding his image went black, softly, a melting.

The thermostat lay open on the tailgate. Oscar prodded it with a screwdriver, one of the small ones used for sewing machines and other intricate motors. He had removed the brass hemisphere of the dial, popped off its clear center, and exposed the internal silver plates of the rectangular frame. Rita had taken some shots of Oscar's dark hands delicately turning the screwdriver, separating parts. But there was nothing there to see, and her camera now remained still.

"It's just a thermostat," said Oscar. "Old style, real brass. It wasn't even active, wasn't even being used. The motel switched over to cheap central heating. Probably left these up so guests could spin them and think they had control."

"You checked on that?" asked Klinsman.

Oscar nodded.

Rita put her fingertip through the empty center of the dial. Oscar, with his fingertip, slid the clear glass toggle switch along the top edge of the frame. "And this, too," he told her. "See? Like a miniature periscope. But it's just a slide switch. Nothing more. What I thought."

"But you took it," said Klinsman. "Anyway. Just in case." He said this because he could see that Rita was getting lost in the thought, the idea of what it could be. It seemed odd to him, to see her touching the instrument rather than taking photos, to be looking at it so directly rather than through her lens. The disassembled pieces didn't appear empty and benign. They fit. They matched his whole impression of the room—a place of what could be, from its veils and tape pieces to its mysterious occupant. To Rita and him.

"The tape pieces, then," said Klinsman. "They're markers, covers, or shadow points."

"Or thoughts," said Rita. "You know? Forethoughts." She dialed the thermostat. "Afterthoughts."

He kicked the soccer ball with Artie for a while, caught sight of a couple more sensors hidden in the desert scrub. The desert just before evening held a calmness, a gathering sense, the afternoon heat survived, predator night yet to arrive. The air was quiet and soft. Oscar and Rita leaned on the truck tailgate and watched, their voices sounding close. She was asking things about Artie, simple stuff about school and food. Oscar made fun of the way Klinsman played soccer, the *guero* way he kicked with the toe of his boot.

After, Rita took some photos: Oscar with Artie, then Klinsman in there, then her in there, too, with all of them, the camera propped on the tailgate, the timer set. It fired a series of three shots, the desert tea-colored in the backdrop. Klinsman didn't feel ready for any of the shots. Their last days working together, he thought. They were just getting started.

In the stillness, the repeating shutter sounded like scissors.

21.

There was only one Klinsman family picture containing Aracely Montiel. It was taken by Aaron's sister Mary after a high school dance. Ara had not gone to the dance. She never went to dances and didn't date boys from school. She did not date boys. She had called Aaron at the hotel where she knew the prom was being held and asked him to come help her. "Please come," she said, and gave him the location of a downtown club.

Aaron abandoned his date, who was milling about with a post-dance crowd, and went to fetch Aracely. To this day he cannot remember his date's name but can remember almost everything about how Aracely Montiel looked when he arrived at the awning for the downtown club. Her black hair was up in something she called a Gibson Girl. It showed all of her neck, and its gentle loop shadowed the delicate curve of her jaw. Her gown was something he had never known existed. A color he could not name, it shimmered in the neon lights like a gift rolled up from the surf. It clung to her torso, somehow without straps. Her shoulders, lifted with sad anxiety, shone with a kind of wisdom and turned to his arrival. She looked at him with such relief he thought she might laugh, though her mascara was smudged with tears. In his rented tux, offering his arm to her, he felt like a bellboy.

Mary had been assigned to wait up for Aaron, to make sure he came home sometime before dawn. She was waiting for him by the living room fire, dozing with a chemistry book and hot chocolate. When he arrived with Ara, Mary was speechless, all scolding about missed curfew caught behind openmouthed wonder. She pleaded for a picture.

At first Ara refused, then obliged, lifting her chin, her fingers clasped before her waist. She told Aaron to straighten his shoulders, to place one hand at the small of her back, and to gaze someplace just above his sister's camera. The photo, which one of Mary's daughters posted fifteen years later, looks like something taken onboard ship a century ago. Ara's gown is the color of the fire.

That night she made love to him for the first and only time in their friendship. She had him drive to the top of Silver Wing, where other cars were parked. The borderland lights sparkled all the way to the Pacific. He assumed she just needed, as usual, to sit quietly some more. But she told him plainly and softly that she wanted him to make love to her. "Here, in your car," she insisted. "Like them. Like kids. Please," she said. "I want to. I need to."

Beginning in junior high, she had shown him things. She taught him the right way to kiss, to hold back his tongue for awhile, to then only brush with it. How to use his teeth and how never to press. She showed him this in the noon sun, hidden in the church-yard rose garden of Mt. Carmel. Once as high school juniors, alone in her aunt's apartment, she showed him how to caress a girl's breast, how it would feel much better to him if he thought about her. See, she said as she guided him by the wrist, thought and touch together. His thoughts at the time were a roaring whiteness.

A week later she told him something about her life. They were at her aunt's apartment again, where Ara was supposed to wait alone after classes. On the couch she sat with her legs crossed and her hands folded in her lap, the way you might imagine a woman at a very formal party, someone who knew she would always be viewed.

She told him she worked as a model in TJ. He said he knew this, that he had recognized her picture over the perfume counter at Sara's and on a billboard over Revolución.

"Yes," she told him, holding herself still in a way that made the background view restive, trying to hold her. "But we do other things. We go with men. The sons of very rich men, or sometimes the men themselves. They treat us nice. But sometimes they also trade us, back and forth. We're like their wives, only younger and prettier. The wives know us, go to the same places and parties. You see?"

He saw. Whenever he walked Tijuana, he felt he was only ever on the very surface, on the thinnest of skins, like a water insect. Trollish men, dressed in silk, would shoulder their way against the heavy foot traffic of Revolución, strange smells on their heavy breath, fleshy, spicy smells. They moved and looked as though they lived by another clock, a dividing of the day that did not fit the rest of the city. Aaron would notice things in the gutters, things tourists would step lightly over, dark oozing liquids. He would see taped to street walls papered with ads for strip shows—first two drinks free—other little posters showing men with broken but bloodless faces, eyes not quite closed, dead men's eyes.

He wanted to believe Aracely could somehow float above all this, hover the way she did on the billboard over Revolución, without suffering, without having to pay. But each time he saw her after that afternoon on her aunt's couch, after that one tremulous vision of her, the pause at the apex, something about her had faded. He knew it came from him, that he was just getting wiser. But he also knew it came from whatever happened to her.

Placing his hand gently on her forearm, watching her eyes carefully to make sure there was no flicker of confusion or disappointment concerning his touch, he told her she didn't have to explain more. He said it didn't matter to him. It was a lie. He wanted to know everything about that life of hers. The only thing that stopped him from pressing was that impression of Revolución, the broken, knobby faces of the dead, the fleshy, cooked smells of men's breath fuming below baleful stares.

Whenever it was an issue in their conversations, she referred to it as *mi vida en Tijuana*.

That night, on top of Silver Wing, she kept things quiet and simple. She climbed over him in the backseat, did not remove her gown. It rustled about him stiffly like sea foam, cloaked them together as they pearled against each other. Border radio played softly from the dashboard, a slow and mournful accordion waltz bringing forth the dawn.

22.

The clothes Rita had gathered from the warehouse piles and tossed into the backseat held a desert smell, heat and powder, as she drove back to the city. The dashboard lights glistened in her eyes and on the skin of her throat and shoulders. Staring into the nightscape of the approaching city, she seemed lost from him.

He looked back to the pile of clothes. "You're leaving soon. Why'd you get those?"

"Because I want to know what Osquí's up to."

"He's covering the clothes mountain again. The assignment Gina left him."

She huffed. "And you're covering the parks again. And the Luchadors again. Why did Osquí show you that spider eye? Out there in the scrub."

"Because," he replied. "Because it's the perfect kind of irony for a journalist. That warehouse is surrounded by things to keep people away. The same people who work the warehouse and the same people who make all the stuff that fills the warehouse."

She bowed into her driving more, glared into the emerging edges of the city.

"What?" Klinsman asked. "You think more?"

"Yes, I think more. Oscar must think something's hiding in the clothes. I knew for sure when I saw him give you that shirt. So I took a pile for myself."

"We know what's hiding in those clothes," he told her. "What's always been hiding in those clothes. The bodies that make them but can't wear them."

She thrust her chin toward the city, the sprawl of yellow lights rolling downward in smaller and smaller hills into the black ocean. "Yeah. But now there's more."

"Like what?"

"I don't know."

He thought a moment. "You think Oscar's right about all those lenses and apertures? All thrown out there, left out there? Abandoned hopes, finished opportunities?"

"I think he really wanted that thermostat to contain more, to be more," she answered. "I think he really believes it's possible that there are even more ways than we realize for us all to watch each other. He wants us to believe that, too."

"Why?" he asked.

"Because he wants us to explore the possibilities." She straightened her back, leaned toward the steering wheel. "He wants it to be of some good. New eyes for old lenses. He doesn't want it to be just *mozos* having fun."

"What do you think?"

She thought, glanced quickly back to the clothes pile. "I think he's on to something. I mean, look at the way we just throw out those fancy clothes. How we just leave them."

"For the *mandros*," he said.

She shrugged, gripped the wheel, getting her knuckles over the top. "It's funny. Amazing really."

"What?"

"How Gina works us. Races us like this. Osquí gets ahead, then I catch up. We let you catch up. Then Osquí gets ahead." She looked at him, letting them soar blindly over the freeway for a moment. "And so on."

"You let me catch up?"

"Yeah. So we don't get too far ahead of ourselves. So we stay on course. So we stay in the middle of stuff. Stuff that matters. At least stuff that matters to Gina."

"This amuses me," he said. He sensed her bristle.

"Why?"

"Because," he answered, "Oscar says the same kinds of things about you."

"What? What does Oscar say about me?" She rubbed her chin to her shoulder as she held the wheel, stared deliberately ahead, not at him.

"He says for me to be careful around you. To try to stay up with you."

"Isn't that contradictory?"

"I don't care," he told her.

"You should. He's saying I'm dangerous to you and that I'm ahead of you on some path. Lying in wait."

"I don't care because I want to be around you."

"*Around* me? How touching. How sincere. *Que resuelto.*"

"With," he said. "I want to stay with you tonight."

"Louis might be there."

"Might?" he asked.

"Will," she answered. "He will be there. He thinks he's coming with me. To Manzanillo."

"You want that?"

"Maybe," she said. "He wants to set up practice there."

"Pretty far from the border. For immigration law."

"More than a million fly to the states from there. To LA and Chicago and New York. Every year. Labor brokers from here, looking for the prettiest waiters and waitresses and *nanas*, send them on their way. Bodies bodies everywhere."

He barely knew her words, but the sound of her voice rang clearly, inside him like a tumble of shells. He thought of things he could do in Manzanillo. He could rent a room for two dollars a day and do nothing.

"Then drop me off downtown."

"No," she said, bearing her chin downward, glaring further into the city lights that were now enveloping them. "I want you there, too. Around."

She put him up in the studio. At the foot of the daybed she dropped the pile of clothes she had mined from the warehouse. The desert air still clung to them, the peppery waft of the sage conjuring thoughts and sensations of heat and stone. He hadn't seen Louis, but they could hear him creaking around somewhere in the little

Victorian. They couldn't quite tell which floor he was on or what he might be doing.

Klinsman sat on the end of the daybed and fingered the top layer of clothes, some linen dresses, so fine you could see your hand beneath the gauzy colors. Never had he seen her wear anything like this, be a woman wandering casually in a garden or secluded courtyard, touching edges of sunlight and prisms on a stucco wall. He caught himself imagining Rita's brown skin under the linen.

"He know I'm here?"

"Of course." She put the remote to the blinds on the nightstand along with a glass of ice water.

"You want me to go say hi?"

"No," she said. "I want you to try to sleep. For once, just sleep."

He took hold of her wrist as she was turning to leave. She looked down at his gentle grasp, a skeptical rise in her brow.

"What are you doing, Rita?"

"I'm saving you," she said, snatching her wrist away from him.

23.

He fell asleep for one hour, the time in clear blue readout above her studio desk, the numbers hanging in darkness. The end number flipped each minute, winking at him. What woke him was a rise in the air, something at first more barometric than aural. And it pulled him out of sleep, loosening him first. The pressure shift in the air became a sound, Louis moaning low and long, his voice sifting ghostlike through the wood of the house, coming from somewhere in its center.

Then there was a wooden tocking, the rhythm changing quickly. A silence, like just before rainfall, embraced the house. Louis cried out three times, each cry louder and longer than the one preceding it. The final one ended in a sob, an echoed drop of water.

Klinsman tried to sleep in chisels of concentration, mocked by the blue wink of her clock.

He reached in the darkness for his ice water, found the remote instead. He pressed the button, and the blinds hummed and let moonlight into the room, a limestone glow, a light that appeared young, damp, not yet ready. It fell across Rita's photo wall, where the imprint of the woman from room 9 shimmied in the moon's tremble.

He played with the blinds, opening and closing them, pulsing the light on her form. He imagined Rita hearing the hum, the one-two rhythm. That might have been his intent, but what he did was make the woman come more to life. As the peripheral curves faded in and out with the fluctuating moonlight, the figure seemed to sway her hips and shoulders. You could imagine her hair tumbling with her walk.

He got up naked from the little bed and walked across the room. As he neared the photo, her form flattened, backed into the wall. He stepped through the moonlight until his shadow appeared on the wall next to her. He moved his shadow across her.

The door to the study opened and Rita slipped in.

"What exactly is your plan?" she whispered. She pointed to the shadow of his erection on the photo wall.

"No. No," he whispered. He found his jeans and pulled them on, stumbling in the moonlight. He gauged what Rita was wearing—a long t-shirt, no jeans—and maintained balance, no shirt. "That," he pointed to his shadow. "That was from before."

"Before?" She looked over to the anxious tangle of sheets on the daybed.

He shook his head and hurried to the wall. He touched the impression of the woman where her shoulder would be.

"Why?" he asked. "Why are the lines so distinct? So deep? So high?"

Rita joined him beside the photo, put her hand next to his on the impression. "Because I'm a really good picture-maker."

Her hair was up, piled in a cluster that was already snaking loose around her ears and neck. She smelled of soap and faucet water.

"Come see," he said, leading her back to the daybed.

She hesitated, then followed. He pressed the remote and let full moonlight fill the room. He pointed to the surface of the day-bed sheets. She peeked cautiously toward them, tucking a lock of hair behind her ear, holding it.

"That's me," he said, motioning to the wrinkled sheet. He cleared the bed of everything but the cover sheet. Then he pulled that tight, smoothed it, his canvas. "Lie down," he instructed.

Rita tucked her lips, then let them swell back into fullness, shook her head slowly. "Not after what I just saw. On the wall."

"I heard you and Louis," he said. "That's all. Actually just Louis. I heard Louis."

"Louis?"

"No. You . . ." He rubbed the back of his neck, firmly, trying to untwist thoughts. "Why did you come in here?"

"I couldn't sleep." She put one knee to the bed, paused. "I heard you not sleeping." She eased herself onto the bed, lay faceup, hands clasped beneath her breasts, legs stretched and together. "You're contagious."

She wriggled herself more into the mattress. "This do?"

Her skin was dark in the moonlight, her nightshirt bright. The moon shone white in the coils of her hair. She looked almost like a negative, even her lips catching a kind of frost about them in the moonglow. The sheet tightened and smoothed beneath her as she continued to wriggle herself in, understanding.

"Now get off," he said.

She lay still for moment, gave him a quick black glare in the moonlight. Then she swung her legs together over the edge of the mattress and stood up beside him. He waved his hand over the wrinkled pattern she had left on the sheet.

"See?" He turned to watch her look. "It's not right. Not at all. The wrinkles are all over the place. *You* are not there."

He resmoothed the sheet. "Do it again. Just like before."

She glanced once at him, opened her lips to maybe say something, slid her jaw. Then she eased herself over the sheet again, settled in. She lifted her legs together, feet pointed, a kind of calisthenics. Her night shirt rolled back to her hips, caught there. Then she lowered her legs over the sheet. She clasped her hands beneath her breasts and closed her eyes.

"Now hold still," he said.

She opened her eyes deliberately, gave him a skeptical look. Without disturbing the surface of the sheet, he gently hooked one arm beneath her neck and shoulder and one beneath her knees. "Stay asleep," he whispered. He lifted her smoothly from the bed.

As he held her, they looked down together at the ripples in the moonlight, as though he had just scooped her from drowning.

"*That's* you," he said. He felt her thigh against his bare stomach.

Rita's imprint lay beneath them.

"We can do better," she said. She hooked her arm about his neck, as though to kiss him, then flexed her legs and hips from his hold. Freed herself.

Crouched in the moonlight, she dug through the pile of clothes near the foot of the bed. She pulled free a satin kimono, silvery in the night glow of the room. It stretched ropelike from the pile until she unfurled it and held it high with her hands, standing on tiptoe.

He helped her stretch it across the bed, tucking it like a sheet. The satin cloth felt liquid-cool on his fingers. "What is this? It's huge?"

"I just took it," she said as she smoothed a corner. "For the cloth. In the pile, I could see it was something. It probably went for two grand a year ago. I got it for a dollar a pound. It doesn't even weigh that much."

He had stepped back to watch her, to wonder. She was setting things up, like a photographer. Or like someone who had fixed a perfect meal, laced.

She climbed back into his hold. His arm scooped across the back of her thighs. She clasped her hands behind his neck. Their faces were close, her breath on his neck.

"This would be hard to explain to Louis," he said.

"This would be hard to explain to anyone," she replied. "Now lay me down."

He eased her back onto the bed, let her settle there, counted carefully to three. Then he lifted her from the satin. For him, she had no weight, only feel and movement. He could have carried her up a mountain.

Below them lay her form on the satin cover. The peaks of the whorls lifted and held like cream in the moonlight. Even the small cups left by her elbows and heels were distinct. He could have poured anything into them, to the brim.

He set her down carefully, kept his hands on her shoulders. After she looked at the pattern in satin a moment longer, he twisted her gaze toward the poster on the moonlit wall.

"She could be you, no?"

"No." She turned her face to his, the word shaped on her lips, and pulled him down into a kiss.

He removed his jeans and she removed her nightshirt and they crawled onto the satin. They didn't think which way was up or down and pushed the satin cloth in swirls between their skin. With the satin over him, she took him into her mouth. Underneath, he did the same with her, the satin a thin layer, only a taste really, between his tongue and her. When she began to come, she pushed herself down against his nose and mouth, suffocating him in the pearly cloth. She muffled her cries on him, biting through the satin, until he had to roll her over in order to breathe and to stop the pain.

The satin robe wound between them as he moved to lie on top of her. She stretched her arms back over her head and he kissed her there, in the pale cups of moonlight. He thought he had entered her, feeling the silkiness, and began to thrust gently. She laughed softly in his ear. "That's not me," she whispered at the end of her laugh. She reached down and untangled him from the satin, aimed things right.

"That's me," she said as he pushed into her.

24.

He left her sleeping on the daybed, a flaunting rise in her hip and shoulder as she breathed deeply, smoothly, an impossibility for him. He caressed the tumble of hair away from her face to watch the moonlight on her skin, dreams aquiver on her eyelashes.

Quietly, fearful of waking anyone, he showered and changed into the shirt Oscar had given him, the one with the orange trumpet vine and clear yellow snaps. He hung his other shirt on the towel hook, for Rita, for Louis. Outside, in the moonlight scuff across her tiny front yard, he couldn't immediately recall where his car was, whether it was here in the Heights, back at work, or near his place.

He walked downtown, hoping to catch the last—or the first—trolley. The safest way through the barbed-wire neighborhood between the Heights and downtown was E Street, where the police station stood in a wash of sodium light. Oscar had shown him how to navigate beneath the string of surveillance cameras along the edge of the Heights. New gulches and passageways were forming all over the city, Oscar told him. People were setting up shop along surveillance strings, like towns beside rivers. Like Tijuana.

Klinsman thought to get home on the night trolley but overrode his stop. Gazing at the harbor lights, he was swimming in notions, not without direction, not without speed. But if he paused, he would sink.

The woman in room 9 had been lifted from the bed by someone tall and strong, or by someone who loved her. She was a pretty Mex who stood in places as though she owned them. Pretty as cactus pear with dew on the needles. She could have been Rita, saving him.

He had fallen in love with Rita. When? Seven years ago? Two nights ago? Four days hence, when she would leave? He was now in the first hours of day three. Day three of seven—*seven days is right for us.* He needed to go home and think, but he had no home. The city, his city, the one he was born in, had erased it.

"If you stay, you'll see our home fall away," Connie had told him before slipping back to her clinic in the Brazilian Amazon. "Like those ice shelves that crumble, sheer by sheer. I think of icebergs a lot down there, Aaron. Come see sometime."

She hugged him, kissed his cheek, the damp wood scent of the rainforest already about her. She had come to look Brazilian, tan all year, her dark hair stained ruddy at the edges by the sun. Her arms had become thin and strong, hewn by her work, the lifting of equipment and children, the starvation of a long workday, the torque of her procedure, the mending of clefts. "Concepción," they called her down there, returning her to what she was supposed to be.

On the Klinsman ranch, anyone would have guessed her to become what Jo and Liz became, an animal researcher. Dogs, horses, goats, cows, birds, snakes—horned toads even—nuzzled her. They visited her before their deaths, it seemed, pushing their snouts into the crook of her arm, the palm of her hand. But animals brought her along further, that was all, to people. "Animals are easy," she told him. "They're always honest, even when they're getting ready to bite you, throw you, hurt you, die on you. That snake that took you down, Aaron. It shook its tail at you first, filled the sky with its rattle. I even heard it, felt it.

"People don't do that. They kiss you before they betray you, hurt you when they need your help."

This she told him at the park that now covered the ranch. Klinsman felt the trolley klatch around a slight bend and realized with a brightening, wakening snap that he had been dozing. He had now ridden far past his stop and was in the borderlands again. Thinking it was the closest manner of getting home, of clearing his thoughts, he got off the trolley at the Iris Station and walked the night mile to Ranch Park.

From a stone picnic table not far out of the single security light, he gazed at the distant South Bay Drive-in screen, blank, waiting for dawn light to fill its pale bend. With his laptop, which cast light onto his face with the upward push of a blue torch, he tapped into the park cameras. He found the empty courts, the white lines barely visible in the darkness. He found himself, a monk atop a stone table, in dying candlelight. But he was there. A sudden shimmer of static passed across his form. Klinsman shivered with it.

He clicked along the other cameras in the series. Beneath the sweep of the third one down from his position, three dark figures were moving toward him. When he looked into the darkness of the park, he couldn't see them. But there they were on camera, only shadows, swaggering and smooth.

He clapped his laptop closed, cinched his shoulder bag, and ran. He carried himself with an odd faith, drawn from the grounds of his youth. He convinced himself that he could outrun them because this was where he had scampered barefoot as a boy, quick as a goat. The light glowed in the center of the park, where the barn had once stood. He made it safely through the light, felt confident on the dark slope up to the far side of the park, where the big house used to be. That was where he headed.

That was where they caught him.

Two flanked him and one got ahead of him. Their sweat smelled sugary with meth and rum. One on his flank leg-whipped Klinsman, slapping him to the grass. Lying still, Klinsman let everything settle. He took one long breath, his mouth to the grass, the green taste of melon rind. They gathered round him like pallbearers looking down.

He rolled slowly over, gazed at the moon, thinking it looked like a jellyfish in dark water.

"He looks high," one of them said.

Another one told him to put all his stuff in a pile—wallet, cell, and notebook—and get the fuck lost. Or they would break his ribs with their boots.

"And the shirt," one said. "I want that shirt."

"Leave the shirt," said the one who was giving orders.

Klinsman felt hopeful. He sensed no desire to keep any of his stuff. He wanted very much for them to have it all. From his knees he began to make a pile for them. One unzipped.

"I'm going to piss on him."

"Wait till I get the stuff away."

"Wait till he gets the shirt off."

"I might do more," the one with the open fly said.

Klinsman began to shiver. He had trouble with the button snaps of his shirt because his fingers were numb and shaking. He was fingering one of the snaps, trying to somehow go into its miniature clarity, trying to catch moonlight in its yellow glass.

Then the button lit up magically in his fingers, seemed to burst with light that spread across him, them. Their black boots and gray jeans appeared statuelike in the sudden light, silent as granite. The one with his fly undone stood holding himself like a boy.

Klinsman shielded his eyes with his arm and tried to peer into the source of the spotlight creating the dazzle. Like the morning star, it shone ridiculously bright, aimed, offering. It appeared to come from a rooftop amid the dark sea of housing tracts aligning the park. But it vanished, or seemed to jump locations, sweeping upward from the end of the park where a patrol car had appeared, blue light strobing.

His captors hurried away, their boots thumping like heart-beats against the grass. Klinsman gathered himself and his things and stumbled out of the spotlight, thinking the cops would not give chase, that only if he stayed in their light would they come to help. But once he was farther into the darkness of the park, standing where the ranch water tower had stood, he felt directionless, homeless.

He remained for a moment, not wanting to feel run off his own land. The moonlight cast the dimmest of veils on the dewy grass. He found another small repair site along the northeast edge, where Connie had once strolled with a bull snake draped about her neck. Workers had drilled beneath the sod, bringing up that red hardpan. He could tell they'd had to use an auger, soak the ungiving strata, lifting it in muddy chunks and swirls that had already reset.

Klinsman knelt and picked a clod from the pile. This was the stuff, the brick-hard subsoil that would catch plows, extend digs, delay plans to lay pipe. His grip on the dirt clod helped him ease away the final shudders of his escape.

In the darkness he couldn't see the sketches he had made on his notepad earlier, when he had been here with Douglas Cook. But he scraped the clod over the page, imagining the red streaks it would leave across the owl, the pig, the goat skull, the cow skull, the imprint of the woman from room 9.

He followed Douglas Cook's sidewalk route, leaving the park at the southeast corner, strolling and veering left into the housing tract. Why, and what he hoped to find, Klinsman did not know. Dogs barked as he got deeper into the neighborhood, so he moved to the center of the quiet street, away from the direct glow of the lamps, navigating a middle distance between the yards. All houses were dark. Some kept porch lights on.

When he had gone about the distance he gauged for the spot-light—the one he might have seen, the one that flashed from button to rooftop to patrol car—he chose a house and walked to its garage door. A security light flicked on, and he hurried away. At the next he ventured more to the side, stood for a moment beneath a dark garage window, got his boots tangled in a garden hose.

What would he see if he took hold of the window bars and pulled himself up, peered into the garage? If this were the right house? If this were any house, in any of these tracts? A *mozo* with a gringo name might be at play in his own corner, in only the glow of his PC. He could have Klinsman captured on screen, caught in the security light from moments before, scurrying back into the night gray of the street.

Klinsman lifted himself, gripping the window bars. Fatigue trembled in strings from fingers to biceps, night heavy on his shoulders. What he saw as he raised his face to the black window was his reflection, an expression paled and hollowed by moonlight, eyes empty dark sockets, mouth frowning in exhaustion. A paint-ing, what he would look like if sleep were never able to find him again.

25.

He used the trolley to get to the *Review* before dawn. He did not power up the lights but worked and thought only by the glow of his computer at desk 5. The 360 he'd taken of room 9 rotated slowly on his screen. Klinsman felt compelled to work, but his fingers waited above the keys, thumbs trembling. Examining room 9 was enough like work in this predawn quiet, this blue light. He never felt guilty about time wasted in these hours. He could do anything and it would be more productive than trying to sleep: watch Santo on Channel 12 and feel as though he were learning, read *Madame Bovary* by the *giallo* light of Edwige Fenech and feel he understood women.

He watched the scan of room 9 for several minutes before he noticed the music. So quiet was the saxophone, so brooding, it seemed to be coming from him, buried in a pocket somewhere. But it was coming from his desktop, a low, lulling saxophone, a tune he knew he'd heard before but could not name. He had not put any music to the 360 of room 9. The horn blew so softly, so quietly, the notes almost broke at the beginning, twitching to come alive.

What caught him, what dropped his hands from the keyboard, was not anger toward the person who might have done this. He did think of Rita and Oscar, all of them together, messing with each other's stuff, stories, lives, trying in these last days to get one another finally, understand one another. But those thoughts only brought him to a further surfacing, an extra little waggle on the shoulder by a waking hand. No. What cast fear into his thoughts was the rightness of the music, its perfect fit. It rolled in time to the slow rotation of the image and lingered here and there with the camera's scan, right along with Klinsman's perception of the room, of things. As though the saxophone, singular above the lightest of high hats, knew what was inside him.

He leaned away from his screen, pressing himself back into the dimness. To remain careful with his suspicions, he kept to the very edge of the glow, in the membrane. As a kid and as a teen, he had often lived as though Aracely were watching him, bound by venom light, vain to her interest. So here he was en garde with his own imagination along with Oscar, Rita, *los salamandros*, and Gina. Only one of these would show.

Klinsman drew his notepad from his satchel and thrust into the light the page full of sketches and crossed with the red dirt slash. With both hands he held it to the eye of the desktop, to the push of the music.

A quiet popping seeped through the saxophone lullaby, as though the record were scratched. Someone was calling his PC. He clicked the green button on his screen but kept himself stretched back into the dimness.

Regina Cruz Montoya appeared. Gina. He clicked her to full screen immediately, and her image covered the pan of room 9. She had chopped her hair short; it was spiky and sunburned on the feathery ends, like cuts on copper. Her skin was taut and darker, drawn and unspared about her bone and muscle. She was visible from the shoulders up, and he could see patches of dried salt, like thumbprints, in the small impressions of her collarbone and throat. Her delicate eyes and lips held him like a cupped bird.

"Is that you, Klinsman? Back there in the dark?" She squinted playfully, her voice a game of hide-and-seek. "Lean forward."

He leaned into the light of his screen.

"You called my desk," he said. "Who else would be at my desk?"

"No one else," she replied. "In that shirt."

"Where are you?"

"Here, of course," she said. "With you."

"You've just been swimming in the ocean," he told her. "It's just about dawn there. Like here. You look more Mexican. Your freckles have almost disappeared. That light behind you looks Mexican."

She looked over her shoulder, lifting her form enough for him to see the edge of a towel over her breasts. "What does Mexican light look like?"

"A tequila sunrise."

She laughed as she turned back to the screen. "They serve those in Peru, you know."

"Oscar—Oscar will show me how to trace the call records."

She flinched with the mention of Oscar, amusement dissolving from her expression for a second.

"Let him try," she said.

He stared into the tiny rectangle above his screen, instead of at her, so they would be eye to eye.

"What are you doing, Klinsman?"

"Working," he replied. "For you. I'm looking at room 9 of the Motel San Ysidro. Where you sent me."

"I know that," she said. "I see that. Those shirts and towels draped over the mirrors. Those seem the strangest to me. Of all."

"They're like shrouds," he said, staring flatly into the lens, trying to stay shivers.

"Yes." The word extended; she was considering the images, maybe on a corner window of her screen. "Like Good Friday shrouds. Or those to keep souls from realizing they no longer have reflections."

"Like in Oaxaca," he said.

"Or Lima," she said.

"You hear the music?"

She nodded.

"Know it?"

"I don't like jazz."

"What do you know about room 9?"

"I know what you know, Aaron. It was a legitimate call. I gave it to you because of where it was."

"That's Oscar's kind of story," he replied.

"I couldn't tell what kind of story it might be. And that's your home court. And that motel of yours."

"It's not my motel."

"You seem frayed," she said, "despite the shirt. You look like a guy going to a Mexican wedding, who's in love with the bride. And those sketches on your notepad, with that red scrape across them."

She appeared very pleased with her assessment.

"Are you watching all of us?" he asked.

"I'm not that good."

"Only good enough to get me."

"A little better than that," she said.

"Who's good enough?" He relaxed, tilted his look, mimicking her a bit. "To get anyone? Everyone?"

"I'm hoping you'll find out. You and Oscar. You and Rita—together." She cinched her towel. There was a tremble in her fingers, and she knew he could see, so she smiled at him. "Maybe only everyone—everyone together, together in the accident of desire—can do that. You know?"

You and Rita together. It played with the saxophone in his thoughts. She made the phrase sound separate and intimate, that halt of discovery before the final word.

She did something with her hands below screenview. The newsroom hummed as though the heating system had been activated. Klinsman looked around as the dark room filled with the light of sixteen screens. Even desk 11 came on. All held the image of Gina, looking at him.

"Oscar already showed me that trick. A variation, anyway."

"I know." She raised her hand, her intricate fingers holding an invisible wand. "Did he show you this one?"

He heard two clicks. All other desks in the room went dark.

"This is child's play," she said. "I only wonder what others can do."

A room in broken light appeared on his screen, mostly gray. Ashy dawn fell in sticks across a floor and a narrow bed. On the bed slept Rita, the satin in a rope around her naked form. He could sense the color of her skin like the softness around a warm stone. In her sleep she rolled toward his view, hip going over, arm reaching across pillow, breasts nuzzling into the satin. She was in a final dream, a murmur on her lips, a twitching in her lashes and fingers, about to wake.

"Turn it off," he told Gina.

"You turn it off, Klinsman." She ended the call, leaving him with Rita.

The saxophone lullaby still played, looping along with the 360 of room 9 running behind the live view of Rita's studio. Rita turned completely onto her stomach, the satin cloth twisting around her waist and weaving between her legs. Her shoulder blades rolled beneath her skin as she brought her hands to her face. Her hair was tossed to one side in a black hovering wave so that he could see her profile, pressed to the edge of the pillow.

To see her wake, that was what Klinsman feared. We're not meant to see that most intimate moment of a person's day. When she would gather, in a few seconds, the span of her life, the consequences of a night, the unveiled and jagged surface. When she would gasp into consciousness and he would see her thoughts flash undistilled across her waking expression. He would know how she felt about her life.

She woke toward his view, fully, suddenly, in lines of clove-colored light. He leaned back, caught unaware. She drew herself up into a sitting position, hugging her knees, setting her chin there. The saxophone began anew, with the first six notes rolling forth, low and deliberate. She wiped her cheekbones, said something to herself, a vow, a curse, but soft and plain, something easily come true.

She rose, gathering the satin robe, wrapping it around her as a blanket. Edges of the brown light brightened to yellow in highlights along the robe and in chevrons over the floor. She moved toward him, her feet tracing these footsteps of light. Her hair kept tumbling over her eyes, and she kept trying to push it back. It wavered in a dark balance over her forehead as she swooped close to his view. Her eyes seemed to consider the corners of his screen a moment before she looked directly at him.

26.

When Aracely took him to the church rose garden to show him how to kiss properly, she first tried to explain herself. They were fourteen, lunch boxes beside them on the stone bench. They could smell the dank tidelands, with close tongue-licks of rose.

"In confession, Father Patricio cries," she told him, pursing her hands in her lap. The breeze flapped the rounded collar of her uniform blouse, white moth wings. "He tells me the sins are not mine but that they're around me, that they'll affect me. For penance, he tells me to help others survive those sins."

Aaron felt pulled from his world, swung into the deep life of Father Patricio, where, out of respect, he could only remain mute. He and Aracely were the only students who liked the priest everyone called Father Picasso. In their art history texts all pictures of Picasso looked like the scowling, demanding Father Patricio. Several priests had passed through the school to tell the students of their calling, the moment they received God's beckon. Father Patricio's calling was different. It traumatized the eighth graders ready for Confirmation. He had felt called to the priesthood at the age of eleven, when he had been made to witness Franco's officers executing his entire family in their home in Seville.

Aracely did not believe in God. But she believed in Father Patricio. "He told me that I probably wouldn't be able to change my world. That I would have to find some way to live in it."

"You're making her up," Rita once said to him, maybe the third time he'd discussed Aracely Montiel with her, over after-work drinks. "But tell me more."

Klinsman had turned away from her, put a beer to his lips and held it there. He never told Rita anything more about Aracely, even when she asked. She called his brother Az and his sister Mary to verify the existence of Aracely Montiel, though their paltry contributions to the description only added to Ara's mystique.

"You blew your chance, Rita," Klinsman told her anytime she asked, even if she apologized.

Klinsman knew Rita still continued her investigation of Aracely. He knew this when Oscar asked one too many questions about the woman. When he asked about her citizenship, Oscar's eyes widened too much, the clay color and feel of his face pulling against his thoughts. Klinsman wanted to put his hands there, tell him all about Aracely Montiel.

"Rita blew her chance," he told him instead.

The story of Father Patricio's calling was real, too, but the priest did not want to tell it. The nuns pressed him to teach the class, but the nuns did not yet know the story. He scowled at them, then at the class. "Mine is not a good one to tell," he said.

"Father Timothy's was a good one for them to hear. Let's leave it at that."

The one teacher who was not a nun pressed him, a look of intrigue on her young face. He told the story, watching her, sneering it out, looking like Picasso drawing *The Centaur* in the air before him, seeing something no one else could see. They blindfolded everyone in his family except him. They left the eleven year-old boy as witness, as survivor. The officers didn't say why. Father Picasso told the class that his heart stopped and his breathing stopped, that when they walked him from the room he was not alive, that he didn't need blood or breath. He could have slain all the officers. He could have forgiven them.

To this day it was the truest story Klinsman knew. But no one he told believed it. When he told it to Rita, she pretended to believe him, hummed, tightened her lips. Later she tracked down Father Patricio, retired to an easy pastorship in the desert, and got him to admit the story. She called him Father Picasso and invoked Klinsman's name. On the side she asked him about Aracely Montiel. He first said, "No," then remembered and uttered a sad "Yes," slipping into Spanish with Rita.

Rita was doing something with her hands below the screen. She was keeping her face close to Klinsman's view, her dark eyes waking, her hair a black cloud filling the margins of his view. He assumed she was working her keyboard. But she startled him by raising a lipstick tube to her mouth.

She tapped the stick against her bottom lip, sharpened her gaze, almost glared. With the scarlet color she wrote backward across his view, so that he could read it forward.

Ojos ausentes, on top. Then below that, *Salamandro*.

She underlined the last word and carefully mouthed, "*Cabrón. Chingadero*. Motherfucker."

He sensed his view was about to go dark, but it did not. Instead she applied the scarlet to her lips thickly, precisely, flexing them to achieve evenness. She then leaned back, clutching the folds of the robe about her shoulders, staring.

27.

*K*linsman did not know what he was looking through. He assumed, on Rita's approach, that Gina had left him with a view through Rita's notebook camera, the easy little trick Oscar had shown him. He stared back at Rita through the lipstick words. Clutching her shoulders, she remained still, returning his look as though waiting for him.

You can't write in lipstick across the lens of a tiny camera. *Forget cameras. I am watching her through her notebook screen. She knows this. She knew this from across the room, sensed it upon waking.* These thoughts leaned him forward. With two gentle fingers he brushed the velvet warmth of his own screen.

Rita leaned away slightly, angled her look behind the lipstick scrawl. He leaned forward abruptly, testing, trying to make her flinch. She remained still. She would know he would try this. It felt as though she were watching his thoughts, not him.

He called her.

He watched her notice the ringtone, her eyes looking down

and to the side of her desk. What was her ring tone? Crickets? Birds? Frogs, he remembered. The chirping of poisonous frogs, she'd once told him. He muted his desktop, killing the lolling saxophone, thinking absurdly that he might then hear her, the sounds of her room, the chirping of poisonous frogs.

She picked up her cell, brought it into view, clutching her robe with her other hand. He watched her consider the call, his name—him. With her thumb sharply angled, she pressed something on her cell. For a second he hovered in the ether of her whim. In that second might be his deliverance.

"Aaron," she said. She looked at him, edged a corner of her lipstick with her little finger. "Having second thoughts? Wish you were here? Waking me in a better way?"

"Can *you* see *me?*" he asked, feeling himself drop into her reckoning, her scent rising sharply inside him with the cut of a wet knife.

"What?" she asked. She pulled the cell away from her lips, something strange and alive in her hand. "Fuck," she said.

She looked straight at him, disdain a flare over her lips and eyes, shining in the scarlet and black.

They each began in a kind of controlled flurry, the deliberate motions seconds before a race. She closed her cell, the snap beginning things. He began to rise from his chair, though unsure what to do with his screen. She swung the robe from her shoulders, and he caught glimpses of her form, her breasts coming close, before the satin covered everything. He shut off the power to his desktop, barely able to hold his finger long enough on the kill button.

He began a run opposite hers, against his thoughts.

How fast and freely he could move through the heart of this city, because he knew it, because it was his, and he was its child in the early ocean air. He didn't even have to think about the first stretch to the trolley, the path ingrained in his muscle memory, the pump of his knees, the turn of heel. So other thoughts were there for him, for him to jostle through, dodge, grasp.

I am running again. My shirt—my new shirt, a gift from my friend and his little son—stinks from it. It has magic yellow buttons that can save me from my own reck-lessness and stupidity.

He called her from the trolley. He stood holding the overhead bar, crammed in with the first wave of commuters, the workers who opened the city and its workplaces, cleaned the halls and cleared the sidewalks. From the *Review* it was a five-minute ride to her neighborhood.

To his surprise, she answered.

"Fuck you."

"Where are you?" he asked.

"Why don't you just look for yourself?"

"I don't know how to do that." He sensed she was about to end the call, could feel a curl in the silence. "Gina did it for me."

"You found Gina?"

He could tell she was moving. Sounds like things scuffing in-side walls grabbed along the straight line of her voice.

"She found me at work. She sent me to you. I didn't do it."

"But you stayed. You stayed to watch."

"I was entranced."

The two women on either side of him, sturdy *nanas* with arms hooked through cleaning baskets, looked at him with confused and irritated frowns. The sway of the trolley pushed their shoulders into his ribs. One eyed his shirt and asked him in Spanish if he had come from a wedding party. And was he in trouble with the bride? Was he in love with her?

"The yellow buttons mean hope," the other basket woman said, across him, to her fellow passenger.

"Entranced," said Rita. "That's bullshit. Who's with you? Who are you talking to?"

"No one's with me. I'm talking to you. They're making fun of me on this trolley. I don't care. I don't care because I'm telling you the truth. Please stop. Let me find you. Let me meet you."

"You were just *with* me, *chingadero*. You were *inside* me."

The two basket women looked at him as though they could hear her words. Klinsman secured his grip on the overhead bar. He breathed softly into his cell, hoping.

"The Big Kitchen," she said finally. "I'm near there. I'll be there. You have three minutes."

28.

When Klinsman stumbled around the corner to the wide sidewalk of the Big Kitchen, his lungs were spent and his feet felt blistered and bound from running in boots. His shirt, damp with morning mist, slapped against his skin like seaweed. Rita sat alone at an outside table. A big yellow mug of coffee steamed atop the rickety iron stand. The table's umbrella stood wings drawn in, a sleeping green insect. It was too early and chilly for outside tables.

He took a seat opposite her, the wire chair taking him like a spring. Rita wore a jacket with its collar up, her hair pulled inside it. The jacket was a gift from Gina, with several pockets for equipment, waterproof. She wasn't looking at him. She was watching the street, the roofline, the rise of morning light, nothing.

The waitress they called Bob Marley brought him a yellow mug of coffee just like Rita's, delivering it wordlessly, her expression gripped against morning work.

"The yellow cups mean hope," said Rita.

"Last night," he told her, "someone saved me."

"That was me," she replied, still not looking at him, still eyeing the roofline across the street. "Me again."

"I mean after that. I went to the park. I got into trouble."

She finally turned to him. Her face was scrubbed. He wanted to thumb the plane of her cheek, the impression beneath her bottom lip.

He went on, "Someone was watching me. Looking over me. They saved me with a spotlight. A spotlight that shone for only a second or two. They probably alerted the cops, too."

"What were you thinking?"

"It's my assignment," he replied. "Oscar would have done it."

"You're not Oscar."

"But it worked," he said. "And I'm telling you this to let you know what I've found. And to see what you know."

"About what?" She sipped her coffee, mechanically tilting the yellow mug.

"About *salamandros*." .

"I told you."

"You thought I was one," he said. He wrote in the air with his finger. "What you wrote across your screen. Backward, for them to see."

"You *are* one," she said, "apparently. You're certainly starting to look like one. What was best? Holding me or watching me?"

He started to answer, but she took hold of his wrist, gripping, digging in with her nails.

"No," she whispered. "The truth. Think and say the truth."

"Watching you," he said. He turned away from her.

When he turned back to her, she reached for his satchel as though it were hers, rifled through its contents, peered inside, lifting here and there. A young couple, both wearing wool caps and long shorts, walked past on their way into the café.

"What are you looking for?" Klinsman asked Rita.

"Your notes," she replied. "Those notes you always have. For your stories."

"They're on my laptop."

"Not those. The real ones. The paper ones." She pulled his battered notepad from the bag. "These," she said, raising her find. She flipped the pad open to the last page and set it on the table. She ran her finger along the sketches, then along the red streak of dirt.

"These?" She shook her head. "I know these." She tapped the owl. "This is Lechuza. The one who sucks the fingers and toes of newborns left unattended by foolish young mothers. Sometimes takes a digit. Sometimes leaves an extra."

She looked at Klinsman, drew back. "These. These don't have anything to do with the parks and cameras. With the Luchadors. With the motel room." She tapped his sketch of the seaweed woman. "Except her. Why do you have her after the cow skull?"

She scooted her chair in, scudding its metal feet on the sidewalk. "And what is this cow skull? The others I get. Lechuza. And the pig—the Wild Boar that used to haunt the high crops, come out of the riverbed and tunnel through the artichokes and asparagus. Stealing the women who worked the fields. And the Goat Man, the guy with the cloven hoof, who was handsome and dressed nice and stole your heart just before you looked down and saw his goat feet on the dance floor. But I don't get the cow."

Klinsman shrugged. "Kind of a twin to the goat. The goat lures the woman to the cow. Ranch stories."

"Why is he right before the woman? You going to make her a legend? Another TJ myth?"

"I don't know." He flipped the notepad closed, looked around. "Those are nothing. Jots. Me doodling because I didn't have anything to say yet."

"You scraped that red dirt over them."

"It was dark when I did that. I couldn't find my pencil."

He sipped his coffee, enjoying the weight and tilt of the heavy mug, mimicking her, enjoying the idea that together they could guide and balance such simple pleasures. He followed her gaze to the roofline, counted the obvious cameras, the less obvious ones, the hidden, the disguised, the possibles. For the old surveillance story he'd done, Oscar had shown him how to do this, how to look for strategic points and little cups and planes of black glass. The only thing that had saved Klinsman's piece back then was the angle he'd given the story; "the inward gaze of a city," he'd called it. Gina had called it lazy but fascinating, said she would give it to Oscar next time, when it was time to revisit the story. But she had given it right back to Klinsman.

By his count at least fifteen lenses could have been gathering Rita and him at this moment. This meant nothing to either of them as they tilted their heavy cups with fingers poised delicately around hot ceramic. A bank security guard could see that he loved her. A pawnshop clerk could rewind the morning and see the anger waning from Rita's expression. Five years from now the clerk could check again, try to decide once and for all if the *chola* in the field jacket loved the guy in the fool's shirt. A *mozo* who called himself Douglas Cook could erase them from this table, from this moment.

"I think I know who saved me," he told Rita. "Last night at the park."

"Good for you," she replied. "You're really learning how to be a good journalist. Now that it doesn't matter."

She eased her cup away, balancing it chalicelike on her fingertips, and looked flatly at him. Her eyebrows held straight and level, black parallels with her lashes. "This is day three. We're three for three so far. I think it was after midnight, last night."

"His name was Douglas Cook."

She laughed, putting her fingers to her lips to keep from spitting coffee.

"You know him?" Klinsman asked.

"No. I'm laughing at the name. That's the name you got? Some guy in *mozo*land tells you his name is Douglas Cook. Did he even say it right?"

"Not quite. He kind of pronounced it 'Kook.' But I'm pretty sure he's the one who spotlighted me. Thumbed 911 or whatever. Watched me through the darkness. Through the park's eyes. But I don't know how. How he knew *when* to look."

She set down her coffee and curled herself into her wire chair, hugged her knees. She rested her chin there, the same pose of her morning waking, but this time looking straight at him. A slight squint of amusement played on her brows.

"Usually I can tell what you know, Aaron. Almost always I can tell. But now I can't see. I can't see if you're playing with me. If you're trying to see what I know. If you're pretending to be so thwarted by your own thoughts. As usual. Or are you using Oscar's little tricks?"

"What do you mean?" he asked.

"You said 'screen.' You said I wrote words across my screen."

"Yes," he replied. "You can't write in lipstick across a lens. You wrote across your screen. I was watching you through your screen. You could tell from across your room. It came alive or something."

She leveled her gaze as best she could and waited, her hair pulled in a hood about her face but starting to free itself in black twists from her jacket collar. The morning sun shone in a yellow slice through an alley, a splash over her shoulder.

He kept going, thinking the further he went, the more her image changed, clarified itself: "On your desk, beside your PC, you keep your laptop open. It always looks like overkill to me, but then I think, *No, she's a photographer.* At first I thought, when I was running here, that Gina patched me in through your desktop, using work. But then I decided, no, through the notebook, which brings your work home."

"What else is on my desk?" Rita rolled her chin on her knee. "What else do you see when you lie there not sleeping?"

"Lots of moonlight," he replied. Then he felt a stun inside him, the snakebite slamming upward through him again. He saw the moonlight sparkling on her desk as he listened to the rhythmic tocking of wood, Louis crying out.

"A mirror," he said, deeply flexing his brow. "A little mirror, like for makeup. Antique-looking, but cheap. Like something Oscar would hand you."

"Oscar did give it to me. Told me what it was." She hugged her knees closer, dropped her chin in the little wedge between them. "It doesn't come alive. But I can sort of sense it. You learn to sense it. That's why Osquí gave it to me. Said we should all learn to sense these things. But I told him I already knew about that kind of sense." She pantomimed taking a snapshot of him, her index finger crooking sharply, then straightening with revelation.

"These things?" he asked.

In reply she only looked upward, then around, opening her fingers upward, too, as though flicking water into the air. She stood, her chair scraping the sidewalk. "But watch. Watch how I can tell. When I'm on."

She pulled a small camera, the size of a cigarette pack, from one of her many pockets and handed it to him. "I'll turn my back to you. Then you pick from three options. Look away. Look at me—really look at me, with interest. Or take my picture."

She removed her jacket and strode to the edge of the sidewalk. Caught in the whirl of her actions, in the whip of disbelief, he thought, *If she removes the jacket, she will be more sensitive.* She stood, boots slightly apart, arms akimbo. Her hair fell about her shoulders. "Go," she said.

He kept staring at her.

"Me," she said quickly. She looked over her shoulder. *"Mi blanca."*

"Easy guess," he replied. "Go again."

She turned away, held still, boots apart, arms akimbo. He aimed the camera.

"You're aiming the camera," she said. "But not pulling the trigger."

"You're still guessing," he said.

"Only about the second part. Because I know you."

On the third try he looked away, to the sun rising over the city rooftops.

"Away," she said

"Ausente," he said.

"Sí. Ojos ausentes. Because I know you."

29.

She gave him a ride to work. She looked so capable to him. She navigated the morning rush on El Cajon Boulevard as though it were all afterthought, one hand fingertip to wheel, the other propped at her temple, elbow resting on the windowsill. In her jacket with its many pockets she seemed ready for anything, any assignment, any place. They were heading into the low morning sun. Los Abandoned played through her speaker. *Nada mio es fake. Ven y tocame. Nada mio es fake. Ven y hablame.* What the Luchadors were playing at Café Cinema.

"I didn't know you really listened to Los Abandoned," he said.

"I'm shooting them today. A possible reunion. I have to go to LA. For the Juárez benefit."

"Watch out for the Luchadors."

Rita shook her head, squinting against the low sun. "Fucking Luchadors. Probably get into all my good shots." She looked at him, then back to the traffic, whispered something under her breath with his name in it.

"Why do you put me with them?" he asked. "Why curse me?"

"Because they mess up my pictures the way you mess up my life."

They watched a car in front of them hurry through the front end of a red light, saw the flash of the camera catching it.

"Well, you won't have me today. At the benefit." He cleared his throat. "Just you and the Luchadors and Oscar."

"The Juárez benefit is all appearance now," she said. "It's nothing anymore. The movie stars a Puerto Rican and a Spaniard. A dead guy from Chile writes the novel like he's so fucking impor-tant, but he never even *went* there. He left Mexico over thirty years ago. Can't anybody find a Mexican? They hold the benefit right where they should hold it. Right in the Tar Pits. Bodies bodies everywhere."

"Is Gina sending you?"

"It was on my tag last night."

"What else is on your tag?" he asked.

"You'll laugh. It's so old. So done."

"I promise not to."

She flexed her jaw. With her free hand she lifted her hair above her forehead, tilted away from him as though cooling her neck. "Chupacabra," she told him. "Right there with your sketches. Like Gina had seen them, too."

He ignored this.

"It?" he asked. "Chupa?"

"Manifestations of the beast. You know? On t-shirts, artwork, paintings on black velvet, tattoos, people singing about it. Maybe Los Abandoned will reunite and sing a song about it, save me a trip to TJ. TJ's too scary these days, with all the crossfire."

"If you go to TJ, take me," he said without thinking.

"How valiant. But why would anyone take you anywhere?"

"What do you mean?"

She chuckled, lifted her hair above her nape. "Did you really believe you could watch someone through their screen?"

"It made more sense than a mirror. You don't know the things I've seen. Or maybe you do."

"Have Oscar show you some other things he's found," she said. She lifted the point of her tongue thoughtfully to the top edge of her lip, marking her words. "He just shows them to me because I take pictures. He has some more mirrors. Some cheap pens. He has an eight ball. Dangly earrings. Maybe he'll give you one."

He wagged his head in exaggerated disbelief.

She whipped her cell from one of her jacket pockets and aimed it at him while keeping her eye on the traffic. "I have you now. Where would you like me to send you? With your bad border Spanish and your shirt with the yellow buttons of hope? You should find one with Chupacabra embroidered on it."

He leaned away from her, from his image on her cell, shoved his shoulder to the door.

"*Que mosca de picó*, Aaron? You worried that Douglas Kook is watching you through my cell? Or is it just me?"

"Oscar says we put the feed in the air. There for the taking. The gathering. So don't laugh at Douglas Cook. Help me find him. Help me learn how he knows *when*."

"You're more paranoid than your Prague uncle."

"I'm the opposite of paranoid, Rita."

"That's good," she said. "Trust Douglas Kook. Maybe the *mozos* will save us all from ourselves." She asserted herself toward the boulevard, adjusted her rearview. She glanced twice at the mirror, then pivoted it away from her, toward him.

She parked in back of the *Review*, where it was quiet and still beneath the jacarandas, amid the fall of their violet petals. She twisted toward him, hitched an elbow over her seat, checked him for presentability.

"If you could watch anyone you wanted," she asked him, "who might it be? Just them doing what they do? Besides me, of course. Who?"

"When?"

"Let's say right now," she replied. "You and I, watching together."

They both looked at the rearview, which was still aimed toward him. She adjusted it so that it faced between them and then tapped it with her finger, clicking a nail against the glass. He could feel the sound of the taps, softer than expected on glass. "Imagine in there. What are we watching?"

30.

*I*n the car, he used Rita's laptop to show her something his niece had done, Azariah's daughter Molly, who was already applying to college. He called up Molly's web page quickly, propped it on his knees for Rita to see. She opened her window to let in the morning breeze, which smelled musky from the jacaranda bloom.

Molly used an antique toy Uncle Mir had handed down to her father, part of their Prague uncle's collection. It was one of those vibrating tin football games where the players move from the electronic shaking of the board and use magnetic arms to throw and carry the metal football. The idea was for the opposing players to line up their tin teams, ball latched onto the spring-loaded arm of the quarterback, strategies laid out. Then the switch was thrown and you watched as the vibrating platform set everything into crude motion, the tin players colliding and falling, all plans collapsing into sad metallic desperation.

But Molly used the toy to act out small bits of Klinsman family history. The green metal field was now the ranch, complete with painted-in barn and reservoir and big house. The players wore little metal ball caps and sunglasses and had their names painted on their backs. The littlest, number I, was Aaron.

Klinsman showed Rita the scene that acted out the snakebite. When Molly throws the switch, no one moves at first, everyone just vibrates for a moment, as though trying to come to life. The tin Alejandro shakes his forked staff. The tin Azariah leads his little brother toward the fateful doghouse. Little metallic Aaron shudders along innocently behind. Molly's godlike finger looms in to guide everyone correctly, to help Az lift the doghouse. The snake is ingeniously re-created using a dismembered quarterback arm and its spring. The strike of the snake knocks the tin Aaron to the ground, where he quivers for a long while until Molly zooms in on him, then goes to fadeout.

"Not exactly what I had in mind," said Rita as her screen went dark. She readjusted her rearview, getting ready to drive.

Klinsman closed her notebook and slid it carefully back into its pouch in the backseat. "I'm ahead of you in one way. Just one."

Her smile was amused, skeptical. "Not from what I just saw."

"When I asked *when*," he told her, "you answered for *us*. You and I, on this side of the mirror. But I was asking about the other side of the glass. How does someone, anyone who wants to look, find you? Find you *now*—or anytime?"

She shook her head and started the engine, bringing back the music of Los Abandoned. "I don't know. I take the pictures. I do the capturing. I go in person. In the flesh." She fine-tuned the rearview, ran her finger along the edges of her lips as she looked at her reflection. "Take a nap somewhere, Klinsman."

"Not coming in?" he asked.

"No reason to," she replied.

"Then say hi to the Luchadors for me."

"Maybe that pretty one," she said. "If you want to find Douglas Cook, then bait him. That's what Oscar would do. Make *him* find *you*. The real you—in the flesh."

"I plan to do that. But not right away."

She nodded. "Yes. Wait a day or two. What park today?"

"The big one, of course," he said. He pulled his door handle, the sound awkward and hesitant, an incomplete count to three. She reached for his collar, pulled him to her, and kissed his cheek. Her lips felt cool and smooth as coins.

She left him alone beneath the jacarandas, where he sat on a stone bench amid the fallen blossoms. As kids he and his siblings would fit the cupped flowers on their fingertips, then rake the air with violet claws. He did this now with flowers he gathered from the asphalt around his boots.

He was surprised when two interns came out back for a cigarette break. They carried coffees with them, and biscotti, their cigarettes already dangling unlit from their lips. They told him good-morning, cigarettes bobbing in lipstick pinches. They still looked like students, their hair yet to find its color. He would call it blond but feel imprecise.

"We always did that," one said to him, eyeing the flowers cupped on his fingertips.

"They go with the shirt," said the other. "Kind of."

They lit their cigarettes deftly, holding coffee and biscotti together in one hand. They laughed out soft puffs of smoke as they watched him flip the petals from his fingers.

"It's been a while," he explained. "I wanted to see if they'd still fit."

They nodded with exaggeration, their cheeks hollowing as they inhaled. He thought again of Molly, wondered if she would laugh with them, show them her shaking tin rendition of his life. He felt he had no choice but to return to work.

Inside the *Review*, all the pastries and strawberries were gone save for a plate with a napkin marked "AK." All the desks were occupied except Gina's, Rita's, and Oscar's. Oscar had Artie with him and was sitting at Klinsman's desk helping the boy play a game of chess. As Klinsman waded into the desks, nodding good-mornings to those who looked up, the keyboards popped softly around him, like rain on dust. The screens filled the lower strata of the room with a cloud of blue light.

He eyed Gina's abandoned desk, so neat and dark. Often when he stepped into morning work he felt as though he were slipping into her mind, into the soft but relentless grease-pop of her weekly vision. Now he wondered if he stood within her masterwork, for the first time in these final seven days a part of something she was building, not tearing down, something she was about to show, not reflect upon. He thought, *I am the opposite of paranoid. I am one of sixteen desks, all doing like things, pursuing like events.* But it was impossible for him not to imagine them all shuddering together on a tin floor.

31.

Oscar didn't relinquish the desk to Klinsman right away.
As was his custom, he was reading whatever printout Klinsman had left, checking for any crossover with what he was working
on, pencil-nicking any highlights. Artie stood in the bracket of his
father's legs, playing beginner-level chess, pushing his queen and
then his knight around Klinsman's screen in illogical but effective
moves.

Oscar looked up at his friend. His smile was sheepish, but
his eyes held a stern kind of plea, a father's claim. The wishbone
lines around his nose deepened. On one knee he balanced
Klinsman's printout, pinning it there with a pencil. Artie's
hand held his father's other knee as though it were the arm of
a chair. Oscar's free hand rested easily on his son's shoulder.
His fingernails appeared soft and white, pressed into black skin
like pearls. Klinsman could see Artie's reflection in the screen,
the little boy's concentration looming above the chessboard. His
eyes were large but not round like his father's. Lifted by high

cheekbones, they had a Mayan angle to them. You could see his mother.

"Sorry, Aaron. I'm downloading another driver onto mine. And Artie likes your chess program better. He knows how all the pieces react."

Aaron looked around the room. Beneath the soft popping of the keyboards he could hear a low collective buzz coming from the earbuds of several of the desks, a gray mush of trill and bass. Klinsman stood chest-high in the rise of blue screen light.

"What are we doing, Oscar? What does she have us doing?"

Oscar gazed around the room, a melancholy scan. "I know," he said. "Almost everyone came in today. Suddenly."

"I spoke to Gina last night," Klinsman told him. "Did you? Did everyone?"

Oscar shook his head. He whispered something into his son's ear, then stood and took hold of Klinsman's shoulder. He nodded toward the back door.

Beneath the jacarandas the interns were still smoking and having their coffee. They wore purple jacaranda blossoms on their fingertips and waved proudly to Klinsman and Oscar. Oscar didn't whisper or attempt to hide anything from them. In fact, he turned toward Klinsman at an angle that almost included the interns, invited them to step into the space if they wanted, form a smoking circle.

"No one else has spoken to Gina." Oscar scratched the side of his nose. "It's what we all talked about. Just before you arrived.

Everyone came in, just like it used to be. What did she say to you? Do you know where she is?"

The interns watched, waited openly, their cigarettes hanging delicately in petaled fingers. The morning air was beginning to warm, take on ocean salt. The sun through jacaranda leaves lightened their hair in streaks, as on water.

"These are unfair questions, Oscar. From you. I found out about the mirror. The thing you gave Rita."

"Those are nothing," he replied. "Those kinds of things are all over the place. Maybe all over the place."

"I want you to show me some. Give me some."

"They're just trinkets." He opened his arms, turned his palms upward to Klinsman. "I picked them up at that last convention in Vegas. Some of them were even giveaways. Stuff in the press packet. A pen. A snowglobe. Marbles."

He looked at the hands of the interns, then wiggled his own fingers in front of Klinsman. "They even sold stick-on fingernails that they said could work. But those were very expensive. And I was doubtful." He dropped his arms. "I just don't know how far back to go with you, Aaron. I could never tell. It's kind of why I went ahead and nabbed the thermostat. Hoped you'd notice."

"Come to the park with me today. On your way to LA. Pool our resources like Gina wants. Let's give her what she wants."

"No," he said. "I need to get to the Juárez benefit on time. For the start."

"Then go back in there with me," Klinsman said as he nodded toward the back door, "and show me what you see in room 9."

"No."

"Why not?"

"Let me just tell you out here." Oscar glanced at the interns. They were drawing their final inhales, their eyes nicotine razors.

"Fine, then," Aaron replied. "The mirrors were draped. Someone thought they were lenses. Could be lenses. The tape pieces were covers. But maybe selective ones."

"Yes. Maybe."

"So someone was trying to control the room?" Klinsman asked.

Oscar shrugged. "As much as we can control anything like that." He looked to the interns. "No?"

"Fine. Okay." Klinsman smiled at the interns, who stepped tentatively into the circle, coffee cups empty but for crushed cigarettes. "The lights were all removed. For control. Light control."

"Maybe that," Oscar replied. "And maybe someone thought they could be something else. Like eight balls and snow globes and marbles. Maybe they were just being safe. I mean, once you start trying to control a collective effort—a collective system—you drive yourself crazy. And call attention to yourself."

"You see that room as a collective system?"

Oscar nodded, his chin high. "Sure, but unintentional. Without design. A motel as old as that, on the border. *De la Tijuana*. Chances are it's full of things. All things over the years we use to see each other. Old and new."

"You think the *mandros* can use them—those things?"

"I think if there are lenses, they will be used. I don't know how good the *mandros* are, but I bet it's how they spend their time. Finding as many as they can."

An ocean breeze passed, stale from rush hour but still briny. It played the leaf shadows over the interns' eyes, a kind of visual music over their keen expressions.

"Who was on the bed?" one of them asked.

"Yes," said the other. "Tell us."

She flickered her jacaranda fingertips at the two men, knowing they had no answer.

32.

*I*nside the *Review*, Klinsman sat alone on the couch and ate the hard roll and strawberry someone had saved for him. The paltry meal stung him, a nutrient rush. He squared the napkin into the corner of the coffee table, focused on his initials, purple ink slightly runny on the soft paper but carefully scripted. How he might've drawn them. Everyone else was busy at the desks, Rita and Oscar were off to the Tar Pits to cover the Juárez benefit, and Gina—it was easy to sense her at work, too.

He went to Oscar's desk, bringing the napkin along, keeping it neat. Klinsman's flash drive activated Oscar's screen, brought up the El Paso journalist's site, her objective tally of femicides, the pink crosses, the sincere facts and gathered vigilance.

Like a schoolboy Klinsman held the napkin and peeked around to see who would've inked his initials, with such care, in lavender pen. The interns shared a desk, the top right corner, number 13, so others could hurry around and throw stuff on them. One was seated there, the other was roaming, taking on more notes and more work, the collection that always kept them after hours. He knew their names but couldn't remember which was which.

He left the napkin at Oscar's desk, thought better of this and moved it to his own, made the easy end run to the interns' desk. The seated intern looked up at him and smiled. Her lips appeared suffused with little tapers from soda and coffee and cigarette pulls, her eyes the color of her freckles.

She was transferring some of the week's line art onto the screen by guiding a penlike wand along the graphic artist's designs.

"Can't you just scan them?" he asked.

"Victor won't use scans." She returned to the task, pulled her hair to the side so he could see her neck and profile, the flinch of a smile. "He doesn't trust them."

Klinsman glanced at Victor's desk, saw him using the same type of wand, hunched over his work, the spaghetti strands of his earbuds tangled in his long black hair. "But he trusts you? Your hand?"

"Just with this throwaway stuff." She tapped the wand to her lips. "Exploratory scribs, he calls them."

He felt her about to look up, but she remained focused on the line art. It was a sketch of a congressman who was trying to bring the tuna industry back to the city. Klinsman could remember the line of holding tanks big as an oil refinery along the downtown skyline, recall the smell, the collective urban relief when they were finally torn out. Victor had squeezed the congressman's face into an opened tuna can. It read, "Premuim White" on the can label. The congressman, the same one who had successfully led the charge to build the steel fourteen-foot-high border wall, was proposing a carefully written citizen-only workforce for the new tuna industry.

Klinsman offered her his pencil sketches. "Can you do these?"

The intern laid his notepad over the line art on her desk. With a measured flex of her wrist, she tapped the wand along Klinsman's sketches, beginning with the owl. "Gruesome," she said when she reached the cow skull.

"Oh," she said when she reached the seaweed woman. "Her."

"Yes." Klinsman angled himself closer, but with his arm between them. "The woman on the bed. Like you said. Out there under the jacarandas."

"Sure. I can do these." She traced the wand over the red slash across his sketches. "This, too? In color? I do color."

He nodded, and she eyed his reflection in her screen.

"You trust my hand?"

33.

After interviewing the IT head of Balboa Park's surveillance, Klinsman sat midway along the expansive stairs outside the Museum of Natural History, the building holding the park's security center. Back when he'd done the first story on the cameras, he'd been surprised to learn they were nesting park surveillance here, amid fossils and dioramas. Nona Kar, the IT head, assured him that there was no irony involved, and that the location had been chosen because of the museum's central location within the vast and sprawling park.

Klinsman had met Nona twice before, when he had covered the museum's exhibit on skull trephinations from ancient Mexico. She had let him into the exhibit before the opening and accompanied him so he could view the skulls without their glass casings. "You again," she'd said when he had returned a year later to do the camera story, the installation of the Robot MV99 Multivision and the W99 Multiplexer, which could, to quote Nona, "simultaneously record and display events from as many as nine cameras to a single screen."

Now he sat on the museum steps, in the tender noon sun, comparing his old notes with his new ones on his laptop screen. He had found Nona less forthcoming this time around, though just as polite. She had kept asking him about the skull trephinations, about that article, which she'd kept. "Did they knock those holes in the heads to let something out? Or to let something in? You should do that one again."

She wouldn't give him an exact answer on the number of eyes currently installed around the park. "It's not really something we need to divulge. Or that you need to specify. Suffice it to say," she told him, "the Robot MV99 and the W99 Multi and the RC60 receiver drivers now belong in the dioramas with the cavepeople downstairs."

Oscar had installed something he called a receiver driver onto Klinsman's notebook, something different from an RC60. Sitting on the steps, watching the museum goers climb past him, Klinsman wondered if they could see him as a diorama, as a reconstruction of a fossilized journalist, trying to write about something that evolved faster than he could type.

The sun felt nice, but the squinting was beginning to give him a headache, making him feel his accumulating lack of sleep. The thought of a well-aimed skull trephination did not seem too far-fetched an option for him. He pressed his thumb to the desired point, where he would aim the chisel.

From these steps he could watch parkgoers stroll the Prado, the spine of Balboa, from the bridge connecting to downtown, to the fountain whose high spray veiled the distant mountains. This was where Klinsman had said farewell to his brother Azariah. Save Aaron, Az was the last Klinsman to leave Southern California, to complete the family diaspora. The brothers' choice of the location for their last meeting was an easy decision.

Uncle Mir had brought them to the park often, whenever he had visited from Prague. He would take them to the International Cottages, the circle of fifteen tiny stucco houses set aside for selected cultures. The House of Czechoslovakia, back then, was joined with the House of Hungary. Jaromir Kilnsman, who refused to anglicize the family name, was amused by the ignorance revealed by this fusion. Not only were these two nations and cultures very different, but their respective immigrants did not get along well in the steeltown neighborhoods they usually inhabited. Their languages were very different, and they historically competed for space and attention on rough, working-class streets.

Uncle Mir enjoyed demonstrating this lingering tension to his nieces and nephews in the little house of hospitality. He would lead them into the cottage, greeting anyone there in Slovensky, introducing himself and his charges using their Czech names. They would watch the old Hungarians playing *shafkopf* look up from their cards and bristle in their Sunday suits. The Czechs playing pinochle at the other table would keep their eyes on their cards, maybe take a pronounced sip or two of coffee.

Then Jaromir would ease things by bringing to the food counter something wonderful from the Old Country, a poppyseed *kolachi*, a blood sausage, some plum wine. The two cultures did cross over with food and drink, and here at least the arguments softened, shaped by reconsidered recipes and ingredients. "Here, taste this. My *matka* always put cardamom in her breads. See?" And all present would nod while chewing, savoring.

On Sundays he always carried a fedora to match his suit, though he never wore the hat. He only twirled and shaped it constantly in his long fingers, getting the brim just so, the dents perfect. Its felt smelled like billiards chalk. Tall and slim, he had to duck into the Czech-Hungarian cottage and would immediately command attention. He was quick to smile, which made him exotic to the old ones who were used to more stoic expressions. Among themselves, they would refer to him as "the worldly salesman." Young Aaron would catch their powdery whispers as he watched their cards unfold.

Jaromir kept his black hair neatly swept back, but locks would always tousle forward after he ducked into the cottage, and he would leave them so, ignore them like a pianist. He would take the Klinsman children to all ends of Balboa, hiking in its eucalyptus canyons, shooting archery at the range, listening and watching the buskers along the Prado. But on Sunday he wore the suit and twirled the fedora, and that day was for visits to the museums and gardens, for matinees at the Old Globe, concerts at the organ pavilion.

He arrived from Prague always unannounced, and left without warning. He claimed there was some kind of federal warrant for his arrest. Aaron always doubted this. His uncle was an importer and exporter of fine costume jewelry. His argument for this type of jewelry was a distinctly political one, involving everything from facade to the absurdity of precious metals and gems to colonial exploitation. When Aaron began working for the *Review*, he started running little side investigations on his uncle. He discovered that there was indeed a vaguely phrased collection of orders against Jaromir Kilnsman, that most federal agencies had latent files on him.

Then one day Uncle Mir strode into the *Review* unannounced, fedora in hand, and told his nephew to stop the investigations. Gina had to leave her desk to intervene. The two hit it off immediately. "I love your paper," he told her. "We could have used it. Back when."

Gina, who had heard stories about Uncle Mir, looked at Aaron with a lift of amused betrayal in her eyes. "You undersold him," she said, as though Jaromir were only a projection among the news desks.

"You get it," Jaromir told Gina, the room, his black locks, now streaked with white, swooping forward with his words. "I hate fuckups who defy authority. As an excuse to be fuckups. Authority wins every time." He lifted his hat as though it were his manifesto. "I love those who accomplish first, then defy. Authority still wins but looks bad doing it—and eventually loses. Prague is the greatest city in the world. You take this paper there, when you're ready."

"And I hate spies," she told him.

Jaromir took Gina to lunch. While they were gone Klinsman asked Oscar how his uncle could tell he was being researched. Oscar told him it would be easy if he were using the Internet in any way. "He most likely has a trap site, a fake page with his name and picture all over it. He could use that to gauge any searches involving him and then could identify specific search sources through repeated visits. Just like ad companies do. Nothing tricky needed. Just a healthy dose of paranoia."

When Gina returned to the *Review* and Mir did not, Klinsman asked if he hit on her.

"He's a bit old for that," she replied, leaning on her desk, arms crossed.

"That's never stopped him," said Aaron, letting Rita watch and listen, frame them with her fingers squared.

"But your uncle prefers men?" Gina tightened her arms.

"That's never stopped him, either," replied Aaron. "What he prefers doesn't always exclude what he wants at the moment."

"Why so protective, Klinsman?"

"Because he loves us," said Rita, still framing them, one eye closed for accuracy.

34

*K*linsman slipped his notebook into his shoulder bag and walked Balboa, seeking the shadiest areas to ease the tension around his eyes. He tried to find a good place to rest beneath the giant bay fig, a tree he and his brothers and sisters had climbed as kids, but found that the park had reinforced the long branches with rebar and cordoned off the expansive root base. He wandered the Japanese garden, where he'd had his farewell picnic with Az. Several tourists were milling through, sending cell-phone captures and taking movies on their camcorders. So Klinsman walked on, his shoulder bag feeling heavy, the air grainy with static.

He found shade and solitude in the pepper grove. The grass was patchy in the duff of the pepper trees, but he could seek some comfort in the spice of the crushed leaves and seeds. Using his shoulder bag as pillow, he stretched out in the shade, crossed his ankles, and let his eyes lull. On the far stone tables, a few families picnicked, but the wide lawn lay empty except for feathery eucalyptus shadows.

Azariah had coffee and sandwiches with his youngest brother in the Japanese garden on his last day in the city. An hour later he caught a flight for San Francisco to join his wife and daughters in their new home. It wasn't as though Aaron and his brother wouldn't see each other again. It was just a moment of clarity between the two, and they wanted to mark it.

Az told Aaron he seemed ready to succeed at the *Review*, that he had found his vocation. Aaron nodded, a lie. Az said he had spoken with one of the photographers there, Rita, and that she had told him how great it was to work with Aaron and that everyone there liked him. Aaron smiled. He had asked Rita, barely a friend back then, to say just that if anyone from his family asked about him.

That was when Rita found out about the snakebite. Because she'd asked Azariah why Aaron was so moody. "But 'moody' isn't the right word," she had said to Az. "It's more like he's always standing right behind himself. You know?"

Klinsman realized he was falling asleep. He could actually hear Rita's words as the first fingerings of a dream. He let himself ease into the sound of her voice, let the tree shadows and sunlight flicker over his eyelids, let memories of Azariah's departure tug him into the grass.

But these turned out to be tricksters luring him to the waiting dream. Rita's voice gave way to images of the Robot MV99 and grinning skulls with trephinations. Nothing went into or came out of the holes, but his dreamgaze hovered over each black, chiseled opening as it swept slowly from skull to skull. He could hear the whir of the MV99, feel it like a heat scan along the side of his neck and face.

He was awakened by the quietest of sounds, a shuffle of leaves, the leap of a rabbit. It was the sense of motion more than sound that woke him. Klinsman lolled his head to one side and caught sight of a small boy walking the shadow line of the pepper trees. From the back he looked very much like Artie, and he was wearing the same soccer jersey that Artie had worn—this morning, or maybe the one from yesterday.

Klinsman propped himself on his elbows and looked around for Oscar, or any nearby picnic, but he found only open grass and the haunted shade beneath the willowy peppers. He grew concerned for the boy, who seemed too young to be alone and who walked with the erratic pace and tack of someone lost.

"Artie," he called out, careful not to sound urgent.

Instead of looking back at Klinsman, the boy glanced into the upper hollows of the pepper trees, as though Klinsman's call had echoed there. Then he began to run, heading along the shadow line toward the nearest garden. Gathering up his shoulder bag, Klinsman tried to keep an eye on the boy. His foot had fallen asleep, and he stumbled to one knee in his attempt to give chase. For a few strides he had to hobble, troll-like, through the leafy drapes of the peppers. He caught far glimpses of the boy's yellow-and-green jersey heading toward the stone wall of the garden.

The Zoro Garden was a terraced grotto with pathways that switchbacked upward. He had done a story on this garden, one that had endeared him to Gina but gotten him and the *Review* in trouble with the historical society and the park. In 1935 the Zoro Garden, with its amphitheater shape, had been converted into a nudist colony exhibition for the Pacific Expo. The official rendition was that the nudists were not really nude, that they wore body stockings and only acted out what nudists did.

But Rita found some old postcards for him that showed something else. And in some legal archives Oscar found records of an abandoned lawsuit that marked the sudden closing of the exhibit in 1936. Rita's postcards indicated that the nudists were indeed nude, and that they were all attractive young women. There were nine at first, and they were captured in innocent but thoughtful poses: brushing each other's hair, catching butterflies, singing together with songbooks held open. "See," she told him. "Like the Muses."

In one old postcard you see a line of sailors, wearing 1930s hip sashes on their uniforms, pressed to the wooden partition dividing the grotto from the rest of the expo. You see them peering through knotholes and cracks. This was the postcard that led Rita and Oscar to look further into the history of the garden. "They're not looking at people in body stockings," Rita told him and Oscar. She tapped her finger over the contorted positions of the sailors seeking the best views. "Those *mozos* are looking at real live naked women."

Now the grotto served as a butterfly sanctuary, with its climbing switchbacks, lacy shrubs, small pools, and rocky nooks providing the perfect environment. Still, you could see where the nudists had cavorted, the stagelike base, the many little plateaus surrounded by tiny streams and ferns. In the online version of the *Review* Rita organized her new photos with the old postcards so you could superimpose the black-and-white nudes onto the corresponding areas of the current Zoro Garden. This strengthened the article's claims and increased its popularity.

"It wasn't us," Rita said when Gina officially congratulated them amid the desks. "It was the *desnudistas*. Those original nine women."

From where he stood at base of the grotto, Klinsman could see no one. Butterflies flickered in the silent air like sparks above the shrubs and pathways. But he did not feel alone. When he shielded his eyes and peered more intently, a reflection from the periphery caught him like a splinter, searing his vision momentarily, bringing tears. He grew dizzy, as though the tension in his head had suddenly burst.

Some far-off busker on the Prado played a mournful trumpet. The tune, at least the snatches he could make out, could have been the saxophone piece from room 9. There were those six opening notes, stumbling forward, but more elongated and breathy on the trumpet. When he blinked away the pain and water and light from his eyes, he caught sight of a woman hurrying through the ferns in the upper reaches of the grotto. He saw only her bare shoulders and the back of her head before she disappeared. Her skin was very white, as though powdered, and her hair was black with a thin white garland in it.

He couldn't decide right away whether it would be quicker to traverse the grotto or circumnavigate it. He also considered just wandering into its center, to find a cool place to rest, maybe to finish his nap, listen to the distant wallow of the trumpet and know it was some other song he couldn't recognize.

A flock of yellow butterflies scattered about his head as he began a hurried climb through the grotto. On flat stones for sitting by a small pool, he found a filigreed hairbrush made of pewter. He took it with him, thinking he might return it to the woman, that it would give him something to present her. He raised the brush and called out.

"Their names are Calliope, Clio, Erato, Euterpe, Melpomene, Polyhymnia, Terpsichore, Thalia, and Urania," Rita had told him. "Their mother was the goddess of memory. In case you're wondering."

On the broad plaza of the Prado, he searched vainly among the scatter of tourists, buskers, and food carts. He didn't even know what he was searching for. A juggler on a unicycle, flipping a circle of things tossed in by his audience, called out to him, asking him to throw the brush into his mix. He knew this busker. He had done a story once on the park performers, and he knew not to mess with this one, this guy on a unicycle who loved to spar with hecklers, bait them.

Klinsman hurried away, staying close to the edge of the Prado as he headed toward the Plaza de Panama. From the statue of El Cid at the plaza's center, he scanned the parkgoers. He thought he caught a glimpse of the woman with the garland in her black hair. She appeared to be leaning against the wall of the archway that ran alongside the promenade, wrapping herself in a white gauze shawl. She seemed mothlike against the sun-splashed stucco and flitted into the darkness of the archway the second Klinsman sensed her.

But she could have been a busker of some kind, a dancer or actress off to perform somewhere in the park. He noticed formally dressed musicians scuttling with their cases across the plaza and some actors dressed for something Shakespearean, something pastoral.

He strode quickly to the archway, would have run but for the onlookers. The long archway always—ever since he was a boy—reminded him of the inside of a whale, the version you get from Pinocchio. The passageway was dim, and the series of arches appeared to taper like ribs bowing along a spine, ending in a far crimp of darkness. The effect was more pronounced when he ran through it.

It was empty, the parkgoers opting for the sunny walkway. Klinsman saw one figure flit across the far end of the archway. He jogged toward it but was suddenly swept into a group of young women dressed in flowing gowns, hurrying across the archway to the gardens. He went with them.

They were going to a photo session at the fountain. The Alcazar Gardens were formal, squared into neatly kept flower beds that were bright and heady now with red and yellow tulips. The photo session was for *A Midsummer Night's Dream*. He could tell because the women in gowns had joined a man wearing a donkey's head and another holding a lantern. Titania was lounging on her side in the center of the shoot, her hip and shoulder lifting, her flower-filled hair spread all about her. The photographer was using reflectors in this shady end of the garden to simulate moonlight. Klinsman felt as though he were gazing back in time twelve hours, in the moonlight of Rita's yard, or back hundreds of years.

He counted maybe three women who could have been the one he'd glimpsed in the grotto, ones with dark hair and bare shoulders. When the entire group looked in the same direction, at something at the far end of the gardens, Klinsman followed their gaze. But the corner entrance to the gardens was empty.

He walked up behind the photographer and asked the group what they had seen.

"I know you," said the hollow voice inside the donkey head. "You're a critic."

The entire cast looked at Klinsman. His head swam in their collective gaze.

"Good," said the photographer, a young man in jeans and a white t-shirt. "Great. Everybody just like that. Looking at your critic."

Not looking away from his camera, the photographer waved backward to Klinsman. "Keep talking to them."

"What did you see?" Klinsman asked them again. "Back there? Just now?"

"Somebody peeking in," said one, a forlorn youth in a burlap vest, holding the lantern.

"One of us," said Titania. She smiled at him, coiled her hip and shoulder. "But not."

"We know you," said the voice inside the donkey head.

"It was me," said a dark-haired woman with bare shoulders. She looked around at her fellow cast members. "I can do that."

Like flowers, they all turned toward her.

Klinsman held up the hairbrush. They all looked there.

"Yes," said the photographer. "Just like that."

"That's not ours," said the donkey head, nodding toward the brush in Klinsman's hand.

Klinsman walked away, heading toward the far exit of the gardens, the corner where the sun shone brightest. He moved in dreamchase, where pace goes slower than command, where eyes see quarry in the normal, pulse quickening for no apparent reason. From the garden's back gateway he could see through the sparse eucalyptus, across the ravine of Palm Canyon to the cluster of International Cottages.

He walked around the lip of the canyon, past the archery range where Uncle Mir had often taken them to shoot, to venture into the walking section of the range, their bows at the ready, looking for targets in wispy eucalyptus shadows. Connie was the best of the Klinsman archers, able to string her own bow by the age of ten. The bale targets glowed in the shade, windowlike, straw bristling metallic. "I imagine them as doors," Jaromir would say, taking aim, bringing bowstring to nose, two fingers curled. He was an expert marksman but shot only three arrows per excursion, each one a bull's-eye, whizzing exclamation points for his wide-eyed nieces and nephews. His black locks would tumble about his eyes as he watched the arrogant flight of his arrow.

Klinsman continued to the International Cottages, following memories of the Uncle Mir excursions, convincing himself that he was somehow exorcizing the folly of the last few minutes, his run after the boy and then after the woman with powdered shoulders. The cottages were closed, the circle of grass between them empty, quiet with the fragrance of a watered lawn. They were used only on

Sundays now, but on the off days he could sometimes sense the aftermath, maybe in the press of folk dances left in the grass, the soft pop of the breeze through the flags that hung over each country's doorway.

Klinsman put his hands in his pockets and walked through the circle, his shoulder bag riding easily against the small of his back. Strolling across a little grassy vale, he approached the back of the marionette theater, where Jaromir would take his nieces and nephews to the shadow-puppet shows and the Kabuki dances. "Someday," he always promised them, "I'll take you to the real thing."

From a few yards away Klinsman noticed one of Nona Kar's new cameras poised above the theater's back door. No attempt had been made to disguise it. It craned above the door like a small streetlamp, but with black glass. He stood below it, waved timidly at his tiny, rounded reflection. He tested the door, found it locked.

Once Uncle Mir had brought Connie and him through this door to show them the fallen puppets, the collapsed metal shadow figures propped on their guiding rods, the hanging marionettes, their mouths agape in frozen realization.

35.

*K*linsman sought refuge and order in the gardens outside the Old Globe Theatre, in the easier slant of late-afternoon sun, the squared plantings. But even here his sense of place and time buckled. Arborists, gone for the day, were in the process of removing the giant eucalyptus that had for more than fifty years been a part of Balboa's skyline, its elegant reach silhouetted beside the bell tower in every postcard. The tree had survived the beetle infestation that had struck eucalypts countywide. But much of its wood might have been compromised, and park authorities decided the risk of falling branches from such a tall tree was too great. Its unique height and strength doomed it. Another of Klinsman's stories, from a year ago maybe.

The arborists had removed and hauled away all of the tree's branches. What remained was the singular spire, marked with bands of red tape, indicating where the felling cuts would be made. Klinsman sat on a planting ledge near the empty theater, alone with the tree. The intense perfume of the arborists' cuts left the air cooler, bracing.

He could never come to this park without feeling that he was chasing something, running from something. Gina could not have found a worse journalist for this assignment: a man who needed a hole in his head, a man who couldn't even take a nap in the shade of a park without being lured and haunted—by the *desnudistas* of 1935 and by his vague notion of protecting his friend's little boy, just the specter of Artie. Why Artie? Why did Artie, the thought of Artie, lead Klinsman to feel protective?

He resisted sketching the eucalyptus spire and instead took some captures, attempting to be more journalistic about things. He took some more stills of Nona Kar's lenses around the theater courtyard, those he could readily spot, small black caps craning from lampposts or embedded in the old stucco walls like miniature cannonballs.

He returned to the *Review* at that odd hour when those not supplying copy grew wary of the possibility of extra work, of sudden drops by the writers coming back from daytime assignments, of last-minute requests by those heading out to cover the city's after-work hours. The low sun and hunched backs gave the news floor a study-hall feel, the restive and bitter grapeseed air of a library. Less than half the desks were occupied, and those present all wore earbuds.

At his desk he could strive for some objectivity, as part of Gina's grid, number 7, there in the center quadrant. Oscar and Rita were still at the Tar Pits, Gina in absentia. Klinsman drew worried glances. He was the least demanding of the center four, but right now he was the only one. He set to work, hunching in like the rest.

Balboa Park was full of feed, Nona Kar's own little Ring of Steel plus the hundreds of cells, digitals, and vidcams. It was a very old place and so must be filled, according to Oscar, with all types of eyes, ancient and new—peepholes in fences, viewscopes, lookouts, blinds, trephinations. But there seemed things today in the park only for Klinsman: a boy who looked just enough like Artie, the trumpet song, another woman not quite there.

He couldn't imagine Douglas Cook or any other *mozos* salting his afternoon with things that intricate, that fleeting and effective. Finding him, yes. They apparently could do that. Maybe they were still warning him off, needling him with little messages. *Keep us out of your story. Keep us out of this park, too.* They were watching his work, heard the music on that pan of room 9, saw Artie at his desk. With a couple bucks they could pay a busker with a trumpet, hum the first notes of the tune—close enough. How hard was it to find some little Mexican kid in a soccer shirt in Balboa? How hard was it to trick the eye of a man who can't sleep?

He pulled up notes and copy for his three stories, flipped open his spiral notepad and set it to the side of his keyboard. It was his typical series of assignments from Gina: one snippet on a quirky border incident, one cultural event, and a feature on the city's past and future. His insomnia, perhaps, had smeared them together, caused him to drag a bit of one into the other with overlapping nap-dreams. He hadn't separated his sketches as he usually did, had done them all on one common page.

The intern had saved her transfers onto his screen desktop, the icon nicked with the initial C—Caitlin. She was Caitlin. He clicked the icon, and the sketches covered his screen. Hoping to thank her with a nod, he looked to the interns' desk, then around the room. He found Victor over his shoulder at desk 4, looking at him, at his sketches, those on paper, those on screen. Victor returned to his line art, maybe a little worried that Klinsman was about to drop something on him, maybe hiding a laugh.

Klinsman compared the screen images with those on his notepad. The transfers were slightly cleaner, with some of the pencil featherings gone, some of the blackouts omitted, though the intern had attended to almost every brush and shading. Lechuza's owl eyes seemed more determined, the goat skull a bit more reflected in the cow—though the cow skull, on screen, appeared more hideous. Maybe it was the slight size increase, how that brought out human angles in the cheekbones and the beckoning sockets.

Klinsman got up and went to Victor's desk. At first Victor pretended not to notice him, bobbed his head a little to the music in his earbuds. His black hair bent the light in long sheens. Klinsman moved his shadow across Victor's line art, a plane full of little hand studies that was being transcribed onto his screen. At the shadow's passing, Victor finally looked up.

Klinsman made a quick little circling motion with his fingers as though shooing a fly from his ear. Victor removed his earbuds.

"Mr. Klinsman."

Once Aaron had heard respect in that. But by now it was just an exclusion. The graphics people were nervy and tight. Going to one of their parties was always a tricky affair, for Klinsman especially. They needed writers and others to come. But at these parties there was always a collaborative work, a large blank canvas of some kind to be filled with everybody's individual contributions to whatever vague theme was at hand. Oscar and Rita were terrible at sketches and paint, so theirs were easy, untouchable and irredeemable, clever in their ineptitude. Klinsman was just good enough to clip his way into the largest circle of sketching talent, just good enough to be considered with a snicker or a regretful sigh.

"Don't worry," said Klinsman. "I just need to ask a few questions."

Victor gave him a *vato* look, that proud lift of chin and lulling of the eyes. Klinsman had grown to like it, to sense a common echo in anyone who used it, a kind of ancestral nod, indigenous sorrow. *"Tirame,"* said Victor.

"Why do you have the interns—Caitlin—transfer your line art? By hand. Her hand."

"I don't trust scans. They're too . . ." Victor twirled his hand. Graphics people always tried to shape words in the air.

"Objective?" Klinsman offered.

"Yeah, sure. That's it." Victor scrunched his brow and looked at his studies on screen, a tumble of disembodied hands. "I scan my own, then get *her* transfers, too."

"To compare?"

"Nah," said Victor. "Probably not how you mean. I don't do any of the comparing. I just run a differential. I do an image-to-image search of the scans, then one for her transfers. Most finds come up the same. I look at the ones of hers that are different, extra."

"What are you looking for?"

"Originality," he answered. *Imaginando.*

"Hers?"

"Nah-nah. *Mine.*" Victor wagged his head and cleared his screen, bothered by something in the transfers. He tapped the transfer board holding his originals. "*Mire,* Aron. I take a piece, like that tuna-can thing today. The one you were looking at with her. I scan it and image-search with that scan. I get any hits similar to my work. That tells me if I'm copying something or someone too much. *Tú sabes?* Emulation is good, imitation is bad. But sometimes you don't know when you're imitating, stealing. All of us do it. Maybe you guys do the same."

"Then you do that with her transfers? From her hand?" Klinsman watched as Victor brought up a search engine on screen.

"Yeah. That's my own little idea. That gives me this extra little differential. What's in between the scans and her hand. Her hand trying to be objective. Then I can see what my work is doing to her. The influence. You know?"

He showed Klinsman an image-to-image search of the tuna-can line art. It really was a clever piece: simple, tight, immediate. The two dozen hits showed some of Victor's own work plus others kind of like it. The search with Caitlin's transfers offered six more possibilities, line art featuring squished faces, the iconic opened can, the one from Popeye.

Klinsman could see. The can was good. That it seemed to come from Popeye was good. Readers would tune in to that, be tricked, lured by the familiar. But the face in the can was probably too imitative. Victor would have to work on that, resketch the congressman. He wanted viewers to go into the known and be startled by finding something altogether unexpected.

"You use a different search," said Klinsman.

"Yeah," said Victor. "This one's better than Polar Rose and ones like that. Those use text tags. This one doesn't. Only the visual tags."

"Visual tags?"

Victor gave him the skeptical *vato* look, the exaggerated eyebrow lift and dipped chin. "You guys know nothing. Yeah. Polar uses visual and text tags, searches captions and shit. But this only goes for visual. Lines, angles, planes, arcs. We use this one."

Klinsman stared blankly at Victor's screen.

"Fucking writers, Aron *cabrón*." Victor shook his head and brought up a white page with a y and an x axis. "*Mire*. Any line or curve or angle drawn by hand will be totally unique on this plane. Yes?" He overlaid one of his hand studies onto the plane. Using the wand pen on his transfer pad, he drew guiding lines around the angles of the fingers, along the straights of the thumb, around the beginning curve of the wrist. "All those are tags, Mr. Klinsman. Totally unique. To the nth degree. See? It's even more exact, more deep than text. You and your *palabras chingandas*."

Klinsman stared at the bold lines and curves Victor had drawn along the hand. Victor deleted the sketch overlay, leaving the fat black lines alone on the axis, the hand in relief.

"It's the same with photos, then?"

Victor nodded with *vato* chin thrusts.

"Thank you so much, Victor." Trying to sound editorial, in command, center desk, Klinsman felt his words quiver slightly.

"*Bien, bien.*" Victor sighed and got back to his work.

36.

*B*ack at his own desk, in the press of waning afternoon glow, Klinsman ran searches on his own sketches using Victor's crawler. The interns, as usual, had switched off the fluorescent overheads as five o'clock neared, to let everyone know. The lamp from the break area provided the only added light. On screen, sketches of Klinsman's owl and pig brought up the usual hits, gaudy renditions of the border legends he had seen so many times before: Lechuza in airbrush colors poised above an infant's toes, the giant pig scuttling through tunnels of artichoke or asparagus ferns, the goat-skull man dressed in shiny black silk, dancing with curvy young *cholitas*. The cow skull only brought up old album covers from the '70s or ads for Texas barbecue joints.

He sensed the *Review* emptying around him, the peeling away of light and bodies and thoughts. He made scans of his sketches, ran those in addition to Caitlin's hand-drawn transfers. There was little difference in the results, nothing significant. His scan and Caitlin's transfer of the sketch of the bedcover in room 9 brought up the same three hits, each one featuring X-25 from *Santo contra Blue Demon en Atlántida*. The actress's orange-red hair matched her pantsuit and lipstick in an old movie poster and two screen captures. At first these surprised him. Then they made sense. He had drawn the vague seaweed woman after watching the Luchadora dance at Café Cinema, while thinking of the pattern on the bed cover. He had watched the Santo flick several times as a boy, as that *guero mozo* trying to let sleep find him.

He copied photos of himself from his niece Molly's site and from Connie's dormant page and put them on Victor's blank axis. That search produced nothing new for him, just images of himself he had found before. The photos were somewhat murky, stills taken from 8 mm film and videotape, Polaroids, ranch stuff. He could find it on Polar Rose or any generic image search using his name. He looked over his shoulder at Victor's desk. He was gone. It seemed everybody was gone. The lamp above the break area was taking over, the windows graying.

"You're it." A woman's voice, youthful, a yard-game call.

He saw Caitlin standing near the back exit on the edge of the light, about to leave.

"You close up," she said. "Unless you need me for something."

"Just one thing," said Klinsman. "I need to use your desk. And show me how to use that drawing board."

She smiled, went still for a moment, her arm bent to hold up a messenger bag stuffed full of take-home work. She appeared small behind it, as though trying to raise a shield that would hinder more than help.

"Please—Caitlin."

She patted the top of his head before she left him alone in the *Review*. At the corner intern desk, in the half glow, Klinsman felt on the unprotected edge. But he just kept going, with that cold wake of sleep deprivation. He copied the murky photos of himself onto Victor's axis. Holding the wand as a sketch pencil, he traced the curves and lines and arcs of his image, him standing as a high school senior beside the doghouse. His brothers and sisters liked to take shots of Aaron by the doghouse.

He superimposed a slightly tilted line along his shoulders, the curve at the side of his neck, which was cocked in a shy bend, the angles of his stance. The bend of one arm, the odd outward twist of the other, as though he were holding an invisible bucket. He looked for more. He made two brief ticks beneath his worn boots, attempting to convey the impatient foot-rolling of a teenager.

He removed the photo, as Victor had shown him. What remained on the axis were black lines, curves, and angles that did not reproduce him in any sort of virtual rendition but clearly evoked his demeanor—him, a deposed self.

He looked back once to be sure Caitlin had left and not stepped up quietly behind him to pat him on the head again. Then he fired the search, flinching at what might come, nothing—or a huge wash of images from his entire life, a tin boy shuddering on a metallic field.

There were only two additional finds, but they were enough to cast a black spike through the center of his thoughts. One showed him today at the park, hobbling on a sleepy foot beneath the pepper trees. The other showed him sitting at the bar of Café Cinema talking to Blue Demon.

A click on the Blue Demon image opened the photo alone in a field of bluescreen. An abandoned starter page of some kind.

Clicking on the other started a movie, a kind of movie.

37.

On screen was a vision of Klinsman napping in the shade of the pepper trees that afternoon. He was not startled at the picture itself but at its clarity, something he didn't expect from Nona Kar's new installations. The stillness made it appear you were viewing a pan of a photo, the willowed pepper branches hanging like curtains, the tight and dappled weave of shadows blanketing the ground and the sleeping man in a fool's shirt and boots. But Klinsman anticipated the movement about to come, a waking nerve-jerk ready in his legs as he sat on the edge of Caitlin's desk chair.

He paused the screen. This was what he had wanted to be able to do as a boy, watching Edwige Fenech in a *giallo*, or Blue or Santo or X-25 or Juno, to still them for a moment. It was that moment of discovery he wanted to covet and share at the same time. Maybe it came from being the youngest of nine in a close family that lived together in an impossible reality. He needed, in the immediate moment, for the discovery to be explained but to still be his, exclusively his.

But more also collected in him. He considered who might be watching with him. Gina could be there—here—waiting to interrupt, chide, discovering along with him. And if Douglas Cook and other *mandros* weren't seeing this now, they had certainly been the ones who had started it. Cook's *mozo* garage corner would be dark enough now, near sunset.

Klinsman called Rita. She told him she was on the I-5 just past La Jolla. She told him, yes, she was coming there. The thought of her in her car, in low ocean light, gave him some sense of protection. He called Oscar, and he was much closer, already heading up the Boulevard.

"But only for a little while, *cabrón*," he told Klinsman over the cell. "Then I get Artie."

The space behind Klinsman felt loaded, the empty desks haunted. How could the interns work in this corner, with everyone able to watch them with just a slight lift of the head, a thoughtful pause? Alight on his shoulders was Oscar's near arrival. Whatever Klinsman began now, Oscar would catch him doing. He could try for a quick preview to get ahead of his friend, or he could shut it down altogether, transfer everything to his own desk.

He left the screen paused and waited for Oscar. Waiting, too, was his image beneath the pepper trees, dreaming of trephinated skulls, the fluting of a captured breeze.

When he entered the *Review*, Oscar nodded once toward Klinsman, then shed his bag and notebook onto the sofa, getting them away from him—off him—as quickly and thoroughly as possible. In the singular glow of the lamp, Oscar's face appeared even more clay-like, his expression still creased from his thoughts of the Juárez benefit, whatever he'd seen at the Tar Pits.

Klinsman turned more fully toward him but made sure to obscure the computer screen.

"Was it that bad, Oscar?"

Klinsman must have appeared derelict, hunched in the dimness, trolling another's desk.

"It's just that it's getting lost," Oscar said. "It's all getting lost. It was more festival than benefit. I even sometimes thought I was at the Tarfest."

"What's getting lost?" Klinsman liked the throw of his voice over the empty desks, felt his nerves steady some.

"The killings. The women." Oscar hugged himself, a kind of collapse Klinsman had never seen before in his friend. "The ones disappearing in the sand. It's all becoming about the drug war. I mean, the crosses were there and everything. The pink crosses. But the music seemed wrong, the air seemed wrong. Boisterous, you know. Bravado. We have to keep count, Aron. Careful count. We have to help her."

Klinsman almost reached to clear the screen, feeling as though he were caught watching cartoons in newly solemn air.

"But what?" Oscar asked, finally coming toward him along the dim grid of desks. "*Que nos tienes?* What've you found for us?"

They huddled around the interns' screen, Oscar pulling an extra chair close, Klinsman making room but still holding his ground.

As Oscar took in the image on the screen, his expression flexed from slight confusion to open wonder.

"It's this afternoon," Klinsman explained. "At the park. After my interview."

"At least you're sleeping." It sounded like a question. Mexican, too. Oscar nodded toward the arrowhead.

"Not for long." Klinsman brushed the arrowhead, and it vanished.

Klinsman continued to nap beneath the peppers. Movement first appeared in the trees, the pepper's long willows, sad as phantoms, swaying around him in the breeze. The trumpet lullaby played, drifting from afar, coming from the busker somewhere up on the Prado. The boy in the yellow-and-green Team Brasil soccer shirt—clearly not Artie, but with some resemblance—ran through the scene. Klinsman woke up after the boy left the frame.

He hitched himself up on his elbows, looked side to side, spied the boy. Klinsman's expression went from mild confusion, as though wringing away dream thoughts, to concern. He scrambled up, gathering his shoulder bag. He hopped on one foot after stumbling momentarily on the one that had fallen asleep. "Artie," he called, friendly but loud.

As soon as he called out the name, the shot jumped to another angle on the action, and both of them were in the frame, the boy hurrying along the shadow line. There were faint, translucent figures up in the dark crotches of the pepper trees, crouching between leaf veils, wearing gauzy robes, it seemed, holding very still, wings folded. The boy seemed to notice them. Klinsman either did not or didn't care.

When Klinsman gained his full stride, shook off the pins and needles in his right foot, the shot jumped closer again, focusing on him. In confusion and concern, he raked his hair back from his face while he ran, searched for the boy. The sounds from the Prado, mainly the soft trumpet, grew more distinct as he neared the grotto entrance.

But he didn't reach the Zoro Garden, not at first. The shot lingered on the sign to the entrance to the park's Cactus Garden, and this was where it looked as though Klinsman were heading. Then Artie—it was clearly Artie, in his Team Brasil soccer shirt— was running through sage and ocotillo. In the next shot Klinsman was running through the same sandy trails, passing creosote bush and cactus, apparently still chasing Artie. Klinsman appeared to have switched shirts but held the original one in his hand. He could hear the buskers from the Prado, the trumpet player and the shouts from the juggler asking his audience to throw more props into his act. "Your apple, please! That bottle! Your brush!"

Then it jumped to a shot of Klinsman leaning against a wall— the grotto entrance—back in his original shirt, catching his breath, gathering his thoughts. As Klinsman turned to enter the grotto, the shot centered on the sign for the Zoro Garden.

This shot dissolved into a view of the garden. It was black and white, grainy, shuddering in its projection, washed in the light of the 1935 postcards Rita had found. Three ascending plateaus of the grotto were occupied with nude women, three to each level. The view was silent, but it was clear that the three *desnudistas* on the middle plateau were singing together, holding songbooks, garlands in their black hair, their shoulders so white they seemed to glow.

On the nearest level, three were catching butterflies with gossamer nets. Their bodies were partially hidden by ferns and bushes and the spray of a fountain. On the top level, the three women were fixing each other's hair, brushing, stringing in garlands.

They all appeared oblivious to any onlooker, to Klinsman's arrival. Then the one with the hairbrush seemed to sense something, Klinsman, perhaps. She looked up, sunward, then into the camera. She set her brush down by a small pool. And with that small gesture all the women hurried into hidden nooks and passages in the grotto, ferns whipping behind their swift exits.

And Klinsman shouldered into the frame, shuffling in the grainy black and white, his gaze following the upward sweep of the grotto. The contrast and variation were low. His satchel looked black, his shirt liquid white. He climbed the path through the grotto, appeared to catch a glimpse of something near the top, then picked up the abandoned hairbrush.

This was when Rita entered the *Review*, or when they first noticed she had arrived. Klinsman and Oscar looked up when she clunked her things onto her desk. Oscar paused the screen.

Klinsman watched Rita's silhouette approach through the dimness of the room, then refixed his eyes on the screen. Whenever he moved his gaze from the screen, he sensed an unpleasant drifting, a buzz in his nerves, the slow warning of disconnection, his body separating from his thoughts. The stilled on-screen image showed him holding the hairbrush and looking toward the top exit from the grotto. A small waterfall was frozen beside him, everything as he remembered it except for the black and white. But even that seemed right, an easy tumble of locks.

He felt Rita's hands on his shoulders, her breath in his hair as she lowered her gaze to the screen. Oscar's arm grazed him, then pressed in gently.

"Do you see it?" asked Rita, softly into his ear but enough for Oscar to hear.

"What? No."

She reached for the screen, tapped her fingernail against the stilled waterfall. "There it is," she said. "No? Her?"

In the pattern of the waterfall, in the striations of shadow, light, and reflection, was the woman from room 9. Klinsman straightened, his head pressing under the curve of Rita's throat. He could feel her swallow run along the crown of his head, like a brush over his hair.

"Jump it back," she told Oscar.

"Where?"

"Anywhere before this scene."

Oscar jumped to the scene with Klinsman and the boy running beneath the pepper trees. The image froze.

"Do you see her?" asked Rita.

Klinsman was distracted by the murky figures crouching in the branches, the things ready to fly. Rita's fingernail tapped a leaf-veil of one of the pepper trees, long enough to sweep the ground just behind Klinsman. The woman from room 9 hung in the willowy sway, in the Munchlike brushstrokes of brown and green and yellow.

"What?" asked Oscar. "What are we seeing?"

"Something from the motel," Rita answered, interrupting Klinsman's attempt. "Jump back."

Oscar jumped to the opening image, of Klinsman napping.

"At least you're sleeping," she said. She let them find the pattern of the woman.

Oscar found her first, just before Klinsman, in the bark pattern of the nearest pepper tree.

"Please don't watch any more, Oscar," said Rita. "Please."

38.

*R*ita fitted her throat to Klinsman's head, rested her chin there, hugged him firmly from behind, gathering him as she continued to make her case to Oscar.

"Let us watch alone," she said softly in Spanish. "Just this first time. Together."

She said something Klinsman could not follow, so quick and soft, the patter of a moth caught in a light shade. Oscar bowed his head, glanced away, then returned his look to them, down to Klinsman, up to Rita.

"Take a walk," she said.

Oscar stood straight in a kind of agreement but kept his focus on Klinsman. Klinsman touched Oscar's forearm. To let him leave with nothing would have been cheating, only a journalist's breach of faith, but a break nonetheless.

"I can tell you what I did," he told Oscar. "I can tell you how they find us. I mean how they can find us in any time. From any time to now. I used Victor's search. I used lines. Lines and curves. I put them in myself, over photos. Photos give too much. *Tú sabes?*"

Klinsman felt Rita stiffen against him, a swallow stroking his hair.

"If Aaron can do this," she said, "anyone can. Please, Osquí? Take a walk."

Oscar moved from the screen light, glanced back once to the stilled image of Klinsman beneath the peppers, Klinsman in noon light.

"I have to go call about Artie." He nodded to himself, bit his lip thoughtfully. "But I'm coming back. Right back."

Rita hugged Klinsman more tightly, rested over him, put her nose into his hair and breathed in. Together they watched Oscar leave the *Review*, watched his form go from the darkness between desks to the low glow of the rest area and out the door, into the Boulevard night.

Rita gripped Klinsman's shoulders. *"Andele pues,"* she whispered, pushing them both toward the screen.

In the grotto Klinsman picked up the hairbrush and then hurried in a black-and-white kinetic sort of way to the top exit. Rita watched him disappear through the upper gateway, passing between feathery lilacs and beneath umbrellas of sago palms. After the waterfall the figure from room 9 did not appear in the grotto, and it could be assumed he was now pursuing her in some way.

In the expanse of the Prado, sound returned, but everything remained in black and white. The trumpet played, slowing the feel of the scene. Not until the juggler on the unicycle called for the hairbrush did the scene melt into color. The view jumped in close to the juggler. He wore a black bowler and a tight-fitting black shirt with long sleeves amplifying his dexterity. When the view pulled back from the black shirt, everything was in color. He juggled a handbag, an apple, a water bottle, a ball, a banana, and a stuffed animal. All the while his unicycle appeared ready to fly out from beneath him.

But Klinsman kept the brush and left. This gesture made it appear that the brush was some sort of talisman for him, and he carried it across the adjoining plaza to the El Cid statue. The scene changed to follow someone else across the plaza. It was unclear at first who was being tracked because a group of parkgoers was moving in the same direction. But very quickly it became clear that a woman in a gown, one of the actresses from the photo shoot, was the focus.

She hurried past parkgoers toward the archway. Beside the archway entrance she briefly leaned against the wall and lit a cigarette that she had tucked into the sash at her waist, along with the lighter. She took only two drags on the cigarette before tossing it away, catching sight of something across the plaza, maybe Klinsman.

Then she was hurrying down the archway with others dressed like her, more actresses getting to the photo shoot. Their pastel gowns trailed in long folds behind them as they neared the end of the archway, the sunlit turn into the Alcazar Gardens. They turned the wrong way at first, then one realized this and did an about-face, jumbling the others. They all pressed together, laughing, then pushed one another in the right direction, back across the archway and toward the Alcazar. Watching the film, Klinsman could almost smell their powder, the flowers in their hair. As they crossed the archway, following the bar of sunlight streaming from the garden, they caught Klinsman in their whirl, swept him along. Holding the hairbrush, he followed them.

In the garden Klinsman confronted the entire group of actors. They were all in very bright moonlight, that false glow created by the photographer. But the photographer was not there, or could not be seen in the shot angle. So Klinsman seemed to have them backed against the wall.

"I know you," said the one in the donkey head.

The entire cast looked at Klinsman. He took a step back, as though a bit dizzy.

"What did you see?" Klinsman asked them. "Back there? Just now?"

"Somebody peeking in," said one, the forlorn youth in the burlap vest, holding the lantern.

"One of us," said Titania. She smiled at him, lounging. "But not."

"We know you," said the voice inside the donkey head.

"It was me," said a dark-haired woman with bare shoulders. She looked around at her fellow cast members. "I can do that."

They all turned toward her.

Klinsman held up the hairbrush. They all looked there. He set the brush down gently before them, as though offering it to Titania. She smiled at the gift as Klinsman hurried away.

Rita paused the screen. The newsroom had grown considerably darker with full night outside and only the soft overhead glow of the lamp at the back wall. She was now sitting beside him, close enough to shoulder him once. He hadn't realized she had moved, that she was no longer watching over his shoulder, that she had taken Oscar's chair.

"How much has changed?" she asked.

"That's hard to say."

"Try," she said.

"The Cactus Garden. I didn't go there today. I haven't been there for years, never with Artie."

"That was you and Artie at the warehouse. The other day. I got that." She looked at him straight on, then tilted her head back slightly, skeptical lips and eyes. "You didn't. Not quite."

"You don't understand how it is, Rita. Watching this, expecting. Trying to remember."

"Okay." She nodded toward the screen, to the stilled image of Klinsman about to pass through the Alcazar gate.

"The grotto was all different," he said. "There were no women there." He rubbed his eyes. "Except maybe one."

"Maybe? One?" She opened her hands before the screen, spreading her fingers in a plea. "It was an old reel from the '35 Expo."

"I meant the part where you could see me," he told her. "The real part."

She widened her eyes, her only prompt for him to continue.

"The Prado stuff was the same. The juggler. The horn music."

"The saxophone," she said. "The one from room 9."

"Not from the room," he replied. "From the pan of the room. See how it can be? And here it's a trumpet."

She shook her head. She looked tired from her trip, sad. The glow from the screen highlighted her profile as she eyed the stilled image of Klinsman about to pass through the Alcazar gateway. The light edged the curves of her eyes, her face, the stroking of an eclipse.

"Did you ask the busker about the song? Its name? Who requested it?"

Klinsman shook his head. "I was trying to follow . . . to find . . ."

"Who?" she asked.

"I don't know." He realized he wanted to get back to the screen, to get back in there. Not away from Rita, but with her there. He rested the back of his hand on her wrist, and quietly she spun her fingers to take hold.

"What else?" she asked. "What else might be different?"

"The exchange I have with all of them. The words are the same, but they seem different. Like we all know each other. I don't remember offering the brush. But I might have. I left it somewhere. And the moonlight. The moonlight was there."

She tapped the transparent arrowhead, sending Klinsman on his way.

39.

He could imagine how she saw it. The shot looked over Klinsman's shoulder as he stepped into the clearing beyond the Alcazar Gardens; it put you at his ear. The saxophone—no longer a trumpet—began again, and all the images were cast in sepia tone. The eucalyptus forest rimming the canyon was inhabited. The figures were too distant or shadowed to discern clearly, milky negatives in the sepia, but some were clearly archers wearing quivers, carrying their bows. One of the archers was tall, the others children. The vague, crouching forms from the pepper grove lurked also in the high, hooded reaches of the eucalyptus. The woman from room 9 had reappeared also, shimmying in the breeze-swept leaves, dematerializing here, re-forming over there, if you found her, stayed focused.

The next shot, a fade-in, offered a sudden image of Jaromir Kilnsman. Uncle Mir stood about to shoot an arrow. His shoulders and arms formed a perfect horizontal as he drew the bowstring.

The sepia tones almost indiscernibly had run into color, the sometimes gaudy and uncontrolled hues and glows of 8 mm.

All the shots, close and long, blending between sepia and 8-mm color, painted a hunting story in the eucalyptus woods. Rita saw the Klinsman children, the four oldest brothers named for the Book of Daniel, the four sisters named for the story of the Immaculate Conception. Connie appeared several times, shots of her stringing a bow, taking aim. There was a close-up of her drawing the string to her nose, smiling, glancing off camera to take instruction. All the other children appeared only once, lingering pans of them posing dramatically with bow and quiver under the speckled light of eucalyptus. There were no shots of Aaron. The viewer remained with him, at his ear, ready to whisper.

In the long shots of the woods, the distant archers moved among the trees, hunting in pairs. The crouching figures lurked in the high branches above them. Only the tall archer, Uncle Mir, seemed to notice them, looking up once in a while, threatening them with his aim, making them vanish back into the canopy shadows.

There was a long pan over a final image of the children holding a large rattlesnake, long enough to need six of them to display their trophy. Connie cradled the head, cooing to the snake as though it were only sleeping. Azariah held the rattle end, weeping.

Two Aaron Klinsmans walked onto the lawn area of the International Cottages. The audio was ambient. The flags popped softly in the breeze, the overhanging eucalyptus shushing. The two images of Klinsman were reflections, and they eventually folded into one another, became one. Then he turned slowly, looking at the closed and hollow cottages, the breeze sounding hollow, too.

Rita paused the screen.

"Aaron," she whispered. Tentatively she touched his shoulder, then brushed a fingertip along his ear.

"What's he doing?" he asked, eyes on the screen.

"He's deciding," she replied, tapping the screen. "Choosing a door."

"Which one do you think?" he asked. "What's behind the door?"

She shrugged, holding her shoulders up for a long moment. "Maybe nothing yet."

She looked at the real Klinsman.

"But pick one."

Klinsman began to move. In close-up he appeared pensive, a troubled lift in his brow, skeptical, but there was worry there, too. So it appeared he was moving toward one of the cottage doors. There was a shot of the door to the Czech Republic, and the door began to swing open, revealing the room beyond.

The room was in Uncle Mir's Prague apartment. Winter light shone in a heavy and final slant between empty armchairs, casting long shadows of book stacks across an oval carpet. The saxophone music played. The shot was a pan over a photo, but because of the music and the roving eye, it seemed like film. The shot glided to Uncle Mir's phonograph, which he needed to play his 78s, his Decca collection. The collection formed a tower beside the phonograph. The music made it appear the record was spinning, spinning in 78 rpm.

The saxophone was Coleman Hawkins playing "And So to Sleep Again." But on the Decca 78, the title didn't fit, and thus it read, "And So to Sleep." Hawkins was reinventing the instrument, testing its limits on the low end first, finding how far back he could pull the notes, how thoughtfully he could release them, how painfully. He was taking a 1952 pop tune and cutting into people's memories, people's hearts. It wasn't jazz, it was a man living, Uncle Mir once said.

After Klinsman returned to the clearing he quickly chose the next door, the House of Italy, knowing. The door swung open. The view faded in. Edwige Fenech walked across the room, leading you. Her black hair was piled high, sweeping upward with her mascara and her stride, the lifted swagger of her breasts. She wore snakeskin pants with a matching halter and walked past Technicolor furniture, a rotating light coloring the walls. She looked back to make sure you were following. But her look was arrogant, either knowing you were coming or that you were a fool to stay behind.

She took you to a scene of Aaron standing with Aracely Montiel, both of them dressed very formally and posing by a fire. Firelight wavered over them, giving the image movement. Aracely's hair was up in a Gibson Girl, and her chin was raised proudly, revealing the elegance of her neck. Edwige Fenech's voice could be heard, her accent filled with French and Tunisian twists, the vowels with extra fluctuations: "When midnight strikes, you must think of me."

The next shot took you back to the clearing amid the International Cottages, with Klinsman alone in the soft popping of the flags and the hushing of the leaves.

Rita paused the screen.

"I thought there would be more in there," he told her. "I was worried there'd be so much more."

Rita looked at him, holding her face still for him. "There will be."

"In everything?"

"In every garden, behind every door, in every scene."

"Those figures," he said. "Those things hunched high in the trees."

"I don't know what those are," she said. "Maybe they're like little tags. Where to put more things. Before digital, we used to smear marks on our proofs. That's what they remind me of. But maybe they're just nothings. Dodges and misdirections."

"But the boy and my uncle could see them. They looked at them."

She shook her head. "It only seemed that way. Those figures were added after. It's just photography, Klinsman."

"This thing has a better memory," he said. "Better than my own."

"No." She shook her head, her hair beginning to free itself from the clasp at her nape. "That's not possible."

"But it knew the song," he said. "The one I couldn't remember. It remembered."

"'And So to Sleep.'"

"'And So to Sleep Again.' It didn't fit on the record."

"Then your memory is more complete. See? You're not so bad off."

She was being kind to him, fighting to be that way. She took his hand, tucked her bottom lip. "I bet you even know that line. That line Fenech says. That cryptic thing, from one of her *giallos*. Your *giallos*."

"I do know it," he told her. They hunched closer in the screen light, as if in front of a fire. "It *is* a line from one of her movies. But not a *giallo*. She was in *Madame Bovary*. She played Madame Bovary—*giallo*-style, yes, with eyeliner. That's a line from that book. That's her dubbing Flaubert. When midnight strikes."

Rita lifted her chin. "You must think of me."

They continued to watch. Klinsman left the cottages and headed along the edge of the park to the puppet theater. As he neared the lens, the light gradually changed. Spilling his shadow over bright grass, he passed from afternoon sunlight into shade and then into an evening kind of shine, of reflected sunset and neon. The shot jumped to a side view of him as he neared the back door of the theater. The stucco wall was deep yellow. The shot closed in, up over Klinsman's shoulder, the view becoming grainy as it sacrificed resolution for zoom. The door, with Klinsman's hand on it, had a number 9 and a peephole.

Rita paused the screen.

Then she turned it off.

40.

*R*ita's shutting down of the desktop plunged them into a deeper night this time. It took a while for them to get accustomed to the dimness, to blink their way into the room and the present moment. The lamp at the back and the slate glow of the city through the windows provided the only light for them.

"*Mandros* make these," he said. "They don't just watch."

She had spun her chair away from the screen, was facing the dark maze of desks, resting her eyes there. After a moment she nodded.

She called Oscar, told him they were finished. Oscar sent her his view of the street where his walk had taken him. He fanned the view of the El Cajon Boulevard sign presiding in pink neon over the street. The taillights of the cars formed red streaks across her cell screen.

"And this will keep . . . growing," Klinsman said. "Backward and forward in time."

Rita looked up from the glow of her cell, the colors like swimming-pool reflections across her face, making her appear newly surfaced. She waited for him, just looking.

"Yes." She held the cell light between them like a candle.

He tried to think of what to ask her before Oscar returned, questions he had for both of them and questions only for her.

"I want to go through that door. That one we found."

"We will," she replied. "Together."

"We'll discover who was on the bed."

"*We* were on the bed, Aaron." She sighed deeply, raising her shoulders with it, then bringing herself down, her face closer to his. "You know what we'll see, what anyone will get to see eventually."

Rita kept looking toward the door, watching for Oscar. Klinsman felt safe with her at this moment, a tremble before letting go of a hand.

"I want to see yours, too," he told her.

"You'll be able to find mine through yours. Or Oscar's. Or Gina's. Or yours through hers. All sixteen of these desks. One through the other. All eight of your brothers and sisters and their children. All one through the other. *Una celosia.* You see how it will work?"

"How long have you known?" He nodded to the dark screen. "About this?"

"Half a day," she answered. "Just after I left you this morning. After talking with you. Driving into LA, catching the high view from the ramp. Right at that moment, seeing that fucking endless city, thinking about you in my room. Thinking about that silly tin thing your niece made. I thought—I realized . . ."

"At the festival?" he asked. "Did you see some of them?"

"Them?"

"The *mandros*."

She looked toward the door again, a hitch in her sigh. "Games are no fun for them. Not when you can make these, with real lives. The *mozos* call them *vidas*. I found one guy—a Mexican in a turtleneck. He told me about *vidas*. But I had no idea they would be like this. This involved, using everything."

"What did you give?"

"What do you mean?" she asked.

He looked at her and waited. .

"I gave him two pics," she said. "One of Osquí. And one of you."

This time he checked the door, eyed the entire room, the empty sofa at the back cowering beneath the single lamp. With her fingers on his chin, she adjusted his gaze back to her.

"But things you did," he said. "Certain things you did in room 9. You seemed to know more. Then."

"Certain things I did?" She leaned away from him, parted her lips thoughtfully. "I did know more. I knew how you felt about me. Which was more than you did."

He shook his head. "You took that piece of tape. You lit the room. You controlled the light."

"I always control the light. That's what I do."

"The tape."

"The tape?"

"The tape pieces," he said. "They were covers. Lens caps. Not markers for staging or lighting. Not any of that other stuff you let Oscar and me talk about."

"You're being paranoid again."

"I'm not paranoid," he said. "I'm right. What we just watched proves that. The person who put the tape up was paranoid." He swiveled his chair a bit. "Maybe."

"Maybe?" She undid her hair, shook it free so that it bloomed about her face. She started to tell him something more, leaning back, her look searching, seeing something in his expression. Then she stopped herself. She eased forward in her chair, their knees grazing, and put her face close to his. Her scent like steel shavings screwed into his thoughts, up into his gasp.

"Okay, *chingadero*," she whispered. "Yes, I felt eyes on me in that motel room. Eyes on us. I did not feel in control of the light or anything. I took the tape just to fool myself a little bit, to give myself a point of reference. One I quickly forgot about."

"But you went ahead?" He spoke softly, his voice breaking a little with the effort.

"I was okay with it. I'm okay with all of this."

Instead of waiting for Oscar, they decided to go find him. They walked the boulevard, heading through North Park toward the sign. The sky was amber, deep, embedded with near and distant glows, yellow swells in the night. Their shadows kaleidoscoped on the sidewalk around them as they passed beneath the colors of 7-11 signs, traffic lights, marquees, and the neon arrows of clubs and bars. They did not hold hands but did stay abreast of each other, he sometimes watching her, she seeking glimpses of him. Both were trying, trying to sense their path together, maybe where it would divide.

They would sometimes look up together into that deep amber sky, one leading the other. What lay behind the door they had left closed played in their thoughts, shone in the hard and soft planes of their expressions, lit by the array of colors from the Boulevard. He stopped—it seemed for no reason—and she sensed his pause two steps on, then turned back to join him there in the middle of the sidewalk, other pedestrians hurrying by like lost shadows. They embraced, his arms wrapping tightly about her waist, her arms reaching high around his shoulders. She buried her face deep in the crook of his arm, and he pressed his eyes to her nape. Whatever space and openings compressed between them, filled with their breath, remained unknown and unseen to the rest of the world. Just those spaces, slivers of air, where they whispered to each other.

41.

Oscar paused the screen. He sat on top of Klinsman's desk, beside the keyboard. The street light through the window curled like smoke along the contours of his dark skin, carving him from the night. He faced them, watching the effect of what he had just shown them, the turn of anger in Rita, Klinsman's hesitation.

"What did you expect? From me?" Oscar stared at Rita, nudging her knee with his foot. "I needed to see how quickly it could be done."

She thrust her chin at Oscar. "You needed to show us how fast you could catch up."

Klinsman hardly cared about who was first, who was fastest in this race Gina had started. And none of it was that simple. He found the *vida*—his *vida*—using his transfers, then Caitlin's hand, Victor's differential. "Help me find Douglas Cook," he said, looking at the stilled image of his embrace with Rita.

"Who?"

"He's some *mandro* Aaron's fixated on," explained Rita.

"He's the one," said Klinsman.

"There is no *one*," said Rita. She nodded toward Oscar, a little push of disdain in her jaw. "See? Oscar just made his contribution." She clicked the image off the screen, then looked at the two men as though she had just covered herself.

"I only gathered what Douglas Cook can gather," said Oscar.

Oscar waited for Rita to return his gaze. She glanced at him, anger in the quick flash of window light in her eyes. It remained, that crawl of light on the edge of an eclipse, as she shifted to Klinsman.

"You found this using sketch overlays. So they use visual signatures. You can find anyone. In a crowd, at any time. Anywhere in all files, all online feed. You would start with clothes probably, the way someone dresses. But then their angles. Their gait. The slant of their shoulders. I have to use my eyes. But with this," she nodded toward the screen, "you could use settings."

She focused on Oscar, raised her shoulders.

"Clothes," said Oscar. "Yeah. That's usually enough if you're actually watching. But angles are best for *searching*. Shoulder angles, posture, neck angles. The gait, yes."

Still sitting atop the desk, he lifted his boot for them to see.

"You're such a fucking Mexican," said Rita.

"Foot pronation," said Oscar. "The angle of your heel. After it's worn a little. Just a little, after just a week or so."

"You're still a fucking Mexican. Fancy words and clever thoughts can't hide you, Osquí. Aaron got ahead of us on this one. Ahead of you."

Oscar ignored her, looking intently at Klinsman. "We're walk-ing fingerprints. And the more lines and patterns you gather on someone, the easier it is to find them. Pull them out of any time, any place, like you said. Frame them."

"Then *why?*"

But Klinsman could feel the answer in the silence and shrugs, in Rita's look away, Oscar's searching gaze, his wide-eyed scanning of the darkness of the newsroom, the loom of the sixteen desks. It's what people do, what they have always done. You build the Tower of Babel, always, because it's in your head and heart. It is always torn down, and it is always being built. If you wrote a word or drew a picture on a blank wall, in a day the wall would have ten more. In a month it would be covered. Half your brain is committed to it, wired for it.

"Gina," said Oscar. "She would know we'd find something like this."

"We should try to tell her," said Rita. "Show her. You, Klins-man. You're the one to do it. You're the one she picks. For what-ever reason. Whatever the hell the reason."

Klinsman looked at Oscar.

"What?" Rita asked them. "What, *cabrónes?*"

"We're pretty sure she's seen," said Klinsman. "She saw what we just saw."

"Or she will," said Oscar. "Very soon. She's watching, staying with us."

Rita aimed her look, a look of anger and betrayal, at Klins-man. Her lips remained set and full, her eyes stilled, lulling. He closed his eyes to it, remembered it, feeling it as something from long past. When he opened his eyes her expression was gone. Seven days, seven years, seven lifetimes. He felt time in the breathless and gathering silence, could taste it like parchment on his tongue.

"I have to go get Artie," said Oscar. He slid himself down from the desk and touched their shoulders. Klinsman sensed his grip, the same maybe for Rita, a kind of taking in it, fingers hooked into muscle.

Klinsman and Rita went to her house. When he asked she told him Louis had already gone to Manzanillo, to start that life whether she would be in it or not be in it. After last night, she told Klinsman, that was what he'd decided. "Leaving it to me. He's down there now, setting up shop."

She led him up the stairs, past the holy-water cups filled with paper clips, keys, and chocolates, toward the studio. He had hoped for the bedroom this time, hers, with Louis away, waiting, forever waiting. She must have divined this hope. She turned midclimb, twisting at the waist, and lifted one brow sharply, halting him on the stairs, prompting him to change the direction of his thoughts.

They would go to the studio, where the moonlight would be cut into slices by the blinds, thrown across the floor, the daybed, the desk, the mirror. She would leave in three days. She would be with him forever.

In her moonlit studio they opened the door to room 9, let it swing with the gentle push of his hand into black fade-out, fade-in.

Coleman Hawkins played, his graceful stumble of opening notes leading them out of the blackness and into the room filled with the softest glows, neon peeks through splits in the curtain, a snowy light from somewhere overhead.

They let themselves be led to the door three times, cursoring different paths for each search, different traces through Aaron Klinsman's faltering, fractured, yearning imagination. He could feel Rita's doubts each time, coaxed by Edwige Fenech on a *giallo* saunter, Aracely Montiel in a chameleon dress, Jaromir Kilnsman drawing his bow. They could not seem real, or none could appear more real than the other.

Each time on the bed seemed different and unreclaimable. Once they seemed to be tearing each other into nakedness, gripping and biting each other, always about to cry. The view shifted naturally, as though moving around the bed, keeping an eye on the most intimate space between them, where their pulls and thrusts felt most urgent. When their bodies arced away from each other, that was when they seemed most desperate, the most searching, a bending of shadow and flesh.

Each time was like nothing they had seen before. There was nothing movielike or tapelike about it because the view felt singular and collective at the same time, traveling along a series of eyes around and above the room. None of their expressions appeared borrowed, and all were lifted in a kind of understanding sadness, even when they smiled. In the most languid of versions it was clear that he loved her most, that she was offering parts of herself she knew he needed. She watched him, assuring herself that he would be all right, at least for a while—that he might find sleep one day.

In the version where it appeared they were almost swimming, he found her with movements slowed by water. In the end they stood in a spray of light, their bodies slick, not touching but wanting to touch. When she closed her eyes and leaned her head back into the flow of light and water pouring from above, he began to break from within, and it was visible.

42.

While she slept on the daybed he used the search to find Rita in LA. He didn't care if she woke and caught him watching. He felt as though he were now living his life several moments at a time, fingering back into the past, ranging into the future, slipping into foregone chances, shuddering through doubts. In this he experienced a clarity, a falling kind of knowing, a quickening.

He saw her face up close for a long moment as she drove. He could tell she was driving because her focus sharpened and relaxed with the roll of the freeway. The daylight—an ocean light, redirected light—played across her eyes as she traveled the marshy section of coast, the narrow break between cities. Then, as the light thinned to the palest of yellows, he knew she had climbed the high bank of the freeway and was catching sight of the northward span of LA. He was getting to see her realization, the knowing. The look in her eyes, the widening, the brimming, compelled him to turn from the screen and gaze at her sleeping form naked and uncovered in the iron dimness, curled into herself.

At the La Brea Tar Pits, sometimes he was there with her, in clear reddish October, and sometimes she was there without him, in a fuzzier spring light. He had covered the Tarfest once with her, three or four years ago. He remembered—suddenly, strangely—that Los Abandoned had played that festival as their last show. Pilar, their lead singer, had announced it, looked right at Klinsman. "You're not from here anyway," he told her later, backstage with the rest of the press. She was sweating in the sunlight, shifting her boots on the grass. "You're from Chile or someplace."

"We all end up there," Pilar told him. She was pointing toward the biggest pit, Tar Lake, where a family of mammoth sculptures bathed.

After the festival died down, Rita showed him how to get to the edge of the lake. "Care for a swim?" she asked, offering the green-and-black surface to him. A methane bubble plopped, releasing the smell of fresh asphalt.

She moved through the crowd, at times pausing to capture an image, selecting from three cameras slung on her hip. She moved, too, through time, with the same stride of confidence and purpose. At each of the two events—the Juárez benefit and the Tarfest—someone gave her a bandana, which she wore capped over. One was in the colors of the Mexican flag, the other in the colors of the Chilean flag, no doubt handed to her by Los Abandoned, a going-away present. Her outfit was almost the same—one tank top was dark green, the other black—so it was difficult to tell if he was watching her today or three years ago.

When Klinsman was with her, walking with her, or standing at the tarry shore, or lifting her onto his shoulders for a shot over the crowd, it was clearly the festival. The sun shifted slightly, the grass reddened, the colors of her bandana and tank top fluctuated, Klinsman vanished, and he stopped caring which was which.

They moved among life-sized saber-tooths, dire wolves, giant sloths, and mammoths. The sculptures all appeared poured from tar, crawled free of the pits and come alive. Two saber-tooths loomed above him and Rita. They were meant to be fighting, but with Rita and Klinsman shoulder to shoulder beneath them, the cats seemed to be in an embrace, up on hind legs.

Oscar sometimes could be seen in the background, on the crowd's edges, clearly dodging Rita, Klinsman. With close attention, reviews and reconsiderations, it became clear that he was at the festival and the Juárez benefit, dressed exactly the same for both, as though he knew. The Luchadors were at both, moving through the crowd, stopping to chat or playfully wrestle. Blue Demon and Santo, only identifiable by their masks, wore business suits. Beneath a giant sloth, the sunlight gleaming against its oily coat, Oscar stopped to speak with one of the Luchadors, the one masked as Blue Demon. Blue nodded. He pointed. And then there were Rita and Klinsman, alone together at the shore of Tar Lake, away from the crowd, gazing at the late-afternoon reflection of the Miracle Mile on a surface of colors swirled in oil.

Along a very white corridor in La Brea's museum, a hallway set aside for touring exhibits, apart from the permanent displays dragged from the pits, the view—Rita's eyes—followed a series of black-and-white photos, an exhibition Klinsman had covered, but somewhere else, maybe in Tijuana. They were German expressionist photographs that from a few steps away looked like wide brushstrokes of gray and black and flickering white; only up close did the downward faces and mournful shoulders and wanting hands come into focus.

Then, from beside the curve of her nape, it seemed, appeared black-and-white photos of the *pardos* Klinsman had once covered at the Cultural Center, where he had met Oscar, caught him for Gina. But it was difficult to tell where the expressionist photos gave way to the *pardos* because some in between could have been either, and her view moved in so close at times, right up to a line of contrast or the gray cloud of an eye, the swirl of lips that could have too been a purse between thumb and finger.

And there was Oscar on the wall, cradling an infant Artie. Oscar's worn wedding shirt glowed clean and white, and the wriggling Artie looked like spilled black in the bleached crook of his father's sleeve. Oscar's look glared at and pleaded with the world. The view, a breath on her neck, moved close to his eyes, over an abyss.

The view drew back, and Klinsman appeared, captured in a series of black-and-white photos. Always a sense of the Tar Pits remained, in the deep black lines of the portraits, the suspended sense of motion. In one he was taking notes on his battered spiral-bound pad, pen and paper up close under his chin, his eyes not believing whatever was being said. In one he was having a beer with Blue Demon, the two leaning close and conspiring. In two others he was sleeping, his shoulders bare, his lips tenderly together, almost parting. Her hand reached up, hovered as though to shoo away dreams.

Klinsman looked back over his shoulder to catch her sleeping form.

But he found she was sitting on the edge of the bed, naked in darkness, a stroke of moonlight beside her, just missing her, spraying some scales into the tangle of her hair. Black curves seemed to push her, shape her, the angle of her knee and foot shying away, her shoulders spread. Her eyes were focused on him, her lips parted, breathing in words.

"Salamandro. Ven y tocame."

He let the screen continue and joined her. They were mirrored in two. In a light so atomized it could have been the feathering of water, they did not quite touch. In a darkness hard and clear, they gripped one another, her skin a darker shade of gray, her hand sculpted almost angrily into the back of his head, hooking him downward. Their hips were pressed together forming a thin black membrane in between, vanishing, reappearing, bending. There was a static sound. And the camphor scent of tar.

43.

The next morning it was Oscar he chose to follow. The image haunted Klinsman, had always haunted him, so much so that he had almost forgotten it was a photograph. It had become his sense of Oscar: the crook of his freshly laundered sleeve cradling the wriggling infant Artie, their dark skin alive and warm against the crisp white of his wedding shirt, the collar and cuffs of the shirt slightly frayed, making Klinsman want to finger the edges. And then Oscar's look—a plea and a challenge in his eyes, everything on you.

Following Rita had not only reminded Klinsman of the photo's existence; it had released the image upward to the clear surface of his feelings. It had been his first view ever of Oscar, a *pardo* in an exhibit. Then there, suddenly on the reception floor of the Tijuana Cultural Center, was the living man, walking among the other journalists as though he had lost what he had been holding.

Klinsman's thoughts and vision were still sliding, like wrong magnet ends, with last night's impressions of Rita. Downtown with Oscar, along jacaranda-lined Ash Street, the morning light appeared still stained with neon, on the points and edges of things. The shell of El Cortez Hotel—condos now—loomed at the end of the street, a ghost building shouldering through the skyscrapers in bold sunlight.

"What do you want on Douglas Cook?" Oscar asked him as they stood on a corner to wait for a crossing. "Exactly?"

"Just a photo." Klinsman looked up toward the tops of the newest buildings, his vision swimming in their altitude. Oscar and Rita hated when he did this, made himself look like a tourist.

"Wait." Oscar held Klinsman's forearm, kept him from crossing. Many of the pedestrians hurrying around them, getting to work, were slipping on the jacaranda petals blanketing the sidewalks. Klinsman could hear the walkers cursing the flowers, their violet, their innocence.

Oscar continued, "That's all you need?"

Klinsman nodded, looked at Oscar's grasp on his arm.

"Then why did you bring me down here?"

"It's where his records will be. If he has any."

Oscar shook his head, smiled, almost chuckled. "This guy," he said, "this *mozo*, this *salamandro*. He's a Mexican all the way?"

"All the way."

A fresh group of pedestrians gathered about them to wait for the crossing, later for work, more snap to their breaths, less patience with the slippery flower petals beneath their heels.

"Then you don't go here, *guero*," said Oscar, his arms raised to the high buildings. "You won't find anything *here* on him. Go to the schools. You think we want to come here so we can put ourselves in your fucking records? We want to learn, *guero*. So we can absorb you like we did the Spaniards. Turn you all brown and beautiful."

Klinsman recalled Douglas Cook, his asthmatic breaths, the jumble of his clothes, his skinny smile and seashell throat, the newly sprung smell of him. He remembered his own dream of Montgomery's flight, the run down the green Otay slope, the hush and lift over the borderlands. He thought of the first quick spotlight that had saved him that night in the park, where it had come from, the rooftop in a housing tract.

He took hold of Oscar's shoulder and began steering him to the nearest trolley stop.

They rode the trolley south to the Iris Street station, then backtracked a mile or so north to Silver Wing. From the overlook, where Montgomery had begun his takeoffs, they could see across the park to the high school named after the aviator. Oscar eyed the camera clinging like an insect to the bottom of the wing monument. Klinsman looked toward the impression in the steppelike sweep of tract homes, where Ranch Park interrupted things with its thumb-press, where his home used to be.

"We should go to the registrar first," said Oscar. "If we start there," he nodded toward the high school, "we'll just be digging through random files. We'll have to get permission or talk our way around them. And there's no way his name's Douglas."

"He said it with some pride." Klinsman started walking down the park slope toward the high school. "And I'm not looking for his name. Just his picture. You'll see."

Klinsman led Oscar into the school library. No one was there except for the student librarian, who was thumbing her way through a game, earbuds in. Her expression hung like a spent towel when Klinsman asked her where the yearbooks were. Her earrings dangled jewel-framed pictures of Elvis, one version lean, one Vegas.

"You get those in TJ?" Klinsman asked her.

"I can't go there no more," she answered, returning to her game, her eyes coming alive, glittering. "Mama says it's too dangerous."

"Someday it'll be okay again," Klinsman told her, but he could tell she wasn't listening, that she had already forgotten him.

Oscar appeared unnerved by her, a crimp in his brow as he hurried away from her desk. Klinsman watched him move in black and white across the overhead monitor. He was surprised to see the view click over, staying with Oscar, his movement. When Klinsman began to move, he appeared, too, but in split screen.

The far corner of the library, where all the yearbooks were tucked onto reference shelves, smelled of banana peels and cough syrup. When Klinsman cracked open the first yearbook, the sound cut the fluorescent air. The scent of open pages rose like a perfume swept in by someone new to the party.

They started three years back. They looked together through the same book, Oscar scanning for the hopeless name, the many possible faces. Klinsman started with the names, then scanned the faces, students grinning or trying to grin in front of blue netherworlds.

"Chingalo todo," whispered Oscar. He pressed his finger to a photo, guiding Klinsman's eyes away from a portrait that reminded him of his sister Connie.

There was Douglas Cook, his skinny throat loosely circled by a tuxedoed collar and bow tie, Adam's apple restive above the knot. His spiky hair aimed this way and that above leveled eyes. His name was Douglas Cook, and that was all the caption said about him—no likes, no clubs, no teams, no favorite teachers, no dreams.

Klinsman took three digitals with his camera and captured another on his cell. He sent that one immediately to Rita, before Oscar could finish returning the yearbook to its dusty slot.

Oscar gazed at the book spines a moment before looking heavily to Klinsman. Klinsman glanced away, spied them both on the split-screen monitor, looking like troublemakers at the back of the library. When he looked back, Oscar was still staring at him.

"Why you follow me, Aron?"

Klinsman led Oscar away from the campus, across the park, and back up the grassy slope to the wing monument. There they could sit and view the Pacific, the distant bullring, and the Tijuana mesa in the breeze-cleared morning light. Gulls vied with crows above them, in the half circles of kites.

By looking toward the mesa, Klinsman appeared—believed he must have appeared—to speak of that sweep of land and humanity.

"I followed you because last night I saw you holding Artie, wearing your wedding shirt, which had already become worn. But it was clean. And you were looking. You were looking. And you were at the Tar Pits—the festival, then the Juárez event. Not covering them, just there at both of them."

A rogue breeze, as though thrown from far out at sea, swept over them, cooler and heavy and damp with the cling and scent of kelp. An orphan mist crept from the sea end of the Tijuana mesa, hovered over the bullring. Even from this distance they could tell the surf was high, walling up with the backflow of the sloughs. The waves must have been crashing behind the distant row of beach houses, surf shacks, and condos, forming an isolated bar of fog.

"And for the first time I really thought about Soledad. Did you make her up? You hid her from us, and we let you hide her because we could tell that's what you wanted. But for the first time I thought maybe you made her up. A quick and easy explanation, an ex who didn't matter, who left you with a kid. And such a great kid—who would ask anything more?"

Oscar shook his head, gazed at the Tijuana mesa. The dog fires were being lit where the ridge swelled highest because of the dump. At this distance the landfill looked like a white-tipped veil spilling down the mesa. You could mistake it for snowcap even, a ski run in summer. Unless you knew what it was, that the black smoke billowed from the week's haul of dead dogs from the streets, hundreds burning.

"I did not make her up. No one could make her up. Soledad Campaneo is Artie's mother. Like I told you all. Her family called her Luz. I went to Juárez to see her family, show them Artie. But I left her there."

The dog smoke crawled into the sky, ink in water.

44.

At Ranch Park Klinsman sat at a table with Rita. He unveiled what he had brought for lunch. The sea breeze flapped the plastic store bag. Shouts sounded in two-step from the game of Mexican Nines on the nearby court. He and Rita sat side by side on the granite bench, facing the ocean horizon, very near the spot where *Crotalus lepidus* had struck from beneath the doghouse and buried its fangs in Aaron's shin twenty-seven years ago.

"This is one sad picnic," she told him. "*Picnic patético. Tortas* and Jarritos and a table right over where a snake bit your ass. A bunch of *mozos* close by, checking me out from their game, the ones who are no good, who never get the ball."

She poked one of the *tortas*, fingering beneath the wilted iceberg lettuce. "What is this? Some kind of *carne cabeza?*" She leaned closer to the sandwich, eyed it. "It *is*. Fucking *head* meat. *Picnic patético, con* Ah-rohn Kleensman."

"The view's good." He tucked the *tortas* back into the plastic to keep the bag from blowing away.

"Sure," she said. "If you ignore the dog smoke."

"On our swing set—right over there, where that drinking fountain is—Connie and I used to swing when we were kids and watch the smoke go into the sky. We'd name the different kinds of dogs we could see in the smoke patterns. Poodles mostly."

"Nice," she said. "*Chingaderitos*. Two kids on this side making fun of that side, swinging away. There are no poodles in TJ."

He looked at the smoke as he twisted open a Jarrito. "Right now it looks like Chupacabra. You need to take a picture of it."

Rita bowed her head, eyed her Jarrito as though it were a beer, gazed into its whiskey color. Her lips held full and morose, and her eyes shone sadly, brows tilted up.

"At least you got me *tamarindo*," she said, still looking at the bottle.

He said nothing, waited, let the shouts from the Mexican Nines bang between them. Her expression darkened further, verged on quiet fear even, as though the amber *tamarindo* in her hand were a crystal ball.

"Chupacabra is gone, Aaron," she said, looking up from her bottle to the distant dog smoke above the Tijuana mesa. "There were no signs of it at the benefit. No stupid t-shirts or bad paintings or fake photographs or songs about it. Nothing. Vanished. Like your *guero* ranch here."

"So?" he asked, waiting for her to look at him. He wanted that look on him, that most unguarded of gazes spilling over him.

"Elvis was still there," she replied, holding her gaze on the horizon. "Santo and Blue Demon. All that kind of shit. On shirts, and drawings and paintings and fakes. Even candies. Like usual. But no Chupa."

She finally draped him with her look, a sadness meant for an entire city, ashes in the sky. It would take him days to endure it.

"You know why Chupa's gone, Aaron? I know why he's gone. Being at that benefit, I knew why. He's gone because he's real now. We know he's real, and he doesn't kill goats. He steals women and girls and eats them. Whether he's an owl, pig, goat, or your fucking cow head. We knew all along, but now it's too much to horse around with demons. And the benefit accomplishes nothing for Juárez. Just makes it an excuse for another Tarfest. Puts a fucking Chicano bandana on it." She sipped her *tamarindo*, winced at its fizz. "Gina *chinganda*. What she get me into?"

"Maybe she's just trying to show you what you're getting into yourself. Moving into Mexico to take real shots." Klinsman meant it, but he could taste a desperate plea in his words. He sipped his *tamarindo* but tasted smoke and ocean.

"Don't try to stop me, Aaron." She looked at him, an expression new to her, surprising herself, he could tell. It trembled in her eyes and lips like a hopeful lie. "I'm going."

"I can't stop you."

She opened her laptop on the picnic table, her actions lending an excuse to look elsewhere and maybe wipe away thoughts aflinch beneath her eyes. Then she scanned the park, upward to some of the cameras.

"Let's just catch a *mandro*," she said. She entered Douglas Cook's yearbook photo into Klinsman's story, added the sketch-over he had done to the portrait.

They waited. The dog smoke formed a check mark over the Tijuana mesa, one short flurry rising against the ocean breeze, one long tail going with it. When the dog corpses melted together, reached a critical mass in their molten core, they ignited a kind of interior torch that blew out the side of the pile. Klinsman had done a story on it. Rita had taken the pictures.

"Chupa was gone, Aaron. No Lechuza, either. No Goat Man, no pig." Rita took a slug of her *tamarindo*. "But you know who was there?"

"Santo and Blue."

"Yeah, sure, them." She raised an eyebrow. "But I mean from your list. Your list of sketches."

"Who?" He drank his soda.

"That skull thing. That thing you drew. I saw it."

"On what?"

"Well, I didn't *see* it. I caught it later. It got into a couple of pictures I took."

"Got into?"

"Yeah," she said. "I only noticed it when I was reviewing. It was on the edges. On the back of a woman's shirt. And carved into the bark of a tree. Who is it? What's it supposed to be?"

"Maybe something I know," he told her. "Maybe something we used to know. When I sketched it, I was here—thinking about the ranch, the borderlands, how they used to be. How those myths would get around. I don't know what I was doing—exactly."

He was about to ask her what she knew about Julián C de Baca.

They were startled at how quickly Douglas Cook appeared. He ambled toward them, his noon shadow like a puddle on the grass. He wore tuxedo pants and a white Rockmount shirt with green piping. The sleeves were torn off at the shoulders, exposing his long, skinny arms, taffylike in the sun. He wore a short-brimmed fedora but seemed unsure about it, how to tilt it.

Rita and Klinsman just watched him approach, let him go right to her laptop without a word. But when he hovered his dragonfly fingers above the keyboard, Klinsman stopped him.

"I wouldn't do that. That's hers, and she might snap your fingers off."

Douglas Cook stood upright, tilting his head back to see them better from beneath the brim of his hat.

"Don't touch her pictures or my story," Klinsman told him. "I don't care what you do to me. Show everybody who I am or make me vanish. I'll always be somewhere, won't I? You've seen to that."

Douglas looked at Rita.

"And her either," said Klinsman before anyone else could speak. "She doesn't care. We don't care. We like how we look together. No matter what you do to us. No matter how you might try to create impressions. You can always see how we feel. You can always see that everything is real. No acting, no thoughts of anybody else. No borrowed faces or gestures or sounds. It's all new and pretty." He felt as though he were talking to Rita now. "All new, all pretty," he said in Spanish. "Like cactus pear. With dew on the needles."

Klinsman felt Rita's turn, the lift in her brow, but kept his eyes on Douglas.

"Now I want something from you," he said to Douglas. "For me to leave you—all of you, *ustedes*—out of my story."

"What?" asked Douglas. He took off his hat, squinted at the sun, then put it back on. His hands were long like his arms. "What you want?"

Klinsman took from his satchel the sketches he had done and laid them on the table next to the laptop. He aligned the sketchpad and the keyboard, squaring the battered notes as evenly as he could beside the metal.

"You know what I can do," said Klinsman. He nodded toward Rita. "You know what she can do. What I can do with her work."

Cook gazed dully at the display, breathing hangdog through his lips, just waited.

"I know you saved me," said Klinsman. "That night, with the spotlight. I don't know if that's what you wanted. Maybe you just wanted to put better light on everything. But I want to know what *you* can do."

"You saw," Cook answered in Spanish.

Rita kept things in Spanish, shouldered herself a little between the two men, blended her shadow with theirs on the park grass. "He wants to know if you do anything out there. Outside. If you make things happen. On purpose."

"Only a little," said Cook. He blinked rhythmically, as though clearing his eyes. "That time with the light. I don't do those things. We don't do those things. But we don't want people to hurt. Hurt each other."

"So you stay inside," said Klinsman. "You don't like coming out here. Into the light." He had to work around his Spanish. "Why did you pick me? To focus on?"

"Because you always come to this park. And this is where I started. I just started."

"Others," said Klinsman. Then he switched it back to English. "Others who've done it longer. Who are better. Do they help you?"

"No. We all do it together. Nothing is ours." Cook sought for words. You could see him translating, his narrow brow flexing, words beginning and failing on his lips. "Nothing is yours. Yours alone. *Sólo tuya. Sólo mio.* How you say? Everybody adds. To the *vida.*"

"He doesn't mean do they help you make the *vidas*," said Rita. "He means do they tell you outside stuff. *Cosas fuera de* . . . to do this and that."

"No," Cook answered. "That would ruin the *vidas*. Make them not real. You know? Except for one thing maybe. Sometimes we tell each other how to watch for . . . how you say?" He pointed to the ground. *"La culebra en el zacate."*

Rita laughed softly and turned to Klinsman. "He's more clever in Spanish."

"The hose in the weeds?" asked Klinsman.

"The snake in the grass," she answered. "Fucking ranch Spanish."

Klinsman didn't laugh. He tapped one of his sketches, the swirling figure from room 9. "Like this?" he asked Cook.

Cook shook his head and tapped another sketch, the cow skull. "Like this maybe."

"How many of you are there?" asked Klinsman. "In this city."

"I don' know. I just started."

"Do you do others? Other *vidas?*"

"We all do other *vidas.*"

"How many do you do?" Klinsman felt the need to write, to write on paper. "Do you do Oscar? Oscar Medem?"

"No," Cook answered. "But someone does. That's how I get the boy. You chasing the boy in the cactus. That's how I get him with you." He had become furtive, his arms twitching, eyes blinking. They could see he didn't just want to leave; he wanted to vanish.

Rita looked at the *mozo* with what almost appeared to be compassion, her eyes fully open, swimming over him maybe. "You say, 'got,'" she told him gently. "You say, 'That's how I *got* him.'"

"It's like . . ." Cook replied. "How you say . . . *escopio con colores?* The kind with *gemitas* inside." He fashioned a kaleidoscope with his intricate hands, held it up to his eye, turning it this way and that. "Once you find the lace you want, you can't go back or forward. Without losing it just that way. For always."

"Forever," Rita corrected him.

"Estan las gemitas."

"Yes," she said. "We are the little gems inside."

"I saw you then I turn it," he told them. "Then maybe someone else turn it. Maybe it turn when you pass it, by itself. You know? Maybe it turn when you just try to keep it still."

"You say, 'Maybe it *will* turn,'" she told him, her voice soft, her lips exact. "These *gueros,*" she said, nodding toward Klinsman, "they always separate the present and the future. They haven't figured it out yet."

Klinsman reached for the sketchpad again, thought of another question, of the snake in the grass. Rita put her hand on his.

"No, Aaron," she pleaded. "Let him go now. Let him get out of the sun. Let him get out of this *vida*. You owe him."

She looked at Douglas Cook, lifted a hand toward his shoulder but refrained from touching. "He owes you."

They let him go.

"Why did you tell him that?" he asked Rita as they watched Douglas Cook drag his shadow out the far corner of the park. "Why did you tell him that I owe him?"

"Because then maybe he'll come back to you. In some way. On his own. Like a Mexican."

He gave her a skeptical look.

"It's like when you take an extra picture of someone," she explained. "You tell them it's for you, this one's for you. Then that's the one they wonder about. That's the one they want to see. Their face changes. You start to get better pictures."

They watched the dog smoke curl higher into the sky above the mesa. The black patterns formed an imperfect Rorschach with the hill barrios scarring the slope of the mesa. Klinsman had walked those neighborhoods with his father, who made house calls there, climbing the tire stairscapes with his children, showing them.

A layer of high wind parallel with the flat mesa was tearing the top edge of the dog smoke into gray rags across the blue sky.

"I wonder now," said Rita, "if those are still just dogs."

He looked at her, puzzled, then concerned. Her eyes seemed to reflect the oily smoke.

"Over there," he said, nodding toward an empty picnic table. Glistening in the sun, the table's granite form appeared like something just removed, wet and vital. "My Uncle Mir killed a guy. He killed the man named Julián C de Baca."

"I know that story." But she shook her head. "That's the one where they let the fire burn so there won't be such a mess. Such a mess of truck and flesh. And when they go back and sift through the cold ashes and bones, they find the skull and it has extra holes in it. Holes where horns would fit."

"I need a ride to Border Park," he said. "I'll tell you the story if you take me."

45.

*K*linsman took her to Monument Park, the southwest corner of California. Everyone called it Border Park. It was open only during the dry season. He parked Rita's car by the locked swingpipe, and they walked the gravel road the rest of the way. Several sections of the road were washed out by winter flooding. Detritus left by the Tijuana River clung like cobwebs in the castor bush and mallow scrub. Dried flotsam formed half circles in the sand. Rita checked the camera on her hip, smiled at Klinsman.

They climbed the little knoll, up switchbacks through the brush, barrel cactus and purple stasis. They reached the park at the top. The grass was cut, the picnic tables were cleaned, and work had been started on the restroom building. New paint obscured half a wall of graffiti. The graffiti still visible was too thick to read, just a black-and-gray collection of lines and curves.

They went right to the metal wall marking the border, right to the section that was still just a chain-link fence, so visitors could see the neighborhood on the other side. Mexico. The bullring loomed above the neighborhood. An abandoned lighthouse with a water trough stood just past an arm's length beyond the fence. Parkgoers could reach through the square cut into the chain-link and almost touch the plaster of the lighthouse wall. The buildings nearest the beach were crumbling into the sea, teetering on the soft cliff edge.

He and Rita sat near the square cut in the fence and watched the ocean. The metal wall ran west down the steep slope and into the waves. It went several hundred yards into the surf until it vanished beneath the swells. To the north ran the dunes that divided the beach from the sloughs. The veins of the sloughs were swollen with high tide, their sulfurous stench mixing in the salt air.

He told her the story of Julián C de Baca, the part she didn't know, the reality.

"My dad did tell everyone to just let the fire burn out. You couldn't get near enough to pull the body out anyway."

But the truck engine had a magnesium block, and it caught fire and burned white-hot, like a torch, through the rest of the day and through the night. Aaron and Connie watched the men sift through the ash pile the next day. Alejandro searched the longest.

"They didn't find a skull with horn holes in it," Klinsman told Rita. "They didn't find anything. Just ashes."

"Bones burn," said Rita.

"That's what my dad said."

That was what Dr. Klinsman told the field hands who kept searching the ashes, whispering among themselves already.

He convinced her that this was the truest version he could render. It was how he had come to own, for two months, the Motel

San Ysidro. Some convoluted trail of leverages led from C de Baca's holdings to a modest education fund set up in Tijuana for the Klinsman children by their Prague uncle.

"I owned it," he told her, as though propriety equaled truth. As though the room that had first joined Rita and him was a chamber in the catacombs of his past. She took his picture, pushing her lens up close. He felt himself bend in the glass.

Some kids on the other side were fetching water from the lighthouse trough. Rita hurried to the square cut in the fence. She called to them, friendly like a *tia*, and said some stuff about the water. Klinsman couldn't keep up with her Spanish. She told them some things that made the kids' hands jump back from the water but that also made them smile and peek carefully back into the black surface.

She turned back to Klinsman. He nodded to the neighborhood on the other side of the fence, the one crumbling into the sea, in the shadow of the bullring.

"You said *we*. All the way through, talking to them, you said *we*."

She shrugged.

He went on, "You're from there. Right there. I thought you were from LA. You said you were from LA."

"I am. But no one like me is just from LA." She pointed toward a yard across the fence, one with a gate formed from tires, with an orange Volkswagen chassis on top. "I think my uncle used to run that place."

She handed him her camera and repositioned herself in front of the lens so that the tire gate could be seen in the background, behind the grid of chain-link. "See, Klinsman? Way back then, when this lighthouse worked, when you sat on your barn roof and watched it spin and flash in the night. When you gazed at the bull-ring hovering over the waves. Way back then, when you were a snakebit boy, you were watching me. You were watching me."

He took a portrait of her face. She smiled gently for him. In the immediate background was the chain-link. Its diamonds divided the view of the oil-dirt road and the tire gate with the VW hull on top.

"I thought that's why we came here," she told him as they walked onto the grass, away from the fence and the little obelisk that formed the monument, marked the border. "I thought maybe you found out and wanted to take me here. So I might be unnerved and impressed. By your prowess. Your newfound prowess."

They chose a picnic table that afforded the best view of the beach and the sloughs. But Rita seemed more interested in the cinder-block wall of the restroom, the one half painted over, half graffiti. They sat atop the table, their boots on the bench.

"No," he told her. "I needed to come here because this park has trouble with its eyes. Because of the flooding. And the coyotes busting the lights during the closed season."

"You're using me. You want to know what I feel here. What I sense."

He looked down.

"It's okay," she said. She scanned from the top of the light-house to the floodlights, then back around to the bullring above the waves. "I think everything you and I do for the rest of our lives can be viewed by anyone who wants to or happens to watch. Any way they want."

"Starting that night in the motel?"

"Starting back when this lighthouse worked, back when the big Mexican pit viper poked holes in you. That's what I believe now. That's what I started to know when you showed us that *vida*. When you found that *vida*."

He pivoted at his waist and pointed toward a gulch behind them, to the east. It was an arroyo of sorts, a crease in the mesa. "That's where C de Baca used to park his flatbeds, gather up his treasure, fresh from Mexico. The border was just a fence back then, with lots of sags and holes in it." Klinsman eyed her. "But you know that."

Army-issue floodlights now stood watch over the high double wall of corrugated steel. He turned back to face the ocean. She kept looking at him.

"What do you think, Aaron? That he got up from the ashes in the middle of the night and walked away? Moved east? Tecate? Yuma? Piedras Negras?" She paused. "Juárez?"

He did not like hearing that city's name from her lips. Now that he thought of her across the border. Now that he was thinking of trucks and fires and bodies. Now that he was sketching cow skulls and those cow skulls were getting into her photographs.

"I think Julián C de Baca burned to ashes," he told her. He shifted to Spanish so he could get the tense right. "But what he does and what he believes and what he wants is not killed. My uncle cannot kill that. Other men stand in line. Always."

"I'll be okay, Aaron. Manzanillo's far away."

"Yeah," he said. "Like Gina."

Rita raised her hand and motioned toward the end of the border, the wall dropping into the sea. Then she moved her hand eastward, tracing the rise and fall of the metal wall as it rolled along the foothills of the mesa. "Gina says it fails. That it always fails because you can't build a wall through the middle of desire."

She hopped off the table and took his hand.

"Come," she said. "One more shot."

She led him to the cinder-block wall. She stood him against the graffiti, then placed herself shoulder to shoulder with him. But behind her was the painted side. She held her camera at arm's length and took a picture. They looked like lovers, goofing. Behind him was a dark explosion of words. Behind her was a netherworld.

46.

They drove back to her studio and opened the blinds to let in all the afternoon light. The old house felt hollow and honeycombed beneath them, fragile. In the breeze passing through one window they could smell the bay from beyond the downtown skyscrapers, the scent of warm salt and jetty rocks.

In one version, before the kaleidoscope was turned and the lattice of images was lost for always, lost to a series of endless changes, some patterns almost repeating others, they kissed gently. Klinsman held his fingers delicately to her jaw. Her arms were stretched behind her, as though she were in a headfirst free fall, but soaring upward to him.

They undressed together, taking turns glimpsing one another as they stood in the center of the studio, seeking balance from one foot to the other. They laughed at themselves for a moment in the yellow light, alone and knowing, alone and trusting that one would save the other from falling.

Then their expressions turned earnest again, just before they embraced. They stepped toward one another as though they were farther apart. And this made them almost slam together so that they fleetingly lost their balance, he bracing one foot back, she bracing one foot to the side.

Gripping her from beneath, he lifted her. His shoulders and arms stretched and flexed to gather her up. She wrapped her legs about him as he stood bracing their weight. Her knees bent beneath his arms, her thighs gripped his sides, and her feet locked behind his back. He could see it all, at once removed and within. That it was all he could do to hold her there, but he could stay that way, endlessly.

They lay in the pile of clothes she had brought from the desert. In the tangle was the satin robe, twisted about their ankles. In pockets buried within the slurry of clothes, they could still catch the scents of warm stone and desert sage, release them with turns and strokes and the slow shifting of limbs. They could burrow their arms and legs into the cool pile and feel the soft distinction between linen and satin.

Except for the one enlargement of the bedcover from room 9, her photos were gone from the wall, leaving pinhole constellations across the stark whiteness, around the life-sized seaweed woman. Rita's equipment, too, was gone. Klinsman braced himself in the pile, secured his elbow to the floor and turned to take in the studio. When they had passed through the rest of the house to get to this room, nothing had seemed different. But he realized that part was still her aunt's place, unchanged, undusted. Nothing remained in this studio but the daybed and the table with its desktop, note-book, and little mirror, almost all else packed away.

Rita shifted against his back, bringing satin and linen and des-ert warmth into him. But nothing felt as soft as her skin, her breasts and stomach a heat along his flesh, like something that should pass through the membrane of him.

She swam down into the swirl of clothes and found him with her mouth. She sucked him gently, and then without surfacing, moved her body over his form and put him inside her.

He watched her dress and tried to memorize as much as he could about her body, the curve of her back and the slope of her neck, the point of her foot aimed above her jeans. The bend of her wrists, which hinted at her vocation, saddened him most. Her face was hidden by the fall of her hair.

When they were finished dressing they moved separately about the room. She closed the automated blinds, shuttering the sun-light. He draped a shirt over the mirror, her notebook, and her desktop screen. She briefly left the studio and returned with two rolls of black electrician's tape. She handed one to him.

"Let's do our best," she said, "and see how it feels. See what it shows us."

The newer doorknobs had small holes in their ends; he cov-ered these with squares of tape. She taped the ends of the blind pulls, which were easy to imagine as miniature old-fashioned movie lenses. He removed the lightbulb from the overhead fan and taped over the hole at the end of the pull-chain.

She removed the bulb from the floor lamp, took the other bulb from Klinsman, and put them both in her shoulder bag. He took a pen and an obsidian paperweight from her table and put those in her bag, too.

"Oh, you're much better at this than I am," she told him. He continued to look around the studio. Only a brothy light seeped into the room from around the edges of the blinds. Still, now fully tuned to the shudder of her imminent departure, he found two clear pushpins stuck into her display wall. He removed them and placed them carefully into the waiting crease of her palm. He couldn't decide whether the wincing look she gave him was one of skepticism or discovery.

Arms slightly lifted, he turned once slowly to take in the room while she sat on the edge of the daybed. In his rotation he saw her there on the very edges of the weak light, a light so thin it could not make it to the far corners of the studio. Shadows tumbled around her in geometric patterns, with bits of color and glints finding their way along her edges. She sat straight and still, gaining full sense of the room, him.

He continued to turn slowly. He wavered on the shrouded mirror and screens, noticed the shine on the shirt buttons. He spun quickly to say something to her.

There lingered the most intricate and delicate stack of dark colors—her red lips, black hair, olive skin, the pale bed, a violet end of light—until the tremble in him mistakenly tumbled it all forward, vanishing her.

47.

He walked the Boulevard from her house to the *Review*. He was lonely and omniscient, back in the A-frame of the barn, Rita's absence like venom in him. *Ausente.* Behind him the late afternoon cast long shadows that swept everything forward, and his strides were long, too, desperate and angry. The Boulevard had, he noticed, collected itself into a current, with everyone moving in a hyperconscious rhythm underneath. The heavy flow of cars tooled along politely on either side of the median, lane changes happening as though on tracks, shaken forward. Signs that read "No Honking" were obeyed. He could hear bands practicing inside bars, clerks trying to chat away their final hour of work, mechanics putting away tools.

He saw himself—it was easy. He looked wrong for what he was. His hair had grown too long, and his cowboy shirt hung untucked. He looked like an old surfer, one past his game, come ashore and lost on inland sidewalks.

A hooker, very far down the Boulevard for her trade and trolling very early, bumped shoulders with him. He could know her name—her life, her dreams. Her real name was Emily. She used to love to play board games with her cousins in Chapin, South Carolina, where she had gone to college for one semester, studying drama. She made more money on the Boulevard by passing as Filipino.

"Emily," he called to her just after she bumped him. "Em!"

She looked over her shoulder, her eyes wide with sadness, her pace quickening away from him. This caused her to stumble into a man who wanted to know the scent of her powder. It reminded him of something he had discovered once, a kind of life he had discovered, one with more jags and colors in it, more jags and colors than the life he glided through now. The man removed his sunglasses and looked both ways, up and down the Boulevard, his shadow a long black line just licking the back of Klinsman's heel.

Klinsman paused his screen, then swept it clean.

He had expected to be working alone at the *Review* and had been surprised to find three of the desks occupied. Still, the lights were low. Oscar was not in. Rita's desk, number II, was bare except for the PC. He readjusted his seat in front of his own desk, considered putting Douglas Cook in his final story. He blamed the *mandros*, all *mozos* really, for Rita's vanishing. But he was just a good enough journalist to ignore any personal sense of blame. Yet he could deliver them objectively, convince himself that they needed to see consequence somehow at this point in their collective exploration. To see the snakes in the grass.

Caitlin left her corner desk and brought him a bouquet of yellow-rimmed white carnations, the kind you see at school science fairs. Caitlin was dressed formally, ready to interview somewhere. Her hair was up, her freckles subdued. Though they fit her trimly, her dark skirt and blouse made her seem younger, playing dress-up. As she leaned in with the bouquet, he briefly mistook her perfume for the scent of the flowers, a warm push of lavender.

"These for you," she said. "Too bad they're not jacarandas." She smiled and wiggled her fingertips at him.

The carnations were professionally arranged in sprays of fern and baby's breath. The outer bend of the clear vase was also rimmed with yellow.

"And this with," she said, lightly dropping a ribboned gift bag beside the flowers.

He carefully poured the contents of the bag onto his desk: sixteen clear plastic pens, shaped like cigars, each with a single vibrant stripe of color.

"They're nice," said the intern, still at his shoulder. "Which one for me?"

He handed her one with a violet stripe, almost the color of jacaranda. She laughed, a soft and single sound, in gratitude. She fastened the pen to her blouse as a sort of brooch over her breast. She pushed it forward, modeled it.

"Can I choose for the others?" she asked.

He nodded and watched her step desk to desk, thinking above each one, deciding, then placing a pen carefully in the most open surface, as though setting a fine table. Sometimes she would go back and switch pens from one desk to another, rethinking her decision, who was best for each color. He wondered if he could have gotten it right, so right as she did.

Caitlin was a family name, something he would discover minutes later on his screen while she stepped out for a cigarette. She was named for her Irish grandmother, who smoked a pipe and lived on three acres in Tipperary, where she collected shell fossils and explored the bogs. Knowing her grandmother first prevented him—and that was all that prevented him—from watching Caitlin wake in the morning.

But he did watch her sleep, sheets outlining her form, the dream-twist of her limbs. In the meek light of dawn he could make out a snow globe surrounded by crushed jacaranda petals on her nightstand. Her apartment looked old but refurbished for rental, with cheap new doors, those odd little holes at the ends of the knobs. The hair clasp on her dresser was a clear purple, glinting early before the sun.

He swept around the room, the light and colors tumbling but the focus clear on her sleeping. Close to her nape he feared she might feel his breath. Then, in a violet-hued glow, she stirred, a coy tilt in the plane of her shoulders.

The fullness of her sleep poured through him like good whiskey, a warm guilt. It draped its way through his limbs, almost convincing him that this sleep was his, that he could take from it. But this was when he had to turn away from the flutter and exposure of her waking. Because he swept back too suddenly, became the waking dream.

48.

*H*e returned to Rita's house. Sticks and bristles of the setting sun lay scattered about her tiny, unkempt front yard.
The buildings of downtown loomed above the neighborhood like
ship hulls, letting light pass through narrow gaps, zigzagged reflections. The For Sale sign tilted, as though still leaning with a long-
gone breeze. Klinsman carried the bouquet to her door, paused
like a suitor, then let himself in.

How many days left? How many days were supposed to be left?
Two? Three? When had the count begun?

He had to pass through the deserted lower chambers of the
house before reaching the forsaken studio. Someone had dusted,
maybe the Realtor, so even her aunt's ghost felt gone. The holy-
water cups in the crucifixes were empty and clean, glistening like
scallop shells. Had he not noticed all this before, when he had last
been here with her, watching her? Only her, ahead of him on the
stairs? He felt himself living in dream-time, not giving himself
time to dream.

In her studio remained the daybed, the pile of warehouse clothes, and her desk with the makeup mirror on it. The enlargement still hung on the white display wall, alone, Rita's enhanced rendition of the woman on the bed. Beside her, in her current, Klinsman set up his own laptop, positioning it next to Oscar's gaudy little gift. He found a chair in the kitchen, an old ladderback painted the colors of the Mexican flag, the straw seat beginning to fray. This became his desk chair.

He poked through the pile of clothes but couldn't find the satin robe. This absence comforted him in a way, the weight of it heavy as an unopened envelope. He reset the bouquet of carnations in a clay vase—decidedly opaque—on the desk beside his open notebook. He stacked his sketchpad and his loose papers, then let them skitter around the desk surface on the breeze coming through the open window.

He wasn't sure exactly what he hoped for when he traced over the photo of Oscar, let the lines guided by his fingers and thoughts appear on screen. He added strokes in freehand, a curl of demand in the slope of the neck, a tuck of self-protection in the shoulders. Oscar in seaweed form.

Klinsman sensed from the elusive nature of the *vidas* that more was being done elsewhere, something else was being composed by Douglas Cook and company. They must be overwhelmed by the possibilities, by what they might be able to create. So much was now available, eyes everywhere, online always, feed everywhere. A person couldn't even hide in time, because that was open now, too. You couldn't retract yourself, what you had lived. And there were the snakes in the grass.

Some torn fragments from his spiral pad continued to shift around the desk top, lifted and spun by the window breeze, reminding him of scorpions.

He caught one by its tail.

Oscar was walking on the beach, the sunset hitting him from both sides, from over the water and reflected off ruddy cliffs. His shirt was thrown over his shoulder, the cuffs of his jeans rolled to his knees so he could walk the shorebreak. Around him three boys were riding skimboards, taking advantage of the evening glass. They glided elegantly about him, silhouettes against the orange sky and flaxen waves. They appeared to stay with him, seeking something from his downward gaze, his profound steps.

One boy achieved a handstand on his board, and his silhouette skimmed past Oscar, a circus shadow against circus colors of sky and water. This caught Oscar's eye momentarily, lifted his head, his gaze then turning away toward the cliffs. He was thinking of his son; Klinsman could tell by that pleading and challenge in his open look. The light reflected off the cliffs touched only the most prominent curves and angles of his face, a desert patina.

There was another photograph of him with Artie, taken later by Rita, though it looked as though it could have been part of the *pardo* exhibit. Artie is almost seven, standing in the foreground, twisting back toward his father, who is sitting, arm draped over his son's shoulder. Anyone could see the Mayan lift of his mother's eyes in Artie, could see a sense of fortune in the way he reaches back to stay in some sort of embrace with his father while obliging the photographer. In his eyes you could see someone who has been chosen, a relief, a treasuring.

Oscar turned into the light off the cliffs, the softer glow. He still thought of Artie. He always thought of Artie in the hour before it was time to pick him up from the sitter. He found the obscured staircase in the cliffs and began climbing the wooden treads embedded in the reddish sandstone. As he ascended the escarpment, he disappeared from time to time in the cover of jojoba brush clinging to the sandstone.

At the top of the cliffs he was suddenly in another world. He put on his shirt and the sandals he had bundled in it and rolled down his jeans, smoothed them as best he could. He walked across wide, manicured lawns toward a fortresslike group of buildings facing the sea.

He found his way to the courtyard, where the lab buildings stood like dominoes on either side and where a single channel of clear water, only a half step wide, drew a straight line to the ocean and on toward the sun poaching on the horizon.

The row of lab towers on either side of the plaza formed a concrete canyon with windowless sides streaked with sea stains of rust and salt. The light of the orange sun poured into the thin line of water bisecting the plaza. The open edge of the plaza obscured the shore below, offered sky and ocean. The inward stance of the towers collected the wave sounds into a quiet, pulsing static, the sound heard when thoughts were gone, all demons purged, all tasks completed.

Oscar knelt like a tracker by the line of water just off the center of the plaza. He shouldered into the blaze of the sunset, peered into it, saw the green flash. He then turned to Klinsman and asked him if he saw it, too.

Klinsman crouched across the line of water from Oscar, their two shadows sweeping back into thin lines the length of the empty plaza.

"They say it's just an optical illusion, a burn on our retinas."

"I know what it is," said Oscar. "But did you see it? Right then?"

Klinsman nodded. He showed Oscar the sketches he had been using, tried to hand them across the water. "Rita helped me get stuff from Douglas Cook."

Oscar shunned the paper. "I know." He mimicked Douglas Cook turning a kaleidoscope, aimed it right at Klinsman. "I'm surprised you went after mine first."

Klinsman pretended to be okay, to be well balanced in his crouch. But he had to brace one knee to the ground to keep from reeling back on his heels.

"I chose the one I feared least."

Oscar looked back to the sun, a chip of light on the blackening water. "Your *mozo* should've told you more about—what did he call it? *Escopio con colores?* About how it messes you up. *Gueros* worse than Mexicans. How time gets fucked up. And what you remember. And know. And forget. Instead of telling you some bullshit about gemstones."

Klinsman felt like an amnesiac speaking with someone who had known him forever. For always.

"You know why I come here, Aaron?" Oscar asked in Spanish.

Klinsman looked about the courtyard, the stark lab towers looming above the barren plaza, the thin line of water bisecting everything. "Because it's quiet. You feel nothing here. You feel no one."

Oscar nodded, looking around. "I brought Rita here. When I first started to wonder how big it all was, what we're all doing together, what the *salamandros* might be doing, before you found us a *vida*. I brought her here to test this space for me. She laughed at first. Said she felt like a witch. Called me a fucking Mexican when I used the word 'divination.' But I told her I figured this place, a place like this, might be free. Because the people who built it, who started it, who live in it, would have seen this all coming before anyone else. That they'd take care to make sure a space like this plaza could be kept. Just a little niche. Maintained."

"What did she find?" Aaron felt good talking about her.

"She stopped laughing," Oscar told him. "She took her hair clasp off, put it in her pocket. She said I was right. She felt certain I was right."

"I see her when I close my eyes," said Aaron.

49.

When you close your eyes," he asked Oscar, "who do *you* see?"

Oscar nodded to the sketches Klinsman was still clutching. They quivered in the ocean breeze sweeping through the courtyard. The line of water slid silently between the two crouching men. It turned copper as soon as the last bend of sun vanished below the horizon.

"You tell me, *salamandro*."

Klinsman showed him.

At first he thought the woman on the beach with Oscar might be Soledad—Luz—though he had never seen her before, even a picture of her. And that was odd, a stained chip of quartz in the kaleidescope, that Oscar wouldn't have at least one photo to show them. Even though it was moonlight, he could see that the woman was thin and muscular, a swimmer, confident facing the night-crash of waves. She shed her clothes behind her in a trail, like shadows peeling. The full moon hung along the top edge, twinned by some refraction into a lesser version of itself.

Her hair was cropped short, exposing the long muscles of her shoulders and back. Her hamstrings and calves were sharpened by the sulfurous light. The waves flashed with phosphorescence. Oscar joined her, held her hand as they strode toward the water. Their clothes lay like dark clumps of kelp on the moonlit sand. The shore was askew, with the quizzical slant of a loose button or something fallen from a pocket.

They hurried into the waves together, letting go of each other's hands in order to churn into the break, balance, run. In unison they dived into the first big breaker and emerged smooth as seals from the foam. They embraced immediately, twined together, slicks of seagrass caught along their sides and shoulders. It consoled Klinsman, seeing the kelp on their bodies. He loved Oscar and Gina and could still remember that he had brought Oscar to her, pulled him across the border to her.

"That's just it," he said to Oscar. Klinsman now knelt on both knees in the twilight of the courtyard, the water between them a darkening line. "You don't see Luz. When you close your eyes. You see Gina. And when you hold Artie, either when he is an infant or when he is a boy, you don't look out toward Luz. You look at the lens. You look at all of us. And Artie looks, too, feeling behind him the man who saved him. Who chose him."

There was a small rise of astonishment in Oscar's calm expression, the slightest lift of chin and brow.

"If Rita is right." It felt so good to say her name. "And you really are just a fucking Mexican. Then you would carry a photo of

Luz. You would have it. You would show it. Unless she didn't exist. Didn't exist the way you tell us she exists."

"She exists," said Oscar.

"Oh, that I believe. That I know." He reached across the line of water and took hold of Oscar's shoulder, dug his fingers in, into the clay. "You rescued Artie after he was orphaned. You go to the Tarfest and the Juárez benefit and you wrestle with Blue Demon. You go looking for her there. You go looking for Luz, making us look for her. Because we should all still be looking for her body in the sand. Like you are, and the reporter from El Paso."

Oscar looked at Klinsman's grip on his shoulder, then at him, a little fearful. "Gina told me you'd be different with this story. This story she put us on. That whatever we'd all find together, you'd be different in it. Like no one else."

Klinsman shook his head. "No. I could have seen this on my own. All about Artie. If I had just looked at the photos of you. The simple photos on the wall. My father used to help with the orphanage in TJ, when he worked on the border. He was their doctor. He always took us down there, to show us. They don't call it an orphanage anymore. They call it day care because most of the mothers are still around, out working. The fathers are way up in the States somewhere, working, too. But there are the kids who really are abandoned or orphaned, just mixed in. Some because of what happens in Juárez and Chihuahua. And TJ."

Oscar covered his face with his hands. Klinsman hopped across the thin strip of water and held his shoulders, gripped him. He wrapped an arm about his waist and pulled him hard against him.

He pressed his forehead to Oscar's nape, felt his pulse there, beating against his eyes.

"I only planned to adopt him," Oscar whispered. "Stop there and make up a story for him, a nice story about his mother. But I wanted to put some truth into the story. How she really was, how amazing she must have been to create such a boy. So I went to Chihuahua to find out what I could about her. Her name was Soledad. Her family called her Luz. She worked in a fucking maquiladora. Riding the bus to go sew shirts. No one's found her. There in the sand."

50.

Klinsman took his sketches and notes back to Rita's studio. He lit a single floor lamp back by the daybed and then sat on the edge of its light at the desk. The blue glow of his notebook hovered before him like a stolen piece of day sky. He dreaded this night more than usual, feeling sleep impossibly distant, feeling his body begging for it in waves along his nerves.

Some of his newer sketches were already as crimped and creased as passed notes. The one for Mir appeared the most complex. Oscar's was interrupted by the most guesses, the most experiments, little dashes and ellipticals like flying saucers between more decisive features. The one for Gina was the simplest.

The one for the woman from room 9 took him to another starter page, or perhaps it was that first page he had found, now grown a bit more. It began with the title of an old Santo movie: *Profanadores de tumbas*. Douglas Cook had doodled Santo on it—the *mozo* could draw—and a salamander, too. Next to that was the still of Klinsman conversing with Blue Demon at Café Cinema. Another Santo title captioned this still: *Santo contra Blue Demon en Atlán-tida*. Then there was a sketch, a more careful and intricate drawing of Klinsman's cow skull, more that kind you find in the desert and hang on your wall. And Douglas Cook had written a caption beneath: *Don't use this, I hope you don't have to use this. I try.*

The *mandros* had feed from room 9, but they hadn't instigated it. They didn't instigate anything. They just found room 9 because Klinsman led them there, with his gait, his foot pronation, the slant of his shoulders, his obsessions. They were waiting for him to move more, everyone to move more, find more.

He found his notepad and sketched a new path of images, beginning with the imprint of the woman from room 9. After her he sketched a knob at the end of a curtain pull, aimed it sideways like a movie lens. He drew the outline of a salamander nosing a circle, the trolley's smoky eye. Next was Santo in Café Cinema. Then X-25, Juno, the seaweed woman, all dancing. Blue Demon. Blue's lips speaking the truth. Rita. Rita's lips.

Klinsman felt a kind of pressure crease in the room, heard a cooling creak in the old house, Tia Coco's footstep. He pushed himself away from the notepad, his laptop, and the makeup mirror on the desk. He wandered the room, made his way to the clothes pile. He scooped up handfuls of it, drank in the desert smells, clicked pearly buttons against his teeth. He fished out a shirt that must have been for him. It had her scent on it, the thump of iron steam.

He changed into it, leaving it unbuttoned, and sat on the edge of the daybed. The mirror on the desk stole some of the laptop's blue light, became a smaller, overdressed twin. Klinsman opened his palms to the room, offered all he had done and said and known in its changing piecemeal light and color. To move would take all he had in him.

Finally he strode across the studio and picked up another sketch—Gina's, the easiest. Without sitting in the ladder-back chair, he hovered his fingers above the keys. He was thrown back by a cracking sound, fresh ice into a drink. And then the computer phone surfaced, just a flutter and hum. He clicked the lime button, which seemed to bulge from the screen. Rita, he hoped.

It was Gina. Again she appeared back from the water, a night swim. As though she had just come from the last image he had seen of her with Oscar in the moonlit foam and kelp.

"Klinsman," she said. Her smile and face were tightened by cold saltwater, her eyelashes beaded. The thumbprint hollows of her collarbone held drops of sand and water. Anyone would want to hold her, feel the hard coolness of the ocean, feel it dissolve in your arms like the fading freshness of sheets, the last sliver of mint on your tongue.

"Let me save you the trouble," she said, nodding to the sketch in his fist.

He stepped farther back.

"I won't bite," she said. "Well, I can't, actually."

He came closer, bent tentatively, then sat.

"That's better," she said. "See?"

He glanced at the makeup mirror, saw his neck and jaw in the bluish light, like a shot from a Santo flick.

"No," she said. "Not that. Not this time. I can't do that without some help. I'm not like you and Oscar and Rita. That's why I have you. You three. That's why I've always had you three. No?"

"Why did you send me to room 9?"

"I told you before," she said. "It was a legit call. So I sent you. My border ace."

"You knew nothing of *vidas?*" he asked.

She tilted her gaze, gave him a half smile, water and salt streaking her throat. "Nothing. I knew what you three knew. That people like watching each other. That, more and more, everywhere we go we are filmed. Some of us will deny it. Some will resist. Some will fear it." She lifted her chin. A drop of water dangled. "Some like it."

He leaned back. "Not filmed, Gina. Captured." He straightened his arm from the desk edge. "As Oscar says. It's just there. Everything is just *there.*"

"You are good," she said. "We're good. Together."

"This is together?" he asked.

She nodded, but her thoughts had already raced ahead. "Keep going."

"Is there a positive form of paranoia, Gina?"

"Awake," she said.

"You're more awake than I am," he said.

"No one's more awake than you, Klinsman." She leaned closer, a hint of salt on tongue and air. "What is sleep, Klinsman? A chance to dream? We're always dreaming."

He ignored this. "Did you know about Artie? About Luz? That they are from Juárez? That Artie is a Juárez orphan? That his mother is buried in the sand there?"

She shook her head, her expression going soft and sad.

"Does Oscar know where you are?" he asked.

"Tell him," she said, reaching to switch him off, "that I'm at the bottom of the sea. Without him I'm at the bottom of the sea."

Her face appeared melancholy and pensive as she looked away, as she disappeared. Her vanishing, the swiftness of it, left him feeling not alone, but with Oscar and Rita on the border desert. This side, that side, he couldn't tell.

51.

Rita had not yet made it to Manzanillo. Maybe it was Tepic, somewhere in between, where she had friends. It seemed darker there, more south, more night. She had just peeled herself away from a table, from people she liked, who made her laugh and still smile as she made her way to the door flap of the cantina. She was wearing the linen dress he had never seen her wear, the one he had imagined her wearing, touching prisms on a white stucco wall. She already looked so different down there. Not *chola*. She looked like someone to be reckoned with on another level, a much higher level. If she took your picture you would feel it like a punch, and the reel from it would convince you that you were flying outward, spreading outward.

She still carried her cameras and bag on her hip, slung with a gunfighter's pride. The dress, her hair free, threw you another way until you saw, too late, the camera. His view was from the table she had left, wavering in a tipsy hand. He could almost smell beer on wood—no, beer on sawdust.

And then Klinsman realized she was not visiting on her way down to Manzanillo. She was already working. He knew the paper she was working for, knew it well. It tried to cover all of Mexico for the American expats, the ones who cared deeply. She might never make it to Manzanillo, never really have to go there, just send them her work. He felt her sliding away even farther, grew dizzy with the tilt of the view.

She ducked through the door flap, and he was clammed into darkness.

Mexico was different, not as connected yet. So he stayed with the darkness, watched it. He could still imagine the smell of beer and sawdust, the caw of an accordion.

Then she was there, strolling a sidewalk lit by window displays. She was in a city that stayed up most of the night, like him. It was a border city then, not more south, just more night. The camera and equipment bag on her hip gave her some protection. The worst of them could look at her and think she was an act on her way to work, like she said, a dancer with her props. Smart ones would think to shy away from her aim, not take her on unless they were ready, not call her out.

He wanted to cry out to her. In the brightest light, the downward shove of a golden neon sign, she slowed her steps. Then she paused in the middle of the sidewalk as pedestrians ambled by her, some drunk and swaying like reeds, some gliding straight and jacked up. She peeked over her shoulder first, then turned fully toward the view. It was easy to think she was spinning to greet the call of a friend.

She smiled slowly, putting her lips into it. She smiled for him and stood there for him. For a moment he feared she would bow. She drew her hands along her sides to show him her dress.

Then she dug for something in her bag, a change of lens perhaps. But what she removed was her clear amber hair clasp, bowed like a delicate ear bone. She gathered her hair to her nape, almost getting it all, and slipped the clasp into place.

He tumbled rag-doll into whiskey light.

He fell asleep in her daybed for twenty-three minutes and was wakened by a high moon slicing through the blinds. Using the remote, he buzzed the blinds closed. The room sank into darkness. When his eyes adjusted, it resurfaced with the press of city gray he imagined seeped through every knothole and crack in the old house. The charge light from his notebook hung green like a distant traffic signal. He eyed the mirror on the desk across the studio and thought to buy some lipstick, to write something for her across the glass. *Backward*, he reminded himself. *Write it backward.*

Then, sitting up quickly, he knew he shouldn't have been able to see the mirror. He should have been seeing only its silhouette, dark matter beside the cold green star of his notebook charger.

He approached the desk. With his fingers he combed back his hair. It felt limp and slick, that undryable dampness you get from too much time in the waves, that fear it's turning to seaweed. He remained shirtless in front of the desk, wanting to feel anything there was to feel against his skin. And at first he began to explain what he knew, to her, he hoped, and to the *salamandros* for certain.

But his jaw felt leaden from lack of sleep, his tongue hollow as a spent cocoon. So he spun the mirror and the notebook to face one another, then pulled out the sketch he had made of Oscar.

"You watch yourself there," he said. To her.

Oscar walked with Santo and Blue Demon through the crowd at Tarfest. The Luchadors wore business suits beneath their head masks, and Oscar wore his t-shirt and jeans. Sometimes Artie walked with him, holding his father's hand, sometimes he was not there.

Oscar was always a quarter step ahead of the Luchadors, leading them. They passed beneath the liquidy sculptures of mammoths, wolves, and saber-tooths. They walked the shore of the biggest tar lake. Oscar stopped to let Artie watch the bubbles glop to the surface like mouths carefully shaping words. Beckoning.

Oscar got away from the lake, leaving Artie. Klinsman felt okay for Artie because he could convince himself that the boy was with Santo and Blue. Nowhere could be safer.

Oscar found one of the pits being excavated, off limits to the public. The pit had been carved into, the tar walled back with planks, scaffolds and makeshift boardwalks crisscrossing above a bed of fossils oozing from black muck. He lay on his stomach over one of the boardwalks and gazed down toward the tar.

From somewhere above him, something caught his eye. He looked up. His movements were amazingly quick along the balance of the narrow boards, his muscles showing through his jeans and shirt.

A snip from one of Santo's early films played. The Luchador was making his way through a tunnel, a torch raised high, muscles glistening. It could have been from any of a dozen of his films.

Oscar was moving through the cave tunnel, alone, ahead of or behind Santo, you couldn't tell. He had no torch, so it appeared as though he were staying on the edge of someone else's light, or tracking something bigger, something that dragged fire.

Oscar appeared to step from the cave into a clearing on the banks of another tar pit, a smaller, more desolate pool with no lawn or sculptures along its shores. It was dusk, and the lights from the Miracle Mile mixed in the distance to form a false sunset, one blended from neon and traffic signals and taillights and the shimmer of exhaust.

Klinsman thought Oscar had reached the oily pool too late, caught only a vanishing glimpse of bubbles on the surface. But the view swung up and around him, gliding along a series of eyes, and settled just off his shoulder, as though to breathe his sweat. Klinsman watching imagined it would smell like the barrel spills on the warm Tecate cobblestones.

On the far shore of the lake he could see the pink crosses standing like angels beside the tar. They seemed to have wandered away from the benefit. They were tilted this way and that, pensive. Whoever had placed them there had done it quickly, in a stolen man-

ner. Or they had carried themselves, ambled like crosses do
sometimes, when no one is watching.

The bubbles on the lake surface, close to Oscar, began to in-
tensify. They surfaced large, with deliberation. Each burst left a
gaping tar mouth. But the final swell was not a bubble. It was an
emerging thing, coated in glistening tar, with broken horns and
eye sockets. Klinsman could imagine the lowing that shivered
across the black lake, and he hoped like hell that Santo and Blue
were close behind.

Someone paused the screen. Klinsman's cell buzzed. At first he
thought it was a moth caught beneath paper. He answered without
speaking, chewing his tongue to life, his thoughts.

"Why show me this?" It was Rita. She was crying. He had never
heard her cry before. It only put pauses between her words, gave
her an accent, gave it back to her.

"Because I fear for you. Down there. I think I know what you're
doing." He sensed his own cry trying to rise, a crimp between his
lungs. "What we are doing."

He heard her sniff and the click and rattle of a phone cord
against a desk, or a nightstand. And this made him want to be in
Mexico, with her in Mexico, where they didn't use shower curtains
and they still had phones plugged into walls.

"Why does it make you cry?"

"Because—*chingadero*—I think he's going to die." She released a
quick, hard sigh. "He's braver than we are. So he will die first.
Maybe, because he has Artie, not so soon."

"That thing, hiding in the lake . . ."

"Yes," she said. "Hiding in the tar of old stories. That's where it hides. Lurks."

"But you," he said. "You're the one who's down there. On that side. You're the one in danger."

"No," she replied. "No. I die last. After you. I get old like Tia Coco. Hmm? Because Oscar is one, the easiest target. You are two." She laughed sadly. "And I am nothing."

"I—"

"No," she interrupted. "We shouldn't even be talking like this. It's all I can do not to talk to you. Not to be with you. But you understand, yes? No one talks without many listening. Without someone listening. These words will play like that saxophone, yes? Maybe in what we were just watching. We all were just watching. It's awake, Klinsman. It's awake to us now. To the *mozos*, too. And they're just boys."

He said nothing, but breathed, tried hard to breathe.

"Now to sleep, Aaron," she said, more softly than anything she had ever spoken. "That chance to dream. If you can't. Then let's go to the motel."

The click of her phone sounded from inside him, the parting of bone and membrane within his ear.

52.

*R*eversing himself on the daybed, he slept in scattered tiny captures as he watched, bathed in the glow of the notebook, which he had dragged close by on the floor.

It was good to see her smiling after hearing her cry. She smiled in that spray of light and water, laughed at him, especially when his eyes were closed to let the flow rinse his face. It increased his desire for her most, when he saw her like that. It was still the most difficult series of images for him to release, to feel beneath a thousand eyes at once. When his eyes were closed and hers opened, you saw a tender prescience in her expression, a readiness highlighted by the beads and rivulets of light and water on her brown skin. In him, you saw what he imagined.

Their motions and expressions on the bed bothered him least in this way because the two of them seemed more equal in their passion. What he saw in the waking dashes of his furtive sleep kept changing back and forth between the light and water and the satin sheets.

Newer images were in there, too, of the two of them entwined on the daybed, wrapped in the twists of the satin robe. She was selecting as well as she could what they were seeing, going back and forth, searching for what might be best for him, what might best help him sleep.

No dreams found him. He never fell that deeply into sleep and the screen finally went dark at 4 a.m., the witching hour for insomniacs. She had fallen asleep, he knew.

He showered and dressed, found the shirt he had left days before laundered and folded for him. She had left a razor and soap for him, too, and a new toothbrush in the bathroom cabinet. It was clear, with a yellow strip inside it. In the studio's fridge was a single bottle of *tamarindo* soda glowing like an amber jewel in a museum display. This was his breakfast.

It was too early to go to Oscar's, and the first trolley hadn't started yet. He felt a deep need to see his friend in person and that shared compulsion to compare notes after speaking with— being with?—Gina and Rita. And sliding heavily at the base of these thoughts and feelings like a slinghammer was the dread for Oscar in the cave tunnel, Oscar tracking the glow of a dragged fire.

Klinsman's car was somewhere—somewhere in the city between his new flat and his old rental. One apartment was off Highland Avenue, the other near Old Town, and for a long, blank moment he couldn't recall which one he had been moving to, which one he was leaving. He didn't care long enough to decide. Notes in hand, he walked the predawn Boulevard to work.

At work, alone among the desks, lights off, he used a sketch overlay to find his uncle.

Jaromir Kilnsman lay dying. He was alone on his bed in his Prague apartment, late-morning light, spring light, sifting in through the leaded windows. He was dressed in a gray suit and black tie, his fedora on the pillow beside him like a sleeping pet. Coleman Hawkins played; the turntable beside the nightstand was spinning at 78 rpm.

The room showed itself with the coo of the saxophone, with the same pace and course of any of Mir's explanations, any of his instructions on how to fix your aim. In one corner leaned a quiver with a bouquet of colorful arrows. Beside this were four family photos, and each was lingered over. The first was Mir's brother, sun-splashed and grinning on the ranch, tall and still gangly with a touch of youth. The next was Connie as a girl, a bull snake looped about her neck like a shepherd's hook, her hair short as a boy's.

Klinsman released a quickened breath moving over the next two photos. They were both portraits of him, one old, one new— one confident, put out even, and the other, the newer one, wild and searching, windblown.

Lining the room were shelves of Mir's collections, what was left of them after many handouts to his nieces and nephews and their children. Some antique toys remained—a mechanical monkey he claimed had once been owned by Ravel and two sad marionettes with no strings. They stared at you, asking for life.

But Klinsman sensed something wrong, something moving

against itself, mirrored actions hesitating the wrong way, magnets flipping. The saxophone went sour on a couple of notes, almost imperceptibly—he wouldn't have noticed had he not had the tune memorized. There was a brief shimmer, a ripple in the lens, the colored circles of old film over Jaromir's black shoes.

He sensed—not hearing really—a groaning, coming from where he could not tell. Foolishly he leaned forward. He was thrown back, heart stopped, by a cattle skull that filled his vision. It had feathers tied to it, like those precious skulls decorated with turquoise paint and hung on cowboy walls. But this one was not genuine, not the real kind found bleached in the desert, but one of those fakes made by burning the flesh off newly butchered heads. He could see the scorch marks, the dig cuts around the horn and eye sockets, bits of hide and meat caught in the cracks. He could still see the terror in the animal's last expression, pouring toward him, disguised in a sneer.

Klinsman staggered back into the darkness of the *Review*. The sudden flare of the last image stung his eyes before it snapped to black. It left him feeling as though the entire building were sinking and shuddering, stern up, into the sleeping city. The waking sounds from the Boulevard outside ended sharply, and he sensed a pressure drop, the opening of a door somewhere. Everything getting up close.

He feared for Oscar, Gina, Rita, but only in the way he knew they feared for him, with hope and trust, an extra little weapon you tuck into their pocket. What he saw unprotected as he rubbed away the scalding colors on his retinas, whom he feared for unabashedly, was Douglas Cook: his yearbook photo, his *mozo* face and mussed hair, his skinny, knobby, innocent throat, that empty space beneath his name. *I try*.

Someone had entered the darkness at the back of the room, in the couch and coffee area. Klinsman crouched amid the sea of desks. He could only discern shadow and silhouette as the figure rustled above the coffee table, a large, wedge-shaped head with long horns angled strangely off-shoulder. He smelled strawberries, to him a border scent, the powder and damp of harvest.

The back light flickered on, a fluorescent stutter bringing the figure into view. It was Caitlin, the intern, carrying a bag of long baguettes and fruit. She set the bag down on the table and put her hands on her hips. An unlit cigarette dangled from her lips, and her long amethyst earrings sparkled.

"It's only me, A. K.," she said. "You can get up. I know you're there."

Trying not to startle her, he stood slowly.

She was arranging the food on the coffee table, setting aside that special plate for him with the hard baguette ends and the fattest strawberries.

"I knew you were there before I came in," she said, continuing to set things up for the morning.

"How?"

"I always check the outside monitor before going in. See what's behind me, what's in front of me." She held a strawberry to her lips as she stood to face him. The unlit cigarette still angled from the corner of her mouth. The white line of the cigarette slanted between amethyst and red: lips, strawberry, earring.

"But it was dark in here," he said.

"I watched you for a while," she replied. "Before it was so dark. When your screen was still on."

He tried to turn things. "Do you usually do that?"

"Only when it's someone interesting. Like you or Oscar." She took the cigarette and tucked it above her ear, lowered the straw-berry. "What about you?"

"What about me what?"

"Watching," she said. She began to fix her hair for work, pulled it into a neat ponytail. With pressing fingers she smoothed beneath her eyes as though applying makeup. He almost asked her about her grandmother in Tipperary, about the fossil shells and the bogs.

"You fell for an old trick there," she said. "The one where they calmly get you to lean close, then spring a scary image at you. A monster."

It took him a moment to realize she was talking about watching him, from outside, before she had stepped in.

"But I didn't laugh," she told him. "You seemed deeply scared. You still seem scared."

She walked toward him, stopped one desk away. "You need to get more sleep. Way more sleep. You know, do all those things they say to do. Close the blinds and make the room darker and don't leave your screen on. Hug a scented pillow. Stop thinking. Imag-ine nothing."

His thoughts became a hum, tilted. She angled her look, her hips, too, as though going with him.

"And don't drink soda in the morning."

53.

*R*ita had already awakened and dressed. She was catching a morning bus off a little *zócalo*, one of those green shuttles with big windshields fingerpainted with indiscernible destinations. But as she boarded, remnants of her waking still, at least, played about her face and shoulders, a thoughtful stare, a ready lift. Klinsman could imagine the breadth of her waking, how tightly she must have hugged herself against it.

The light into the shuttle was more advanced, an hour earlier. She was sliding east, then, not dropping south. Piedras Negras, maybe. She wore a sleeveless blouse, very white against the brown of her biceps. She wore jeans and boots, and one camera was out, strapped above the bag riding on her hip. The other riders collected in the shuttle appeared dressed for the desert, too, warehouse and road work.

She vanished into the press of the morning, marbling in, a stir line on a thick surface.

She stood alone in the desert brush. The landscape was similar to that surrounding the Tecate warehouse, yet with the brush a little more sparse, the spring bloom more faded, the rocks and arroyos bigger, laced with darker patina.

She had crossed back over, for the time being. He could tell because he was a sweep of a hundred desert eyes, gridded like those of a spider. He flew around her, level with her knees, swirling up a gentle whirlwind. She rested one hand on a camera and held still, waiting.

That night she would be a green silhouette slinking over the dark landscape. The liquid green of her movement would be very light, almost yellow, on the cool edges of her. The warmest parts—her heart, between her legs—would be darkest, blue, almost violet.

What light would she have to work with? A wedge of moon, the filter of stars, the veil of the Milky Way, the distant slumbering glow above twin border cities? The trailing edge, the ruffled hem of dragged fire? Delicately grazing along precious light, her aim would have to be released between heartbeats.

54.

On the rush-hour trolley toward Oscar's neighborhood, he imagined his movements tied to hers, both of them riding and pushing themselves around morning current, easing in among people shrugging off the night, the past, and getting to work. Tonight he would make sure to find someplace where it was flat and dark and he could see a few stars, where he could fathom light and color.

Salamanders drawn in black marker surrounded the trolley's embedded eye, their tails out as though drinking from a watering hole. He had little doubt that Caitlin was watching him, keen to the angle of his shoulders, the filigree on his shirt. But how much could she imagine with him? Could she see the white-hot coal in the scramble of his thoughts, the immediate idea of getting to Oscar? Was she privy to his boyish notion of Rita moving and thinking in distant tandem with him? Could she smell the desert, the scent of warming stone, the pleasant bitterness of rust and sunscorched wood?

Were gauzy figures crouched among the upper racks of the trolley or perched like crows along the upper handrails? Uncle Mir might be in there somewhere, seeming to ride a couple seats behind, aware behind the cover of his *Jednota* newspaper. Because Klinsman knew he had died, there would be something ghostly about Mir. Nothing common—no transparency or pale skin or drawn look. He would be wearing his fedora, finally wearing his hat, crimped and brushed to perfection over a lifetime, and that would be enough. He would look like a Cold War importer. But when Caitlin peered sharply, considered everything, she would see a spy on a train, someone who could save you with one deft motion, a quick foot in the aisle, a perfect quiet memory.

As he walked from the Logan Heights stop to Oscar's apartment, he called Connie. He was careful to picture her day first. It would be just a little later but an entirely different season. Her mornings were filled with the most physical work, when she had the most energy. This involved the setting up of the surgery tents, clearing rocks, logs, and brush, then fashioning makeshift planking over the muddiest footing.

Early afternoon was for surgery, when the light was most direct. She had invented a kind of focusing mirror that served as a surgical lamp, coning overhead sunlight passing through a tent flap. She needed light to repair the most extreme clefts—hard, clear, dependable light.

The rest of her day was for lighter work, conventional work, the cleaning of gums and filling cavities. She also taught others how to do these minor, routine procedures, gave them the tools when she had collected extra. She skipped them over eight years of higher learning and showed them how to clean a child's teeth and numb a molar with clove oil.

Klinsman grew hopeful when the phone croaked against his ear. It was ringing there, at least, at that last number she had sent him. Often nothing resulted from the numbers she gave, just empty silence. He could hold his ear to it forever and not even sense the hollowness of a shell. It was an outward flowing quiet, a leaf on water.

He imagined the phone on a post tilting in mud, a single wire trailing across a clearing, like the call posts in the TJ *colonias*. He imagined it bleached bone-white in the subtropical sun, cut and scuffed and relentless.

Someone answered, a boy. Hope lifted to thrill.

"Concepción Klinsman," he said. Then he remembered how to ask for her in Portuguese, to say "please." To say who he was. Her little brother.

A breath cut into the receiver, sounding like falling books, then the phone seemed to go dead. Klinsman took his cell beneath the awning of a pawnshop and huddled against the closed door. He turned his shoulder to the sidewalk, closed his eyes, held the cell delicately to his ear, floated on the surface quiet.

He felt shadows. He turned, still cupping the cell to his ear with both hands, and found himself trapped in the doorway by three teenagers, all sporting Frida Kahlo mustaches. He told them that, mixing Spanish and English, the way Rita would have done. He told them it was a nice way to show that they were together and that they liked her work. Their scent, an up-all-night, crushed-flower smell, filled the doorway.

When the tallest one took a step toward him, Klinsman nodded up to the security camera tucked into the awning's frame. Then he showed them their image on his cell, the three of them together, shoulder to shoulder, with their feathery mustaches. He waved the image at them, cocking his thumb above the send button, only frightened that he was losing whatever connection he had achieved with Connie.

The boys left. They threw insults from up the sidewalk, out of range. Had he not been tenderly holding a possible connection with Connie, Klinsman might have followed the boys, caught them minutes later, named them, accused them of their sins, reveled in their dreams. He would name for each boy his girlfriend's favorite color, her biggest hope. And then Klinsman would offer them everything he had, all of his stuff, right there on the morning sidewalks of Logan Heights.

He held still beneath the pawnshop awning, fearful of stepping out of his connection, imagined the fragile beam of a satellite zigzagging like a spider's single windblown strand. The cell fluttered beside his ear. He could hear people speaking another language, a dog barking, insects trilling, the sound of a shovel cutting into mud.

He heard his name, no louder than a waking thought.

"Aaron?" It was Connie. Reception was clear, unmuddled, but very quiet. Like threading a needle.

"Con." He felt a great lift through his chest.

"I can't talk long," she said. "There's a line here. People waiting for scheduled calls. Understand? I want to talk to you forever.

But I can't. Call back at 9 tonight. Your time. I'll be alone by this phone."

"Wait," he said. "Uncle Mir."

"Uncle Mir?"

"He died."

He heard two breaths, shorebreak through a window, her crying. "When?"

"Yesterday. I think."

"You think?" she asked. "Who told you?"

"No one," he replied. "I saw him."

"Saw him?" She spoke quickly to people there with her, some Portuguese mixed with another language. She shushed them. "Is he there?"

"No. In Prague. It was okay. It was nice. He knew. He had a picture of you. His quiver, too. He was listening to his records."

"But . . ." Her breaths crashed softly again, her cry.

"I just wanted to tell you," he said. "To be the one to tell you. Like he wanted."

"Yes," she said, but it sounded as though she were talking to someone there next to her. "Call me at 9."

55.

*T*he door to Oscar's street-level apartment was open. The music coming from within was wrong, that border polka stuff Oscar hated. Klinsman knew it could have been Oscar's cousin, already come to take care of Artie, mindlessly playing a morning radio show.

He stepped into the apartment. Artie sat alone at a table in the kitchen area. The boy looked at Klinsman, then returned with fisted pencil to some schoolwork he hadn't completed. It was as though Klinsman were coming from across the room to get a cup of coffee. A box of chocolate-flavored cereal stood on the table. Oscar never allowed that kind of food for Artie. Beside the window a Siqueros print hung upside down.

Not quite knowing what might be the most normal thing to do, Klinsman opened the refrigerator. Three Jarritos sodas stood on the upper shelf, one *tamarindo*, one lime, one strawberry. Oscar hated Jarritos and did not allow them for Artie. Klinsman took the *tamarindo* and went to the kitchen table to sit with Artie.

"Need help?" he asked the boy.

Artie shook his head and kept penciling his workbook. He was spelling words three times each. But Klinsman noticed he was writing the wrong words beneath the given word. Beneath "giraffe" he had printed "gorilla" three times, perfectly. Beneath "gnu" he was printing "cow" for a third time.

"I always did my homework right before school, too," Klinsman told him. He kept his voice steady by telling a truth. He measured his breaths. Artie continued to work.

Klinsman poured himself a bowl of the chocolate cereal, stood and took that and his *tamarindo* with him to the living room area of the apartment. Using his foot, he closed the front door as he passed it. He turned on the TV and pretended to watch it. It was set to Channel 12 showing a morning soap. He waited for the first commercial, a pitch for Nivea face cream featuring a woman who reminded him of Edwige Fenech. Then he stood and went to find Oscar.

Klinsman opened the door to the hall closet and went inside. Oscar greeted him with a smile. He had converted the space into an office by punching out the wall dividing the hall closet and the bedroom closet. "Why you *gueros* need so many closets?" he'd asked Klinsman when he had first shown him the little room.

They called it the Paper Room because no computers were allowed in it. It was decorated with prints by Siqueros, Viaud, and Kahlo. The shelf was stacked sideways with books, magazines, newspapers, spiral notebooks, and folders. The small desk was bare except for a pen, a notepad, and an old phone shiny as candy. And new to the desk, in one corner, was a twine sculpture, a board randomly crisscrossed with hundreds of strings fastened to brass pins lining the sides. The overhead lamp was a single blue cone hung from the ceiling by a black wire.

Oscar sat at his desk silently and watched Klinsman enter. Klinsman removed his cell, switched it off, and slipped it back into his pocket. He took a seat on the stool Oscar used to reach the top shelf, where he kept his maps. Klinsman leaned forward, elbows to knees, and eyed the Viaud—*The Left-Handed Barber*—liking how the gaze of the young barber was aimed somewhere between his work and you, the fingers of his right hand pinching a lock of black hair, the left hand wielding scissors.

Oscar spoke as though they were midconversation.

"Deadline is tomorrow at 6 P.M. They moved it up so the interns and ad people could finish their follow-ups on the last day. Drop-deadline is midnight."

"I haven't missed a drop-dead yet," said Klinsman.

"It's your last chance to make first deadline. For once."

"I write best between the two."

Oscar leaned away from his desk for a moment, then drew a gun from beneath. The gun startled Klinsman because it was the kind his father had used for mass inoculations at the orphanage. It was gray plastic with a pointed muzzle.

"I put a chip in Artie," Oscar told him. "Behind his left shoulder. I want you to put one in yourself. For Artie." He slid the gun across the desk toward Klinsman.

"If you don't want to, that's okay," said Oscar. "But here is the number for Artie and the site you use." He handed Klinsman a scrap of yellow notepaper with the word "SafeKids" on it. "It's the same thing they use for prisoners."

"You're leaving."

Oscar nodded.

"North?"

"The networks are older in LA. Stronger. I'll be able to work better, and Artie will be a little safer. Both of us farther from the border. Where I need to be. Rita is already where she needs to be. Still ahead of me, yes? And Gina is where she must be. And you are where you need to be. Where you've always been. On the border."

Klinsman shook his head. He was looking at the Viaud, the stare of the left-handed barber. "I'll have no one."

"You'll have us all."

"No one to touch. No one to hold." Klinsman reached across the desk and took hold of the back of Oscar's wrist, then moved his grip up his forearm.

Oscar put his hand over Klinsman's, smiled.

"Why can't we be with each other? Why can't you be with Gina? She says without you is like living at the bottom of the sea. Why can't I be with Rita? And now us? Why us, too?"

"I'll just be in LA," said Oscar. "I have more network up there. For help with Artie. And for what we're doing. You, Rita, me. Going after Juárez."

"Still. I've seen you every day for seven years. Why do we have to work this way?"

"Because we'll be faster, harder to see, hungrier, crazier, closer—better. You know."

Klinsman injected the chip beneath his left biceps, wanting the quick, sharp pain, then slid the gun back to Oscar. "Tell Artie he won't need this. Tell him he'll always know where I am. Everyone will always know. What I think, what I don't know, what I don't remember. What I love."

He flexed his arm, trying to feel the chip, set it.

"Rita's getting ready," he told Oscar. "Down there. She's moving around, zooming in."

Oscar delicately pushed a black-and-white photo across the desk toward Klinsman. It was the reporter from El Paso, the author photo from her book. But it was different from the usual glossies. She is looking back over her shoulder, as though called to from somewhere back on the sidewalk. The sun shines harshly on her features, and she appears preoccupied, annoyed even.

"She's real," said Oscar. "She is so real. A journalist in the sand, right in the teeth of it. She names the two men. She *names* them. Juárez knows them. There's no mystery, no detectives needed. All of Chihuahua knows them and what they do, their kill parties, their harvests. She names them. She knows they'll never be tried."

Klinsman stared at the woman's photo for a moment. "We can't go after something this big. *I* can't."

"We're not going to go *after* anybody. You are such a fucking *guero*. We're just going to adjust the focus." Oscar slid the journalist's book across to Klinsman. The cover showed a photo of blood-pink crosses in the desert. He patted it with an open hand. "Over the last fifteen years over four hundred women have been murdered in Juárez. Anyone who cares just a little knows this. Apparently it's an acceptable number for us to go about our days, buying shirts and bagel toasters. But what's getting lost in all the cries and stomping about drug armies doing the killing, about a violent society that allows femicide, is the fact that two men—known men—have killed at least a hundred and thirty-seven young women and girls for blood sport. Who knows how many more they've buried. They get to hide inside the mass of hate and murder they inspire. And now they get to move farther because it's spreading. Tijuana beat Juárez in this year's body count."

"So we just fix the aim?"

"We do our part. What we can do. What we're good at."

Klinsman stared at the cluttered shelf, then down to his hands, surprised to find his palms softly opened. *What we're good at.*

"Rita's going to take two pictures," he said, finally looking at Oscar. "Exactly two perfect pictures."

Oscar returned Klinsman's gaze, his cheeks hollowed, eyes still.

"And leave them for the *mandros*. And you."

Oscar nodded. "And then maybe everyone will get to see those two men, how they really are. Their ugly, weak bodies. Their shriveled, impotent selves. The blood on their chins and throats. Instead of what they let us see. What terrifies us.

"It's just a start for us." Oscar tapped the overhead lamp, making the blue cone swing between them. "This will be nothing. Right? Another old story. Refocused. Unearthed. Up north I can find witnesses who'll talk—at least after the *mandros* get their stuff out. I've met people at the benefits and festivals up there. I can tell what they know, what they've seen. What they're ready to say. About harvesting. They go to those things because they need to feel something."

"What am *I* supposed to do?" Klinsman asked.

"You'll know."

"How?"

"Stay on your toes. Stay awake."

Klinsman looked at the string sculpture on Oscar's desk. The sculptor's name, Luhmann, was carved into the side of the wooden board.

"Gina sent it to me," said Oscar. "From the bottom of the sea."

"It's ugly." Klinsman gave it a more sideways glance. "But in a nautical sort of way. Does it measure barometric pressure or something like that?"

"Push a string," said Oscar. "Anywhere, along any string. Like a guitar."

Klinsman pressed down on a string, taking all the strands down with it to the board surface. A startling spiral formed, spokes twirling out of a snail shell. He tried another string. Another spiral formed, different from the other. He tried three more, each one producing a uniquely patterned swirl of lines.

He picked up the board and hefted it. The wood felt heavy and rare, the heart of something. The brass nails were antique; you could see minuscule forge marks in the heads and shafts. The strings were unidentifiable, a material spun from another world, another time, the color of Santo's mask.

"This is a toy," he told Oscar.

Oscar opened his fingers beneath his chin, a kind of shrug.

"You don't understand," said Klinsman. "This was my uncle's. He must have given it to her."

"I'm leaving it with you," replied Oscar. He looked around the tiny office. "All of this to you, Aaron. Until the lease runs out."

Klinsman looked down at the toy in his lap. He pressed down on the uppermost string. The grandest of spirals formed, a whorl of strands like a forever descending staircase, pulling everything in, everything together. But only until you released your finger, and only at this very specific point on this unique string.

When Klinsman lifted his finger, Oscar would be gone.

56.

Oscar sat at the breakfast table taking notes while Artie diligently completed his spelling assignment. The upside-down Siqueros on the wall above them had been righted. The yellow sun shone through the dark honey of the *tamarindo* Klinsman had left unfinished. The boy glanced up from time to time, to see that it was still time to keep working, to see that his father was with him, full of answers.

Klinsman stood at the southwest edge of Ranch Park. He felt taken there by some dream, a sleepwalker come awake. This was the space where Aracely Montiel would sometimes meet him, at the lower fence corner of the tomato field, beneath the cloudlike eucalyptus. Had he come to finish his last story? To ask her more questions?

Her giant image used to loom above Revolución, selling perfume, or clothes, or jewels from Sara's. In the TJ nightclubs she played the elegant lily on the floor, holding a clear and glittering drink, her stillness, the bend of her neck, making all the dark silk and dancing around her appear frantic. And then he would see her walking toward him on the blacktop of the schoolyard, his smiling friend, in uniform like him.

Back then, at that fence, she'd had the answers he needed now. *How do you exist as a body, a living body, as flesh, among thoughts, memories, hopes, sorrows, dreams, feelings, desires? How do you not let yourself be sloughed away, lifted on a breeze? Will we be able to live this way?* He could lift her in his arms, carry her innocently, as though she had sprained an ankle, her arm about his neck.

He sat at one of the stone picnic tables, near where the barn had been. No search found Aracely anymore. He tried some new sketches, overlays of that one photo he had of the two of them standing by the fireplace. This only brought him to his own *vida*, the photo doubling back on itself. It was impossible for him to believe that someone whose image had been so widespread and so desired could have vanished. He used to be able to find pictures of her easily, some from the past, a few from the present, those of her at fund-raisers, his age now. Worn from what she had known all along, she had become more striking, her dark features deepened with sadness, knowing.

Klinsman walked to the game of Mexican Nines, wanting to feel the players' shouts, smell their sweat, inhale their glares. He imagined Rita watching him, taking a break in the shade, checking to make sure he wasn't pouting somewhere, that he was staying on task.

He set his shoulder bag courtside and joined the game. He slid into the middle of the crowded key and raised his arms for the ball, suddenly the tallest player. It took him a few jogs up and down the court to figure out which team he was on. "Hey, *guero, guero*," they called to him whenever he grabbed the rebound, which was often. He never took a shot, only rebounded and passed.

The ball sometimes surfed over a sea of raised hands toward the hoop. The ocean air brimmed within his lungs, knifed the center of his chest. The noon sun blinded him whenever the arc of the ball led his eyes into it. Sweat peeled from him, and his feet began to blister inside his boots.

The game disintegrated rapidly around him as lunch hour ended and players headed back to their jobs. The last couple rested a moment with Klinsman, their mechanic's shirts opened, hands braced against knees. According to their shirt tags they were named Larry and Charlie. They were both short and muscular, a little too big for jockeys. One had curly hair and Olmec eyes; the other had very thick, very straight hair, skin as dark as his eyes, all lending to an unnerving quickness about him.

"Larry," said Klinsman, nodding to the name sewn onto his shirt. "From Tabasco, yes?"

The player raised his brow, dissolving the quickness and darkness a little. "Yes."

Klinsman tried Charlie. "Oaxaca, yes?"

"Chiapas."

"Close at least," said Klinsman in Spanish.

"Someone was here earlier, *guero*," said Chiapas, "looking for you. Asking for you."

Klinsman tried to appear calm, kept his hands on his knees for a moment, catching his breath like the other players. Then he stood upright.

"Who?"

"We don't know," said the other one. "A man with two men behind him."

"Did he say his name?"

They shook their heads.

"What did he look like?"

"He was small and skinny and old. Mexican maybe. Almost. Nothing to be afraid of."

"The others?" asked Klinsman. "The two behind him?"

"I would be afraid of them," said the one from Tabasco. He smiled, and his friend smiled with him.

"Don't worry, *guero*. We just told him the truth. That you weren't here today."

Klinsman scanned the park through the chain-link fence, clenching the galvanized steel. His shadow lay in a net of diamond patterns on the grass.

The two mechanics started to leave, then one, the one from Tabasco with Olmec eyes, turned back toward Klinsman.

"They don't fool me," he said.

Klinsman gave a puzzled look.

"They don't come here to find you. They know you won't be here. They just want to ask. To show themselves to us. Not you. But to let you know."

Klinsman nodded. "Thank you."

They nodded in return, first one, then the other, single fare-well lifts of the chin.

"Maybe you play again," said the one from Chiapas. "You don't play like a *guero*. You play good. Straight. Loose. Like a Mexican."

Klinsman stood in the very center of Ranch Park, where the pump shack used to be. Eyes closed, the sun on his face, the ocean breeze in his hair, he could picture the ranch. The long slope of tomato rows would be at its spring height, its greenest, the fruit ready to ripen. He could smell the tomatoes reddening from within before any color showed. That was when the harvest would begin.

In his hand he held his notepad: *woman from room 9, salamander, Santo, Blue, and cow skull.*

57.

From the park Klinsman rode the trolley to the Motel San Ysidro, hoping to catch whatever remained of the building, maybe to speak to the day clerk one more time. He hoped also to catch the right *mandro*. There were only three stops between the park and the border. He switched cars at each station in order to survey as many passengers as he could.

He saw several *mozos*, riding to nowhere among the afternoon commuters, all choice targets for one of Rita's tongue-lashings. At the border stop he remained on the trolley and backtracked north. After the second stop he switched cars and found himself in a crunch of passengers, men and women who had just crossed, holding tool belts and overnight bags, starting long commutes to North County for evening work.

Two *mozos* stood near the door, though not together. One was a pretender, wearing a fashionable leather jacket, a blackish green, with wide pockets and belt. He was very pale, like cool ivory, and his black hair was swept into low bangs evenly across his eyes.

Two passengers over from him, standing free, surfing the rhythm of the trolley, was another—a *mandro*, clearly, even though Klinsman could only see him from the shoulders up. His hair was unwashed, licked in all directions by thoughts and puzzles. He wore an oversized blazer with some nautical crest on it. His skin was marbled, white and caramel, visible all the way down into the open collar of his shirt, a crimson blouse cut for a woman. His eyelashes were thick and long and black, except where the white curls on his skin cut across their ends, staining them blond. One of his side-burns, too, was stained this way.

He returned Klinsman's gaze for a moment, then continued scanning the rest of the passengers. He stood just underneath the car's smoky eye. Klinsman paid a man five bucks for an aisle seat so he could work his notebook. The *mandro* watched him openly now, peeking through the forest of swaying passengers, sometimes glancing out the trolley window, trying to anticipate the next stop.

The *mandro* jumped the trolley at the next stop, the Iris Street Station. Klinsman followed him across the concrete platform, then hurried up beside him on the sidewalk. He took hold of his shoulder, pulled back on the loose blazer. It was like reaching into a dream, the way he sometimes tried to stay in the dream, in sleep.

The skinny *mandro* let himself tilt back against the cinder-block wall, the barrier built to protect the housing tracts from the rush of the boulevard. He looked forcefully away from Klinsman, shrugged himself free of his grip.

"You know me," said Klinsman softly, just above the traffic wind.

"I don' know you."

"You know me like you know most people on that car. Like you'll know everybody on that car. Like that other *mozo*—that fake. Yes? The one named Hector, after his father. Yeah? He wants more than anything to ride that trolley all the way out to El Cajon, to see his father. To make him come back."

The *mandro* continued to look away. Klinsman put his hand back to the shoulder of his blazer, held it there gently.

"He don' go," said the *mandro*, looking toward the sea, the bullring at the water's edge. "Not this time. Not ever." The blond edges of his dark lashes looked wet in the afternoon sun, candle melt.

"I need you to do something for me," said Klinsman. "Quick and easy, for you. At the park."

He looked at Klinsman directly. "What do I get?"

Klinsman answered in Spanish, using the plural *you*.

"You get two pictures. Two devils."

At Ranch Park two women were power-walking the perimeter together, dressed in yoga clothes and ball caps. A *nana* watched two toddlers dig in the sand of the play yard. Three boys in jerseys and jeans kicked a soccer ball in an expansive triangle over the open grass. A bum sat alone on the basketball court drinking a forty at the base of one of the hoops. There was the thump of the soccer ball and the occasional call and laugh of a child.

It all sounded like echoes to Klinsman as he sat with the *mandro* at the stone picnic table where he had first met Douglas Cook. He turned the screen toward the *mandro*.

"You know my name. What is yours?"

"Victor Saturnino Herrán Bevaqua."

Klinsman drew back. "Like the painter?"

"My mother is an artist."

"You know his work?" Klinsman asked. "Herrán's?"

The *mandro* nodded as he looked over Klinsman's notebook. "They just call me Nino."

"You're not afraid? You don't hide?"

"When you look like me," Nino replied, "When you are painted like I am, *qué más da*. Even you found me."

"How many of you are there?"

"In this city?" Nino rubbed his chin. His long fingers were marbled like the rest of him. "Five hundred. Maybe more. More each day. You know?"

"How many do each of you have going? How many . . . *vidas?*"

"You can't do more than a hundred. That's the rule. But anyone who is any good finds a way to . . . *como se dice?*" He made a circling motion with his fingers.

Then Nino flicked his fingers over the keyboard, at times thumbing the screen like a painter smoothing a brushstroke. He was even faster than Douglas Cook. Klinsman did the math while he watched. Five hundred times one hundred. Each one of the fifty thousand containing how many others? How many other lives does

one life contain? Even the most solitary? He pictured bigger cities. Subways and metros.

Nino took him around the park, one hour back at a time. The
shadows first grew shorter, receding to noon. Then they grew
longer, stretching back into the morning. He watched himself
playing in the game of Mexican Nines.

But there was a jump in the screen between where the basket- ·
ball game began and where the court was empty just before noon,
just before the shadows began leaning east. Nino took them back
and forth, trying to fix the jump.

He shook his head after three tries. "The one you want to see.
I can't get him. Or the two men who were with him. Because he
knows."

"You can do more," said Klinsman.

Nino shook his head. "I don' want to."

He got up to leave, putting a hand on Klinsman's shoulder,
keeping him seated. "I try," he said as he nodded once to the
screen. "You try."

He left quickly, heading to the south edge of the park. He
seemed to gaze often at the distant bullring as he strode toward the
sidewalk. His thin shadow formed a perfect black line on the grass,
barely attached to his heels.

Klinsman was left with a screen showing a blank patch of green. A
breeze brushed the grass tips, flickered the dandelions. He was
about to shut down the notebook when he noticed a swirl in the
lower right corner, a cut against the grain in the grass, a mower's

mistake, or signature. He brushed his fingertips over it as though to comb it away.

The image of the cattle skull leapt forth, stopping his heart again, gears freezing. It filled his screen. The same breeze that rippled the grass and dandelions was fluttering the bits of hide and ash caught in the skull cracks. You could almost hear it fluting in the horn hollows and eye sockets.

"It's even worse the second time," Caitlin had told him. "When you think you're expecting it."

58.

*K*linsman could not find the motel. At first he thought he must have somehow lost his way, gone along a parallel street. But he knew he could have found it with his eyes closed. Just for fun he could have used the afternoon shadow patterns on the Tijuana mesa to triangulate the motel's exact location. He could take anyone anywhere along the riverbed. He knew every brackish pond, any remaining graveyard, every gutted car skeleton teetering over a dry bed, every freshly spun cul-de-sac. It was all he knew anymore.

The motel was gone. All that remained was the lot, roped off and thickly coated with a new layer of asphalt and painted with sulfur-bright parking lines. A kiosk stood at the center, cheap and bright as a circus tent.

He stepped over the rope barricade and walked across the fresh asphalt toward the kiosk. The soles of his boots stuck to the tacky surface, left dust footprints on the unblemished tar. No other footprints were visible, so he was surprised to find someone working inside the kiosk. A skinny old guy was carefully painting a menu on a placard. The placard, decorated in the colors of the Mexican flag, was set on an easel. The menu listed the services offered under the big heading "Park & Ride."

A fan was pumping tar-scented air through the kiosk, and a paint-spattered radio played a Mexican polka, accordion and trumpet vying against a man's mournful pleas for love. The old guy paused between brushstrokes to get in a couple of dance steps. He probably had been pretty good once; he did a little two-step, his knees bending smoothly, his right heel up.

Klinsman moved his shadow over the easel, and the old guy turned around. It was the day clerk from the motel, his horn-rims perched on the end bulb of his nose, his dentures pressing forth like something about to fist through dry lips. He smiled at Klinsman.

"Snakebite," he said, drawing out the last syllable. "Nice to see you."

Klinsman leaned through the kiosk window and nodded toward the man's shirt, a royal-blue uniform with a stitched nametag that read, "Sal." "That really you?"

"Yeah." He finished painting a letter. "They make me wear this shirt. It's part of the deal. The people who sold the place wanted to make sure I had a job. I was part of the sale. Nice of them, no?"

"You going to drive?"

"Nah. Nothing like that. Just work the register. I work a register better than anybody. It's in my hands after all these years. I don't even have to think. When I die they can cut off my hands and I bet they'd be able to ring you up right."

Klinsman fought that image. "It's sad about the motel."

"Nah," he replied, two-stepping to the accordion. "This'll be good. You park your car here, safe. We take you across, stop at the outlet stores on this side, on the way back." With his brush he pointed to the menu. "See? We'll take you all the way to Ensenada."

Klinsman looked at the paintbrush balanced in Sal's bony fingers. "That's good work. You an artist?"

"Once." His upper lip caught on his dentures with the word, sneering it.

"What did you paint?"

"People. But I had trouble with ears. I could never paint a good ear. I always hid them."

"Like Degas with hands," said Klinsman.

"I could paint hands. I loved painting hands. I painted whole canvases full of hands."

"You ever paint a man named C de Baca?"

The old guy smiled and put down his brush. He stood close to the kiosk window. Klinsman could see the Mexican in him, inside the pale and freckled skin, the lightbulb head, the white rim of hair. He could see it in the long line of his jaw, the lift in his cheekbones, the sincerity of his stare above his calm smile.

"Nah. I never painted anything like that."

"They used to say he had a twin. On the other side."

"Yeah." Sal smoothed his top dentures with his tongue. "There was no twin. Mexicans just said that because it was too scary thinking there was just him. Everywhere like that. This side, that side. Mexicans always divide their devils. You know?"

He looked at Klinsman, his gaze measuring him, going from shoulder to eye, eye to shoulder. His expression softened, grew less weathered and mocking, lulled almost to sadness.

"You fooled me good, Snakebite," he said softly. "For a while there. But now I'm just a motel clerk again. Answering motel questions."

"Then answer me like a painter."

Sal leaned close, elbows on the counter between the two men.

"There was only one C de Baca. The one who burned to death on your ranch. But there is always one C de Baca. Divide him as many times as you want. Burn him dead. There is always one."

Klinsman turned away for a moment. Then he eyed the upper frame of the kiosk ceiling, looking for security. The wires were there, dangling, ready. He pointed through the window at Sal's work.

"I bet you were good. I can tell. You were better than you thought."

"Hah." Sal grinned and shook his head. "I was better as a motel clerk. I'm still better. You're full of shit."

Klinsman bowed his head. He needed Oscar. He needed Rita to aim her camera.

"But I'll tell you, Snakebite," the old guy said. "This motel. C de Baca never set foot here. Never had anything to do with it. Never would touch it."

"Why not?"

"Part of a deal," Sal replied. "Part of some deal. Going way back. Way back before even me."

"I don't think anything goes back more than that."

The old guy nodded once, just a quick tilt of his head, his heavy glasses sliding back. "You want to see your motel one last time?" He pointed an angled finger toward a pile of rubble along the far edge of the fresh asphalt. "It's all in there."

59.

He climbed to the top of the rubble heap, all that was left of Motel San Ysidro. The Park & Ride lot, with its new slick of asphalt, lay like a negative of the afternoon sky, the wet streaks of tar mirroring the cloud wisps. Two illegals had made temporary camp on the obscured side of the little mountain, had fashioned a makeshift table and bed from boards and stucco slabs. They were young men dressed in worn flannel shirts.

When they saw Klinsman atop the pile, they merely stood, their shoulders stooped with fatigue. Then they both brushed their fingers down their forearms twice, a sign he hadn't seen since he was a boy on the ranch. It meant they needed a little more rest before they got off your land—and do you need any work done?

He gave them the key to Oscar's place, trolley fare, and directions. He told them not to pocket the fare, to purchase the tickets and not try to jump the trolley. He told them the trolley tickets would be like passports. There was food and water for them at the apartment, and a place to sleep.

They said they were going to Oregon to work the peach groves. They had walked from Michoacán. He said he had once worked with a man named Alejandro who had walked all the way from Oaxaca. That the man had saved his life from a snake. He showed them the scars on his shin.

They told him that the kind of snake that left that mark didn't kill you. That it only ruined your life. They used the same word Aracely had used: *Arrasara su vida*.

Starting from the rubble heap, he planned to do some last footwork for his three pieces for the *Review*: room 9 in Motel San Ysidro, the Luchadors at Café Cinema, park surveillance. He didn't imagine Gina watching; he felt it, a finger graze between his shoulder blades. He sat in the migrants' makeshift camp for a moment, recalled such encampments his family would often find along the ranch peripheries, lean-tos with leaf beds and battered pie tins. As kids he and Connie would sometimes use them to play adventure games, to be explorers in the wild. Rita would hate that if he told her. Little *gueros* playing out their dreams in the hard desperation of wetbacks.

From atop the heap he took one capture of the lot that used to be the Motel San Ysidro, centering it on where room 9 had been but framing in the rubble and the kiosk. Through the kiosk window he could just make out Sal at his easel, looking like one of those animated *calaveras* from the Days of the Dead. Klinsman jotted down a few lines in his notepad, describing the old man like that. He described the deal, too, and the legend of C de Baca.

Off the trolley ride north, he first stopped at Rita's to organize and ready himself. He stacked his sketches and notes neatly beside his laptop on the desk, adjusted the little makeup mirror for no reason other than to acknowledge his reflection in it, the grainy light it cast him in, as though he were in old Santo stock footage. He regretted not taking a souvenir from the rubble of the motel, something more than just that picture of Sal, the *calavera* in the kiosk.

In his peripheral vision the woman on the wall squirmed and shimmied. It made him laugh a little to think that Rita already *had* taken something good and useful from the ruins, better than any of his notes or amateur pics or Oscar's useless artifacts. He left the desk and stood before the woman from room 9, again aswim in her seaweed current. He panicked at the size of her. The panic he attributed to sleep deprivation, then took a measured, steady-handed capture with his camera set to its best resolution. He loaded the image onto Victor's search grid, no overlays, no added touches from him, just the best and purest of what he could get from Rita's rendition. *Come with me or stay with her.*

His own sketches and overlays of the woman had before found X-25, in that old movie poster and that still from *Santo contra Blue Demon en Atlántida*. With Rita's photo, he found someone different, but almost the same.

He found the Luchador X-25, new and bright and clear on the dance floor of Café Cinema. And another of her, stepping in dim window light, in filtered neon, toward a bed in a cavelike motel room, over a caption: *Santo vs Blue Demon in Atlantis*. And another, where she stood in slants of sunlight streaming through sea mist between shadows of high rafters. The Luchador X-25 looked very similar to the old movie version but more athletic, with muscle lines in the tight form of her orange pantsuit, more believable as someone who could take you down with a high kick.

Klinsman knew where to go. He recognized the warehouse light, that fuzzy ocean air and that odd weave of rafters and girders. X-25—the imposter X-25—was in the big warehouse on the Del Mar fairgrounds where they sometimes held boat shows and Cal Expo exhibits. Maybe he could catch the Luchadors in their secret hollow, catch them in rehearsal, before they fell into their impenetrable roles, before they became spontaneous. This time of day would be right: afternoon, when actors and wrestlers did their real work.

The trolley ride from the border to Del Mar was very long, and he was able to get some work done, making notes on each of his three stories, getting some thoughts down. He changed cars occasionally to view as many riders as he could. At one point, under the canopy of the City College stop downtown, he saw three students, almost shoulder to shoulder, watching their notebooks. One was passing among empty morning streets in some far-off snowy neighborhood, one was watching a live shot of a watering hole somewhere on the African veldt, and another was on the hood of a state trooper's jeep chasing a strange-looking beast galloping along a desert road.

Sitting at the rear of one car, he managed to tap into the trolley's eye in the front bulkhead. When he showed the view to the passenger beside him, she looked at him in horror, her blue eyes like deep ice. She hurried away from him, found a place to stand near the front exit. The passengers on his screen all looked at her, the way commuters watch the only one moving, the only one who seems to know anything.

Riding the final leg to the Del Mar stop, he visited the Luchador's site. He watched one of their first time loops, one they had done downtown in Café Lulu. Only one masked Luchador appeared in the loop, a Blue Demon passing by the big front window in his gray business suit as though on his way home from work at the bank. Other repetitions in the loop included a sneeze by the barista, a customer's request for more chocolate, and a chance reunion between old friends.

He watched a hyperspeed version of the Luchadors' eerie appearance and vanishing at a big concert, how they multiplied themselves on the crowded floor below the stage, finally prompting the band to sputter and falter midsong, some members in fear, others in wonder. The sudden complete disappearance of all masks only intensified things. The crowd, fixated on the band, crushed in the volume, knew nothing about masked figures. "You're seeing things, seeing things," they chanted.

Along the short walk from station to fairgrounds, Klinsman felt ready to face them. The scatter and spark along his nerves caused by lack of sleep served him well in the late-afternoon sun. He felt as if he had just stumbled out through casino doors to find it day while expecting night. The smell of high tide hung heavy in the Del Mar air, salty and primordial.

6o.

Warm sea air filled the warehouse. Sunlight fell in precise shafts from the high windows. Klinsman counted six Luchadors as he entered and two female agents. Three of the Luchadors were Blue Demon, wearing dark, short-sleeved turtlenecks beneath their head masks. The three playing Santo wore white turtlenecks. Klinsman recognized the getups from the *Atlantis* movie. The two women wore blond wigs and tight-fitting orange pantsuits, like X-25 and Juno from the same movie.

They were clearly waiting for him. Two Luchadors sat on an overhead beam, one Blue, one Santo, both watching him intently as he approached the others, who stood in a semicircle.

They all had sweat marks on their tight shirts and appeared tired from rehearsing.

"It's hard work, no?" asked Klinsman. "Being spontaneous."

"We usually don't let the press see us this way," said the nearest wrestler, Santo. The one you'd pick out as the real Santo if you were X-25 and you had to decide quickly.

"You could've hidden," said Klinsman. He nodded toward an overhead security monitor showing the outside parking lot and sidewalk. "You could've left."

Santo shrugged. Inside the silver mask his eyes looked moist and vulnerable. "We face our marks. When they find us out."

Klinsman looked at the two women. The one who was supposed to be X-25 was shorter. Her blond wig was coiffed, more waxy, and her false eyelashes were longer, her lipstick red-orange to match her pantsuit. When Klinsman had watched the movie as a kid, he had always wanted Santo to end up with her, even though she was on the wrong side.

"It was you in the bed," he said to her.

X-25 walked over to a cot and lay down. She straightened her legs together and clasped her hands beneath her breasts. She closed her eyes, false lashes lowering into an elegant sleep.

Klinsman eyed the Luchadors. He chose the tallest of them, remembering how challenging it was to bend over the daybed in order to scoop Rita neatly, perfectly, from the satin. It would have been even harder with the motel bed. The one he nodded to was Blue Demon. "But you would've been wearing the Santo mask."

The Luchador walked to a point on the warehouse floor, approximating where the door to room 9 would have been in relation to the cot. He then walked in, stepping like a considerate thief. He stood for a moment above X-25, taking care not to graze his knees against the edge of the cot, and delicately scooped her into his arms.

He carried her to Klinsman. Thoughts of Rita drove through him, images there for him, he knew, if he closed his eyes and waited. He could smell the sweat from Blue Demon and X-25, bitter in the trapped sea air of the warehouse, like fresh cement. And stirring between was Rita's wet copper scent, a soothing cool bar.

The Luchadors regathered themselves, the two above still sitting on the beam, the other four in a semicircle around Klinsman.

"Did you mark the other journalists, too?" he asked.

"Anyone who happened to show up at the motel room," replied Santo, the same one as before, the one on the end nearest him. "We knew you, the *Trib*, and *LA Weekly* would be covering the Café Cinema show. The motel was just an extension—our little extra scene for *Atlantis*."

"And then see what happens?" asked Klinsman. "What forms?"

Santo nodded, his eyes soft inside the silver head mask, like snails curling back into their shells. "We left you a phantom before you came to the show. All we did was call the cops and figured it would get to all of you."

"Why the black tape? Why try to cover all the eyes? Didn't you want it to be captured? Wouldn't you want the *mandros* to get it?"

Santo shrugged. "We called attention to the room by trying to hide it." Then he nodded to one of the Luchadors on the overhead beam, the one as Blue Demon. "We let Sergi try to cover the room and the bath. He's fucking paranoid. He tried to cover all possibilities. But it was impossible. With all these eyes left everywhere. And now, with the *mandros*, we never have to worry about recording our work."

"Did you know about the *vidas?*" Klinsman asked.

"Only rumors. We figured something like that would come about eventually. We had no idea we'd actually find one—yours. Like that. Only because we searched for ourselves, our little motel-room skit."

Klinsman scanned all of them. "It seemed like you knew more. About me. Specifically. A lot of things hit me when I walked into that room. Every time I walked in."

"Like you said," Santo replied, "spontaneity is hard work."

"Did you mess with me in Balboa?"

Santo shook his head. "We were at the Tar Pits. Look, you're all over this city. You've lived here just about all your life. Finding you is easy. Watching you is easy. You probably get into almost everybody's *vida*, like a cat ruining photos. And it would be child's play to salt these *vidas*. A kid in a soccer shirt. How many of those could you find in Balboa on any given day, bribe with an ice-cream cone? Place a hairbrush there. Pay a busker five bucks. Let the crazy park do the rest. *Mire?* See how it's done?"

"Do you have any idea what you caused? With what you did in the motel?" Klinsman looked at them all together, opened his arms. "What you did to me? What you set in motion?"

Santo stepped a little closer. He held his arms open to Klinsman, as though he were carrying someone, a lot like the original Santo. "Look. We do what we do. You know us. What we've always done. But now . . . we're still learning what happens with the way things are now. In this." He motioned to the warehouse, the sultry visible air of it. And to the overhead monitor.

X-25 moved forward from the semicircle, a perfect, choreo-graphed step that shimmered up through her orange pantsuit. Klinsman knew it was her line. He heard it through dubbed and painted lips, Edwige Fenech in one of her *giallos*, throaty and truth-ful—kind, if you let it be, if you knew her.

"Do you regret it, Aaron? Would you undo it if you could?"

61.

*K*linsman let the warehouse door swing closed behind him as he stepped into the sunlight. The vast fairgrounds parking lot was empty, no cars anywhere, stillness all around. From this lot he was beginning his final reinvestigation of the parks. He wondered if the Luchadors watched him on the security monitor as he strode across the asphalt expanse. He felt taken apart, divided like light through a prism. The sensation shot through him. Gina. Oscar. Rita, Douglas. Caitlin. Others even—his niece Molly, people he didn't know yet.

He caught the trolley to begin the park visits in what was for him reverse order, north to south. He hopped off downtown, hiked up Laurel, and crossed 6th onto El Prado. Distance slid beneath him.

Until Balboa loomed before him and he began a more tentative pace across Cabrillo Bridge toward the main entrance. The low sun shone green on the tiled dome and in the narrow hollows of the bell tower. The sides of the tower were streaked with black watermarks, making it seem rocketlike somehow, something scorched on reentry. Beneath him, rush-hour traffic slogged both ways on the 163. Parkgoers along the bridge leaned over the rail and watched the freeway as though it were water.

He wavered as he neared the tunnel entrance. Would even this cursory stroll down the Prado peel him away in layers, fill and fuel the kaleidoscope of Aaron Klinsman? He paused in the alcove beneath the tower. On a stone bench in the alcove, where the exhaust from the 163 collected in sweet blue air, he spun his life. He tried to find more of Aracely Montiel, more than the single image of her in a firelit dress, the Gibson Girl standing in his youthful arms. But that was all that remained of her.

He shot arrows with Connie and Uncle Mir, said good-bye again and again to Azariah in the geometric shade of the Japanese Gardens. He learned to string a bow again, to bring the string to his nose and lips and wait until everything stilled. He tasted the pleasantly bitter catgut, felt the cut in his fingers.

He turned away from his screen to watch the parkgoers pass through the entrance. He saw each one blindly walking into the visual ricochet of their cams and cells and whatever had replaced the Robot MV99 and the W99 Multi and the RC60 receivers. Careful what you imagine in there. Careful what song you listen to, try to recall. Careful what you think, what you dream. If he really called out to them, they would think him one of the dozens of homeless crazies sifting through the edges of Balboa.

When he turned back to his screen, Rita was there, naked with him on gray satin, over him, erasing him beneath brown curve and black coil. He felt a gasp pulled from him, an underwater breath that wasn't there to take.

The sun was setting by the time he reached Silver Wing. The overlook beneath the wing monument was more than empty, a vacuum. But to Klinsman it had to feel that way. The kids from the high schools—his old school and the one at the foot of the grassy hill—weren't coming here anymore to drink beer from soda cans, smoke pot rolled into cut cigarettes, watch the sun set beside the bullring, hook up, screw, experiment with one another, try out each other's cars. Maybe they couldn't stand being watched. Maybe they wanted to do the watching. Someone had left a kite flying, the string tied to an empty bike rack. The kite wiggled its shoulders on the steady ocean wind, its tail softly popping, licking back into the evening sky.

At Ranch Park he traced the perimeter, following the path of the half-dozen power walkers out to catch the last bit of light and safety before going home to fix the family dinner. High school kids played soccer on the widest green, dusk beginning to shimmer like fish scales on their sleeveless jerseys. Klinsman didn't tap into the cameras, still feeling the afterbuzz of this afternoon's jolt from the sudden cow-skull image.

He stood directly beneath the eye atop the basketball cage, opened his arms to it, stared with determination. The power walkers gave him lots of room as they passed him, their conversations halting, their pace increasing.

On the long trek from Del Mar to the borderlands, a ride spliced by quick visits to each park, Klinsman had watched *Santo vs Blue Demon in Atlantis*. Not the version he had seen several times on Channel 12 but the one he'd found using Rita's impression of the woman from room 9. A few other Santo stills were there, too, including a poster from the one Douglas Cook had captioned *Profanadores de tumbas*: Don't use this, I hope you don't have to use this. I try.

62.

tlantis began in reverse, or so it first appeared. A *guero* journalist backed out of a room while Coleman Hawkins's saxophone played, keeping a kind of lullaby time. The journalist had
his satchel and notebook and cheap camera slung on his shoulder.
His backward steps were careful, and soft neon colors bathed the
room in cellophane light. The light, the deliberate back-steps, the
expressions playing about his face and shoulders would convince
anyone that he was a little fearful, intrigued, perplexed.

He went to what looked like a lively party in an undersea ball-
room, where cocktails in little green glasses were being served,
where women in little black dresses danced wildly around the stoic,
business-suited Santo and Blue. They danced to the music of Los
Abandoned, led by the seductive sway of X-25 and Juno. The webby
light of water swam over everything, everyone. The *guero* journalist
was being stalked by a flickering, shimmering figure, a seaweed
woman with lines and tendrils thin as ink in water. She material-
ized only if watched closely, watched without being distracted by

the beautiful X-25 and Juno, or the glitterfall of bright colors, or the Luchadors.

The journalist chatted with Blue, discovered something about the Luchador, that he must be up to something. That maybe he wasn't himself anymore, that someone else, something else had gained control. But maybe that was a feeling carried over from the original, where Blue is hypnotized by the undersea people.

The *mandros* had trimmed away all the stock footage from the original, all the lumbering, grainy wrestling sequences from smoky Mexico City arenas, all the filler. This left room for the real story, the plight of three heroes in Atlantis—Klinsman, Oscar, and Rita. Jaromir was in it, a sort of Ares, a tall figure of strength and knowledge with his tousled hair and confident longbow.

Connie as a young girl, a natural with a bow and arrow, a conqueror of snakes, Ares' favorite pupil, matured into Rita. When you saw Ares die, wounded on his bed but content with his legacy, which surrounds him in the artifacts of his life, Rita drops to her knee in sorrow, her camera slung like a quiver over her shoulder.

From his many movie reviews, Klinsman knew that films were composed of two- to four-second shots. Longer shots, lingering ones, created the illusion of thought, feeling, and imagination. The *mandros* needed very little, could conjure motion and discovery with mere snippets. With Klinsman, they had a lot.

In *Atlantis* the love story between the *guero* journalist and the photographer wove itself within the adventures of the three heroes as they—sometimes together, sometimes apart—attempted to expose the atrocities wrought by the bony men who ruled the undersea city. The lovers appeared driven toward each other by their goal. There were two sex scenes between them, one in the room from the opening, which came to be his place. The other was in her place. There were other scenes, water-filled moments, where they were naked and washed in a spray that appeared more light than water, drops becoming sparks and brilliant photons.

In one scene she kissed him coolly but deliberately as he left her car. There anyone could see she had decided to be with him.

But a larger monster hung invisibly above everything, something much stronger and more expansive than the evil men of Atlantis. You could see the heroes look to it at times, upward glances and gazes, quick turns, guarded stances. While Oscar pursued one of the hideous ones in a firelit tunnel, helped by Santo, who was covering the rear, he also looked back and up to the indifferent one, the one that was just there, always there.

Gina appeared, an underworld goddess, living away from Atlantis, like Persephone. The Santo movies always played freely with the myths, mixing them, using them the way myths should be used. Persephone had run from things, from her plight and her discoveries, ahead of the heroes, but was there for them when needed, to give what she could from her underwater lair, letters expressing her despair. She came ashore once, to make love to Oscar in twilight waves.

Oscar saved a boy from Atlantis, orphaned by the atrocities, by the hideous men who had hollow eyes and trephinations in their skulls where horns could be set. Oscar left the boy in the protective hold of Santo and ventured back into Atlantis.

Rita, near the end of Klinsman's journey on the trolley, shot the two devils of Atlantis with her arrows. But Klinsman couldn't tell if her aim was true. The last two things shown were him looking out over the sea toward a misty, futuristic structure at the water's edge, a fleeting platform above Averno—and then a final lingering shot of a kite hovering on an ocean wind, deciding.

63.

The final scene had already moved on from the kite. He stood beneath the eye that was atop the basketball cage, everything growing murky in the dusk, fading to shadows. But the shadows remained, cast by the lone security light of the park, the half moon, the shotgun spray of city light off the Tijuana mesa, and the backlash of the night sky. Everything, including Klinsman, had four shadows, falling like the directions of a makeshift compass in the sand.

"How many times have you watched it?" he asked Caitlin.

She sat across from him on the sofa at the back of the *Review*. Her notebook was open on the coffee table. Beyond, the sixteen desks rested, empty and quiet in the dimness, screens blind and openmouthed as nestlings.

"Maybe five," she answered. She crossed her legs and spread her arms along the top edge of the sofa. Her skirt reminded him somehow of a nickel, with its colors and texture and inward curls. "I fell asleep to it once. Brought it into a dream. You know how that sometimes happens. I guess maybe you don't. Since you never sleep."

"You watched my *vida* five times?" Klinsman leaned forward, elbows to knees, trying to keep the notebook screen the center of their attention.

"Yes" was her answer. "And sometimes just you, not in anyone's *vida*. And you watch me."

"You can tell?"

She nodded, tucking in her lips. "Mmm. From how you look at me. More familiar. More kind than you used to."

"I didn't . . . I never . . ."

"It's okay," she said. "I'm getting used to it. I guess we all have to get used to it. Running into people who know us more. Or we know them more. All out of balance like that. It's what your story's about, right? One of them, anyway? Are you going to put me in it?"

She looked down at herself, her arms still spread winglike along the top edge of the sofa, her small breasts pressed against the black t-shirt, her nickel skirt. She raised a sandaled foot, to get to the very end of her.

"It's funny," she said. "I don't want to make love to you. Here, on this couch. Even though it would be great. And all right even. In front of them." She nodded toward the sixteen desks. "I don't want to—finally don't want to—because of the way you and her are." Caitlin nodded to her notebook screen. "It makes me want to. And not want to."

He tightened his elbows and shoulders, making him—he knew—appear awkward and stiff. He didn't try for any words, and he understood hers, and in that waiting fold his awkwardness dissolved.

She gave a quick smile and looked downward. "The way you drank that soda she left you."

She showed him with her own sketches and overlays how she could find Oscar. "But only how he is now," she warned. "He seems impossible the other way."

Her way was better. Klinsman could see how she implied more with her shading, feathered in skin tone, shoulder angle, gait rhythm, heel pronation, clothes color, clothes shape. She overlaid a photo she must have taken herself, one of Oscar outside beneath the jacarandas during break. Shoulder to shoulder, Klinsman and Caitlin watched together.

Oscar was fixing something to eat for Artie in a kitchen, something just for a kid after dinner, something he'd really eat. Klinsman could have relaxed on the sofa and watched for a long while. He liked the way Artie peeked skeptically into the bowl his father passed to him. Klinsman closed his eyes to the clean lime-colored tabletop, as though the color were a cooling mist. He watched the bend of Oscar's muscled arm ending with, tapering with, the gentle offering of the bowl.

"Usually with him there's only one angle," Caitlin said. "Sometimes nothing. Usually you can swirl around people. But you know that." Still crouching toward the screen, she looked over her shoulder at him. He had to keep from falling into her, into the V she made in the sofa.

"You're pretending to know less than you really do," she said. "I've learned some things. Working here. Why're you having me do this?"

"I need to watch someone else do it. Someone else. Like you. Someone smart, clear."

"You *are* putting me in the story," she said.

He tried to stay on task, like Rita. But he wanted to find her, or watch Oscar, or just talk with Caitlin. It was how he always was with his stories, what he always fought, surrendered to, the bricolage and distractions.

"And I also need some company," he told her. "I'm afraid. Of what I might see." He snapped the photo of Douglas Cook onto the coffee table like a trump card. "Do him?"

"Give me more."

"His clothes change," Klinsman told her. "His shoes are always different. I mean different shoes on each foot. His shoulders are always disguised—big blazers or torn sleeves, like that."

"Oh," she said. "One of them."

"But, yeah." Klinsman reached for her notebook. "I know his skin. I can do that. His gait, too, yes."

She gave him Douglas Cook.

There was nothing but dark screen, a swimming murkiness, the night surface of a dank pond. Not even a silhouette or impression.

Klinsman leaned back on the sofa and rubbed his eyes, pressing hard to stir the colors. He heard Caitlin's voice, a youthful curl still in it, reminding him of Aracely.

"It's not completely blank. Not really." She waited for him to open his eyes. "They pride themselves, you know, A. K. They pride themselves on how they can hide. They give each other points for that. He must be in there somewhere. In that green. That strange green."

"I know, Caitlin." He put his hand briefly on her shoulder and then stood, stretching. "Thank you. Thank you for helping. Staying late. Trying. I can close up, if you need."

"No," she replied. She leaned back from the coffee table but sat primly on the sofa, fingers knitting, occupying her. "Will I see you here? Again? Before we're all done?"

"I think so," he replied. "If not, I'll see you in my dreams, no?"

"I'd rather be in your nightmares," she told him, looking up, just missing him, as though she were about to think of something else. "But not the nightmarish part. The good part, when you can only feel that something might be about to happen. When you still think you can fly."

64.

*T*he lights of the Boulevard dizzied him as he began making his way to Rita's house, the closest bed, the feel and smell of her. Far behind him the pink neon "Boulevard" script hung over the traffic, the sign a T with its arms spread wide, throwing light from behind, casting Klinsman's shadow in front of him. The shadow melted at his feet as he strode the sidewalk, hyperconscious of his gait, stuttering it out. The huge electronic billboards seemed to be rotating their images more quickly than ever before—an exotic dancer with shiny lips and cleavage, a cardiologist in smock and heavy glasses, a lizard selling insurance, a dry cleaner who smiled as though he couldn't wait to fondle your clothes, all pulsing forth one after the other on one sign. Lightning flashes struck from atop traffic lights, catching cars trying to poach a red.

Sleep deprivation pushed upward beneath his skull like a corroded spade, acid-edged, leaning him, shoving him forward. He felt his delicate sleep pattern crumbling inside him, urging his body to get to a bed before it was too late, before lights and thoughts

scalded away any waiting dream. He looked away from the electronic billboards, fearful of all he might see—the dreams he was
supposed to have that night. *If you won't dream them, we'll dream them for
you, and show them to everyone below us on this boulevard.*

He made it to Rita's studio in time to catch a bit of sleep, the tail
end of a cycle, perhaps. He undressed, curled himself into the cool
sheets of the daybed, and watched her, his laptop pulled close by
on a chair beside his pillow.

Rita was darkness. But he watched anyway, knowing she was in
there, hoping she could feel him. He slept for forty-eight minutes
in that darkness, a deep, stunning sleep, a clear stab into his brain.
Awake, he felt it like the small relief of a removed splinter.

"Call her," he heard just before he opened his eyes. It could
have been an echo from his talk with Connie, his promise to her,
her reminding voice. The voice was that dream-voice, sparkling,
female, what woke Hercules to the snakes. It could have been Gina
calling—or Rita. The sound of it dissolved as he opened his eyes to
the dark studio.

The blue numbers on the clock said he had two minutes. He
used the remote to thrum open the blinds, let in stripes of moon
and streetlight. The blue wink of the clock subtracted a minute. He
pulled on a pair of board shorts and took an ice cube from the
fridge, cooled his neck, his chest, then slid the remaining cold
pebble into his mouth, tasting his own salt.

Sitting on the edge of the daybed, gazing at the bars of light on
the dark floor, he called the phone post in the muddy Amazon.

She answered before the first ring was finished.

"Aaron." Her voice was sunlight on the ranch, the summer shine on a horse's shoulder, the scent of dry grass around your ears as you watched the blue sky, listened to a single hopeful cry of a gull.

"Con," he said. "Is it safe for you there? Like that in the night? It must be dark as hell."

"I'm the only dentist for hundreds of miles. Me and the optometrist. We're the safest people you can find. No one can touch us."

"What about wild animals?" he asked. "Frogs that kill you with just a look?"

"Ha." Then she sighed. "I would risk anything to see an animal. Anything besides a dog or a buzzard. You really need to come down here sometime. See what it's like."

"Is it dawn there yet?"

"Not quite."

"A moon?"

"It set a while ago."

He pictured her looking at the sky. Seeing different constellations, the Southern Star.

"What you said, Aaron. About Uncle Mir?"

"It's true," he told her. "I watched him die. I'm pretty sure he knew I could—that I would. I can still watch him. Watch him live, too. I'll show you next time you visit. We'll watch together."

He decided not to tell about how he had been stopped, thwarted. By what? By whom? C de Baca? What remained of him? What he had become?

"I'm going to send you some stuff, Con. Just some things. Like some pens and a mirror and a toothbrush."

"You're going to send *me* a toothbrush?"

"Just keep them. Keep them around you. Carry them with you. Everywhere. All right?"

"Why?" she asked with an extra lift at the end, an inflection only a sister would dare.

"So I can be with you." He wanted so much not to sound crazy. "In some way."

"Sure, Aaron. Okay. But I have to pack light. I have to stay light."

"A hair clasp, then?" he said.

"I buzzed my head," she replied. He heard her brush her fingers over her scalp twice, once back, once forward, a regretful sigh. "The lice are really bad here."

"Then a shirt. A great shirt Oscar gave me. With beautiful buttons. Just to hang on your wall."

"Sure," she replied. "That sounds nice."

"I'll come down, Con. There. I'll do a story. What you're doing. You and the optometrist."

"That sounds even nicer, Aaron." He heard the muddy wheels of a truck, splashes, some voices. "I need to go, Aaron. Now. When you come, bring Oscar," she added. "Bring Rita."

Rita's heat pattern was a green figure in the darkness, her outline amorphous. She moved as though underwater, past silhouettes of stiff and sparse scrub, along sandy paths lined and dotted with black rocks. He could see her heartbeat, hot and violet, in the center of the green-and-yellow cloud of light that was her.

He wanted to embrace her like that, as that green fire. To pull her into him, press his body through the heat waves of her skin and burn himself in the dark, molten, interior colors.

65.

He checked on Oscar but could find nothing. He must have already put Artie to bed in their new place, fashioned a new space, a new Paper Room. Douglas Cook was in blackness, too, eluding anything Klinsman could try. But they watched him. This he knew.

He let them see how he wasted his life—how he had always wasted it—on finding too much meaning in silly, trashy works. "When midnight strikes," said Edwige Fenech, in her *giallo* getup as Madame Bovary, "you must think of me." *Think of me*. Her false eyelashes were beautiful, her black hair lifted high, her pale breasts pushing forth, filling out the screen.

They saw him try to find sleep, like Caitlin, while watching *Santo vs Blue Demon in Atlantis*. *This is where I belong*, he told them, showed them. *This is as close as I get to giving anything, saving anyone.*

He paced the moonlit studio in his surf shorts, drinking ice water, trying to trick his body back into some right pattern, to some point in the circadian rhythm where it would slide toward sleep. Curled on the daybed, clutching a pillow, he watched Santo carry X-25 off to find solitude and peaceful dreams, watched Rita's infrared pattern melt back into darkness, watched the thought of Douglas Cook shrouded in a pond's green-black surface.

He tried going to the Santo film Douglas had captioned, with his sketches of the Luchador masks and the cattle skull. *Profanadores de tumbas*. There was a bit more now, a few seconds of motion, but nothing in it except jumps and smears of rotten film, the decayed tapes of Channel 12. When Klinsman turned away from the film and straightened himself on the daybed, he saw a streak of color left burned in his vision. When he closed his eyes, pressed them, the color remained, searing brighter along his retinas.

It was red, a red he had once known. It was the color of the dirt just below the topsoil of the Klinsman ranch. The stuff all the ranchers and farmers back then had known, cut into no matter where they plowed. The clod he had given Douglas Cook.

He got up and went to the desk, taking the laptop with him. He pushed aside the mirror and his notes and sketches in order to give himself elbow room. He worked only in the light of the screen. These *vidas* and reinventions were more than games; they weren't impressions for Douglas Cook. They were expressions. They were sincere, perhaps even desperate. From a *mozo* whose language and perception didn't bother with time, didn't bother to separate present and future.

He played *Profanadores de tumbas* again, letting the snippet jump and melt across the screen. The same exact color occurred when Klinsman shut his eyes or turned away to stare into the dark. On a piece of paper he rough-sketched what Douglas had given him with the snippet the first time: the cattle skull, the Luchador mask, the salamander. The caption: *Don't use this, I hope you don't have to use this. I try.*

He put different colors up on his screen, closed his eyes to them, and saw that his optic nerves created their complements, their negatives, when he shut his eyes. He downloaded a color wheel, a very intricate one that an artist would use. Blue, eyes closed, produced yellow. Orange made violet. Red made green. Green, red. It could be as subtle with the negatives as with any of the hues.

This scrap of film, the color it burned, was for Klinsman, one only Klinsman could understand, sent by a *mozo* who knew everything about him, had watched his life, had helped patchwork it together. It was the same color on the dark screen Caitlin had found for him. He spun the color wheel to the reddish hue that came closest to the subsoil of the ranch. That stuff anyone could still see piled up around sprinkler repairs or new plantings in the park. Kids loved to play with it because it looked fake, fabricated for a movie about Mars, and they could throw the clods and watch them splatter on the white sidewalk like meteorites from the Red Planet.

Klinsman shut his eyes to the color and observed the phosphene that melted across his vision. He then chose that color on the wheel, stared it down, then shut his eyes, saw that red. He cut and pasted the green from the color wheel onto a stilled frame from the *Profanadores de tumbas* snippet, saw how perfectly they matched.

Why would the *salamandros* send him this? What had Douglas Cook—they—seen in the other slips for Mir, Oscar, and Gina? In his own? Maybe they were just being *mozos*, playing games, sending codes, giggling among themselves. Playing in the dirt. He recalled Douglas Cook, how he had been with him and Rita that afternoon at the park. How furtive he had been in the light of day, beneath the cameras. *I try.*

What had stopped him? The cattle skull was infecting their stuff, too. Warning them off. *Aim your kaleidoscopes away,* mandros, *back to the pretty colors of our day. Like the boys you are. Like Aaron Klinsman.*

Or else what? In this clip Douglas Cook seemed to know. It was disposable and prophetic as any of his classroom doodles. *I know how to save the world. I know what happens to me—if I try. You shroud me in red.*

66.

The screw worm of insomnia tailed into his heart, into the muscle. He was done sleeping for the night. The next day, he knew, would be one of those jagged gauntlets filled with bright yellow flashes, bursts of directionless energy, concussionlike to the very end, all the way to a sunset whose colors would spill over his parched eyes and racing thoughts.

Ordinarily he would have watched a *giallo*, a Santo flick, or anything Channel 12 had to offer, or read a complicated novel, or do all four together in a rotating attempt to imitate dreams. But on the daybed, gripped in moonlight stripes, he felt worry twisting in each roll of his heart. Worry for Connie, for Oscar, for Rita, for Douglas Cook.

C de Baca was a demon that lived in belief. If you were quick enough to kill him, burn him, he would always rise from the tarry blackness that remained, to lurk, to wait, to want. Klinsman was driving himself crazy not watching what he usually watched, not watching anything, not doing anything.

So he watched the darkness that was Rita, even caught glimpses of ochre stars, silhouettes of her hair fanning like spools of dark matter across the lowest constellations. He remained awake, lurking, waiting, wanting.

Then two photographs appeared on the screen. They were portraits of the two men the journalist from El Paso had named in her book. Rita had captured clear full-body shots of each man, standing alone, spent and panting in the night. Each one stood beneath the baring shine of a porch light. They wore black silk suits, expensive and tailored. But none of the fine, unique cuts could hide their skinny, slumping backs and shoulders, their filled little bellies. Their flesh was the color of the cigar smoke that curled up from their crooked fingers.

He rode the first predawn trolley south. With him were night workers scattered about the seats, each one sitting alone, eyes glazed in clinical light, briefly registering any movement. In a piece titled "Nightriders"—Gina's title, not his—he had profiled some of these passengers. He recognized the guy who baked rolls for the *panadería* on San Ysidro Boulevard. No matter how many he baked, there were never enough to last beyond noon. And Klinsman knew the security guard for the foreign currency exchange on the same boulevard, knew she could shoot the heart out of an ace at thirty meters. She hated the dawn shift. People often found unfortunate courage in those hours, she told him. They misread their lives, found the wrong hopes, lost the right fears.

She looked at Klinsman, her uniform cap pushed back on her beaded hair like a sailor on shore leave. Her full lips were in a pensive frown, her black eyes in a tearless kind of cry.

"If this were my watch," she told him softly, "I'd be marking you."

"Why?"

The baker and the other riders didn't appear interested in the aisle conversation.

"Something about you," she said. "Something jacked up. Like somebody gave you a pill and didn't say what it'd do to you. But you took it anyway."

"What should I do?" He asked the question to curb suspicion, to assure her. He didn't expect an answer.

"Go home," she told him. "Walk it off. Walk all those worn spots in your rug. Have a bowl of your favorite cereal. Drink a glass of milk. Like from that dairy you once told us about. When you were doing that story on us. Just go home and be home. All the way home."

But when Klinsman got to Ranch Park, nothing was familiar. The security light in the center, where the barn had stood, was punched out. The park was a long rectangle of darkness amid the sodium cower of the housing tracts—like a reservoir full of night. He could smell dirt, the bloodlike scent of fallow ground finally turned.

The slope was off. Even in the darkness he could sense a crimp in the beckoning downward sweep of the tomato field. From the barn roof he could follow that sweep and continue on to the drive-in screens, and the bullring, and the night sea.

Whatever calm he had found on the trolley ride vanished with the first rising heartbeats. What he would have given for one of Rita's grip lights. He walked the lower periphery, looking for dark piles of upturned soil. They might have looked like crumpled shadows in the slant of the setting moon. The overhead surveillance was useless without the security light.

Beneath the dead security light he found glass, large chunks glittering like ice under moon and stars. He moved to where the swings had been, where he and Connie would pump themselves up into the wind and watch their older siblings and the field hands work among the tomato vines, where they would watch the dog smoke rise, where he could make himself believe he could see everything.

He knelt by the picnic table, where the doghouse had been, where the big Mexican pit viper had bitten his life in two. The grass was firm beneath his knees, a skin of night dew breaking around him, his heat. He used his open notebook as a lantern, its blue glow reflecting on the dew in an even glass.

He tried not to panic. He watched Rita materialize from the darkness, her green amorphous night form sliding calmly into view, her violet heart beating steadily. He saw Oscar check his sleeping son, touch his hair, dowse the nightlight, before going back into his enclave to write his story. But he could not find Douglas Cook.

67.

A low cloud mass was sliding east across the sky, erasing the stars over the ocean. The first thin membrane of the mass veiled the moon, softened and enlarged it into a white nova. Klinsman watched it vanish behind the thicker layer of cloud that followed. He cast his screen light along the grass in front of him as he made his way down the slope.

He paused for a moment at the stone table where he had picnicked with Rita, had watched the dog smoke with her, drunk those sugary Mexican sodas, told her how C de Baca's death screams had filled the summer air. The table stood almost exactly where Alejandro had taken Aaron and Connie to witness the burning.

He approached the burn point on a spiral, circling his path, tightening it inward, aiming his screen light downward. The glow seemed no more powerful than gathered and focused starlight, blue and cold, pretty and meek. But it was enough for him to see that no night dew remained over this patch of grass.

He dropped to his knees, his heartbeat flipping. The skin of grass gave easily beneath his weight, throwing him a little off balance as he knelt, into a dreamfear that he was suddenly dropping into darkness.

With his shoulder bag he fashioned a platform for his screen on the grass, giving him the best light he could work with. All around him he felt that crimp in the slope, a melt and flicker in the film. Those color circles that used to cue reel changes—he always believed he could jump in there.

Unable to think of anything else to use, Klinsman began digging with his fingers. He clutched at the sod and felt it give easily, rolling into his palms like a thick blanket. A sheet of grass peeled up into a neat rectangle that he was able to lift and place it to the side. At his knees was a squared patch of soil, black in the deep shadow of the grass but red as Mars in his memory. Immediately he knew there would be more sheets.

Calmly, swiftly, he peeled back the segments of sod, stacking them like evidence. His entire body trembled to maintain control as he wavered between purpose and panic. He unveiled a larger rectangle cut into the grass, a little longer than himself. Breathing carefully to pace against the slam of his pulse, he laid himself over the stretch of dirt, felt it ease beneath his weight, imagined its red pulling him under.

He scooped the dirt away in armfuls, raking it into a pile at the end of the rectangle. He pounded the earth, a rhythmic one-two-three, one-two-three. Sobs rolled upward through him as he pulled at the dirt and fought for air. When his hands began to shake too much from fatigue and worry, he took a second to breathe and rest. He glanced at the light of the screen, the absurd and plastic blue.

Tall shadows gathered suddenly about him, hushing sounds from mouths and from boots on the grass. One of them, the tallest, clamped the screen closed, dropping them all into darkness. Klinsman could see only the silhouettes of their heads and thin shoulders against a black wool sky. There were three of them. He recognized the clatter of shovels, then the voice of Nino.

"You dig there. You, that end. *Apurate. Andale pues.*"

He took hold of Klinsman's shirt by the shoulders and pulled him clear of the shallow hole. "Fucking *guero*," he whispered in Spanish. "Fucking amazing. Let the Mexicans dig now, yes? Let us do the work." He shoved Klinsman into a resting position.

Klinsman fell back into the grass and gazed at the blank sky, blinked fast against it. He heard the shovels quickly find wood, begin scraping it free. He eased himself back to his knees. The hole was barely two feet deep. Nino pushed him away, barred his arms, when Klinsman tried to reach in to help.

The two *mandros* with the shovels pried open the lid.

"Careful not to stab him," Nino whispered in Spanish as they levered the shovels and yanked the lid free. "Let him breathe."

The three of them lifted Douglas Cook from the box, held his length in their arms as they knelt in the grass. Nino unbound

Douglas's mouth and hands. He had to pick the tape off carefully around his lips. "Fucking *mozo*," he whispered over Douglas. "Why you try a mustache?"

They let Douglas roll himself free. He hunched over, away from all of them, and released long, painful groans into the night, rocking back and forth on his haunches.

Nino moved over to comfort him, put his arm across Cook's shoulders. "Hey, *mozo*. You be all right. We let you have the honors. You get to start it. Start it good. Make it good."

Douglas shuddered in Nino's embrace. He pressed his face into Nino's chest. The other *mandros* moved in close again, shushing over the grass. They put their hands gently on Douglas's arm. Nino held his embrace, the other two continuing their touch—drawing what they could.

Klinsman leaned back, bracing his arms. From across the dig, he watched them, their silhouettes against the Tijuana lights. He thought of instructions for them, to tell them to take Douglas to the ER, to tell them exactly what to do. But they knelt together, gathered and ready, whispering ideas, far past anything he could give now, ready to vanish into what was left of the night. If Klinsman remained across from them, got back into their screens as quickly as possible, they would continue to believe in him. They would know what to do with him, what to expect of him.

"You have the two photos?" he asked them.

"Yeah," said Nino quietly. "And you, *guero*. We have you."

68.

*K*linsman slept from dawn to well past deadline. A hundred dreams must have poured through him, each one only seconds long but a lifetime in breadth. The commotion of the *Review*'s last full day ran like a downstairs party beneath his dreams. They must have stopped by the sofa, in turns, to watch his eyelids undulate and flicker. "Come see this one," Caitlin might've whispered to the nearest desks, motioning with her arm.

Of course he saw it later in chosen snippets. How at his desk Caitlin wrote up two entries for the blotter page, an inch and a half apiece: one on an odd finding in a San Ysidro motel room that the cops deemed harmless but intriguing fun and the other about damage left by park vandals in Otay playing goth games.

There Klinsman was in the back, stretched across the sofa like a drunken uncle. They stopped to check on him once in a while, watch him dream. Klinsman could have viewed the entire day he had missed.

But that was what would limit us. That was what the *mandros* had learned. We can't live one life while watching another, even if that life is our own. The trick would be to create brief versions that could somehow imply forever, for always.

Despite the twelve-hour nap past deadline, Klinsman made the drop-deadline with all three of his stories for the *Review*. It was the final issue, but it would run indefinitely, gather and grow endlessly, spooling out the weave of Gina's loom. Oscar's stories on the clothes warehouse and the orphans of Juárez spun across Aaron's pieces on the Luchadors, the city parks, and the monster legends of the borderlands.

Rita's photos, which were continuous, could be mixed and matched with each story. One photo of an orphan of Juárez appeared taken through a topaz lens, as though through the spangle on an earring or a button on a shirt. Like the stories, one photo crossed into another, became another, drew on another.

Back at Rita's house, from the desk with the ladder-back chair painted the colors of the Mexican flag, Klinsman chose one reader and watched her. She sat alone in the morning stillness of the Big Kitchen sidewalk, a student at City College probably. The print version of the final issue lay pushed aside on the tabletop. Her coffee mug was green, the postcard color of a motel roof. Klinsman swept in from the back, up over her right shoulder. He could smell the shampoo in her still damp hair, blending with the morning dew on the table and sidewalk. She flicked the shoulder of her corduroy jacket, as though to shoo him away.

Her notebook was all screen, no mouse, no keyboard. She brushed the surface using the tip of her ring finger, a choice that intrigued him. Her screen filled with the front page, reflecting the cover of the print version on the table. The cover showed Rita's photo of the clothes mountain. Three workers stood along the escarpment of last year's fashion. They held shovels, the garden scoops they used to organize the heaps brought up by train from the maquiladores. They each wore expensive silk shirts tied as bandanas around their brows.

Her screen had no frame, images brimming all the way to the edges. So it looked as though the screen was a rectangular opening in the streetscape beyond her table.

"Prada by the Pound" was the headline. And it swept her in.

The student in the corduroy jacket had started with Oscar's story on the warehouse, but by the time Klinsman found her again, at a table in the campus foodcourt, she was looking at photos of an orphan of Juárez. She grazed the tip of her ring finger along the screen face, moving the photo into an upper corner and unveiling Oscar's story.

There were not many orphans of Juárez because most of the women were very young. They would be girls but for the fact that they had to work long hours and take bus rides during the most dangerous segments of the night. There was no need for any kind of detectives—noble, corrupt, exacting, or savage. The two men who had brokered the one hundred thirty-seven killings were known. They wanted to be known. Most of Juárez and El Paso and Chihuahua City and Tijuana called them Los Juniors. They could not be touched.

But now they would be watched. They would be shown.

In the weave of stories that followed, Klinsman couldn't tell which one she might have started. She could even end up well outside the *Review*, watching the Luchadors, for instance. Maybe she would find a better version of *Santo vs Blue Demon in Atlantis* or the much more horrifying *Profanadores de tumbas*. Or maybe she would find her way to her own *vida*, the *mandros'* collective concentrate of her life and imagination.

She could watch the one of the very journalist who had written the piece she happened to be following. Or, if she had the stomach, a *vida* spawned from the two photos Rita had taken in the desert.

69.

Certain moments provide center. He could find this needed moment with different approaches—in his own *vida*, or Oscar's, or just in some *mozo*'s posted fantasy. But to Klinsman it seemed best when he found it as the ending to *Atlantis*.

Only he knew that it was really the desert, because under a weak moon it looked like the deep ocean floor, the sand diatomaceous and faint with heat-light.

A single heat outline moved across the sparse seascape, a green form finding pale channels between rock and black coral shapes. It was the *guero* journalist, transformed perhaps by the underworld goddess. It was Aaron, because right before was a shot of a kite snapped loose on an ocean wind.

He was searching, a measured rhythm to his stride, a traverse to his path, but all softened by the fluid green and yellow of his form. His center was the size and color of a plum.

Just as he passed center view, she appeared suddenly behind him, as if from a shutter, her unveiled form. It was easy to recognize her shape from the previous scenes when she had been alone with her aim and arrows, a green-and-yellow night figure with a violet core. She had him ambushed from behind.

He took two strides further before sensing her. He went still and then turned. They went into each other like cells joining. His violet center expanded first, the outer edges and layers of his form darkening, yellow to green, green to blue.

When they were fully joined, their dark center aswim above the sea floor, she lifted the shutter and they vanished, masked in cool satin.

Thank you to Esme Bajo for showing me what matters most. Thank you to Fred Ramey, my wise and artful editor. I thank Peter Steinberg for his friendship, advice, and representation. To Elise Blackwell—we grew up together on the border, where we will always be in some way, the impossible to translate simpático.